Southern Storm

SPECIAL EDITION

NATASHA MADISON

Southern Storm

The Southern Series Book 3

Natasha Madison

Cover Design: Jay Aheer https://www.simplydefinedart.com/

Editing done by Jenny Sims Editing4Indies

Proofing Julie Deaton by Deaton Author Services https://www.facebook.
com/jdproofs/

One

BEAU

"Tell me that my brother is not Ethan's father," I hiss. My heart pounds in my chest while the tears stream down my face as I stand here looking at who are supposed to be my best friends. The tie around my neck suddenly feels tight. I have the white paper clenched in my hand so tight that my whole body feels like it's shaking. Savannah stands there looking more beautiful than she has ever looked in her whole life, and trust me, I know. I've been watching her for what feels like my whole life.

"Tell me!" I shout, and the tears flow down her face.

"Ethan is mine," says Jacob, my best friend and father of Ethan. Kallie, who left eight years ago when Savannah found out she was pregnant and said it was Jacob's, stands beside him. When I learned the news, I was cut off at the knees. I was gutted and hollow, thinking that my best friend had slept with the only woman I have ever loved. I pretended to be supportive of them, but deep down inside, I died. A piece of me was gone forever.

"Really," I say. Shaking my head, I walk around the big brown desk that belonged to my father for the past twenty-five years. And before that, it was my grandfather's. Today was supposed to be a day I never forgot, and after this, it will be. Jacob and I would always sneak into this office and take a couple of swigs of the top-of-the-line whiskey my father kept in here. More than once, we got caught, but my father would just smile and walk back out of the room.

"Beau." Casey says my name, and my eyes fly to his. Casey is Kallie's brother and another one of my best friends. I look at everyone in the room and wonder if they all lied to me. Was it all a lie? Was everything a lie? "Sit down."

I shake my head. "Imagine my surprise ..." I start, my voice low so Savannah can hear me. She stands there watching me, her face wet from tears. "When I walked in here to take a drink with my best friends." I swallow. "To take one shot of whiskey. Then my leg hits something on the desk, and the sound it made caused me to stop. But it would sound weird since the desk was one hundred years old. But when I bent down, this little box was under there. And if you look closely, you can see it is a hidden compartment."

"Beau." Savannah whispers my name, and my heart shatters in my chest.

"I had no idea what could be that confidential that he would have to lock it up this tight." I laugh bitterly, looking down at the paper. "I flipped over a couple of things and then found this." I hold up the paper being crumpled by my tight fist. "My brother is Ethan's father."

"No," Jacob states loudly. "He's my son."

"Is he?" I ask, wondering how he could stand there after all he's been through. He's tolerated the judgmental looks from the townspeople for the past eight years. He heard all the whispers from everyone when Kallie left. He lost fucking Kallie, and he still takes Savannah's side.

"I, Savannah Harrison, relinquish Liam Huntington from all parental duties."

"I can explain," she finally says. Sobbing, she puts her hand in front of her mouth. Ten minutes ago, I would have been the first one rushing to her side to hold her in my arms. I would have given her anything. But now I look at her, and I can't give her anything.

"Explain this to me!" I shout at the top of my lungs, and it startles her. The music from outside at my party can be heard. A party my parents put together to honor me for being the third generation to fill the shoes of mayor. "Why you would sign this paper?"

Jacob steps forward to stand in front of me. "You need to calm down and let her explain," he tells me. When I push him away from me, Casey now coming forward to make sure that nothing else happens. The anger radiates from me now, and I brush away my tears.

"You lied to me." I point at Jacob and lean forward, hissing in his face. "Everything was a fucking lie." My normal calm and cool demeanor is now out of the door. Suddenly feeling hot, I throw off my jacket. "This whole time, it was all a lie." Laughing, I shake my head and loosen my tie. "What a fucking joke this was."

"You need to stop talking right now." Jacob has tears in his eyes, his chest rising and falling the whole time. "Seriously, you need to just stop."

"Stop," I growl. "After everything." My hand grips the white paper even harder in my hand. "After standing there beside you all this time. Supportive, stupid Beau."

"Stop it!" Savannah yells. "Stop talking!"

"What's the matter, Savannah? The truth hurts," I say. I know I'm going over the line, and that I'll regret it in the morning. "That the whole time, people were talking about you. Can you imagine what they would have said about you?" I laugh. "Guess what? They did say it." I don't even see the fist that comes flying at me, so I can't duck, but Jacob hits me right in the jaw, snapping my head to the side.

"Jacob!" Kallie shrieks, and it takes me a second to realize that he hit me. After tasting the blood in my mouth, I reach up with my hand and wipe away a trickle of blood with my thumb.

I look down at my hand and then back up at my best friend. Savannah's still crying silently. I turn back to look at Jacob. "She isn't worth it." The sound of Savannah's gasp fills the room, and now when I look over at her, she looks down and then up. She never says a word. Instead, she turns and walks out of the room, slamming the door behind her.

"You son of a bitch," Jacob hisses. "You stupid son of a bitch." I feel numb, completely numb. I pick up the bottle of whiskey and take three long gulps, only stopping when the burning gets to my stomach and it feels like there is a fire there. I don't know if it's from the whiskey or if it's because I just lost the woman I love. I slump into the chair, gripping the bottle tightly.

"How could you do that to her?' he asks. I wonder if he's for real right now. "Do you know what you just did?"

"Me?" I point at myself. "What I did? I did nothing."

"You just shit all over Savannah," Kallie says, and my eyes fly to hers.

"Out of everyone in this room, I'm surprised you're sticking up for her." I take another gulp. "She ruined your life."

"She is Ethan's mother," Kallie says, walking toward me and the big brown desk that held all these secrets.

"And God knows who the real father really is." When I look into Jacob's eyes, Casey shoots his arm out to stop Jacob from charging over to me.

Jacob looks down and then up. "It just goes to show the apple doesn't fall far from the tree."

I look straight into his eyes when I say the next words, coming out before I can stop them. "Isn't that the truth. Like mother, like daughter."

He shakes his head, then over at Kallie. "Let's go." He turns and walks out of the room with Kallie right behind him.

"You better get your head out of your ass and go after her," Casey says. Turning, he grabs Olivia's hand and walks out of the room, then closes the door behind him. I look down at the paper I still have gripped in my hand and read the words over and over again until they are blurred from my tears.

I take another pull of the whiskey, and it takes five gulps until the burning starts. After another six, the glass bottle flies out of my hand and crashes against the white wall, shattering everywhere like an explosion while the amber liquid leaks down. The pictures on the wall of my father and my brother stare back at me. The picture of the three of us standing in front of this very house. "Fuck you," I say to the empty room, but more to my brother whose picture I'm staring at. "Fuck you and the horse you rode in on."

Two

SAVANNAH

"She isn't worth it." His words cut me more than anyone else. I knew this day would probably come, but I thought I had more time, or at least I hoped I would. I'm standing in the same office as I was eight years ago when I begged his father to help me. All he did was laugh at me, then toss me two hundred dollars and told me to take out the trash. I was broken then, but nothing could have prepared me for the look Beau is giving me. Nothing could hurt more.

I can hear the music from outside, and I can see the pain in his eyes. I can feel his hurt all through my bones. I want to reach out to him and touch him and tell him that it's all a mistake. I want to tell him everything, but I don't. No words come out. The only thing that comes out is a sob, and then Jacob swings, and it's the final straw. Everything I touch gets ruined. I turn and open the door, then step outside to rush to my car. I'm almost out the front door when I feel a hand on my arm. Something inside me wishes it was Beau, but I know right away it's not. My eyes roam down to my arm, and I see the stupid fucking gold pinky ring, making my blood run cold and the sadness suddenly turn to hatred.

"Now, now." When I hear his slimy voice, I rip my arm away from his touch. You would think he would get the hint, but he doesn't. Instead, he closes the distance between us and puts both hands on my bare arms. "I hope you're not leaving yet." Hearing his voice and feeling his breath make me want to vomit. The smell a mixture of cigars and whiskey. "We didn't have a chance to catch up." I look at him, and I have to wonder how the fuck I ever found him attractive. Sure, he's tall, and his hair is always perfectly coiffed, and his blue eyes just pop with his brown hair. But underneath all those preppy good looks is a spineless piece of shit.

"Get the fuck away from me, Liam," I hiss. Moving away from him, I spin to face him. I look at the man who lied more than anyone I've ever known.

"Now, now," he says, coming down the last step to me. He looks around and then leans his head in closer. "Is that any way to talk to your baby daddy?"

I look around to make sure that no one is around and can hear him. The big white house is filled with people who walk around, but none of them pay any attention to us outside. "Fuck you, Liam," I hiss. "Where's your wife?"

He smirks at me. "Don't worry about that," he says and brings his hand up to rub my arm, causing me to throw up in my mouth. "Besides, we have an understanding."

I step back, and my heel almost gets caught in the rocks, but the last thing I will ever be is vulnerable to him. "Do you both understand what a grade A piece of shit you are?" I ask, and he just laughs at me.

"I like you feisty," he says, giving me the smirk that worked on me eight years ago. "Always did."

"Get the fuck away from her." I hear Jacob hiss from behind Liam, and he turns to look at him.

"Hey there," he says as if they are long-lost friends. "Great seeing you again. I didn't get a chance to see your son."

"I dare you," Jacob says, coming closer to him, "to fuck with me."

Liam throws his head back and laughs. "Calm down there, Sheriff." He shakes his head and turns to walk away.

"Are you okay?" Jacob asks, and right then, Casey walks out the front door, his hand in Olivia's, and he spots us.

"Why did you leave him by himself?" I ask them. "He's hurting."

"He's not going to listen to anyone right now," Casey says, walking down the steps and looking at me. "You got this?" he asks Jacob, and then he looks at me and nods. As Kallie's older brother, he's never really spoken to me, but when shit went down, he was one of the few who didn't look at me like I was the scum of the earth. I mean, don't get me wrong, he was not all flowers and shit, but he never looked at me with disdain the way everyone else did.

"You still shouldn't leave him by himself," I tell them and then look down. "I'm going to get going. Can you grab Ethan?"

"Yeah," Kallie says.

I look down and blink away the tears. "I'll call you guys later," I say, walking toward my truck with my head down. Something that I've done for the past eight years. Opening the door and getting behind the wheel, I look down at my red dress I chose for this occasion. When I got dressed today for the function, I did it hoping Beau would tell me that I was beautiful. When he came over last week and begged me to come, I couldn't say no to him. There isn't much I would say no to him for because I loved him. Bottom line, he was the hero in every single romance book I've read. He was the prince in every Disney movie. He was everything, but he looked at me like he always did—as a friend. I was his best friend, and he was one of mine.

I mean, let's face it, I didn't have many people to choose

from. I was the kid from the wrong side of the tracks, or so I was told my whole life. My father could be one of five people, which just made me shake my head.

My mother tried as best as she could. She was a waitress at the local watering hole, and then one day, she applied for a job for the mayor and his wife. She was their cleaning lady, and she became very close with the mayor's wife, Mary Ellen. Soon, she was doing the cooking and the cleaning, and Mary Ellen got me into the school where Beau and Jacob attended. I started there wearing secondhand boy clothes since my mother could never save enough for clothes, and Mary Ellen always felt sorry for me and gave me the boys' hand-me-downs. I dressed like a boy until I was fifteen and got my own job and could buy my own stuff.

Jacob and Beau ignored me at first, but then when we got back to the house, I would be stuck waiting for my mother to finish, so Beau was stuck with me. Slowly but surely, we became three peas in a pod until that fateful day when our lives changed. I want to say I wish I could go back and change it. I want to say I regret everything, but then I would regret Ethan, and I refuse to allow him to feel like I've felt my whole life. He was never going to be told that he was lucky I kept him. He was never going to be told I had no choice. He will always know how much he is loved and how much he is wanted. I hope that if he ever finds out what I did, he will still love me as much as he does today.

Starting my car, I make my way toward my house. When I walk into the cold house, I take off the new black shoes I paid way too much for. I can't even return them now since I scuffed the heel. I close my eyes, and all I can see is the hurt on Beau's face. My knees give out, and I collapse with a sob, lying on the floor with my broken heart. When I finally peel myself off the floor, I walk to the couch. The same couch I spent every single night watching movies with Beau on. The same couch I bought because he came shopping with me and said it suited me. I grab the blanket hanging over the couch and cover myself with it. The smell of Beau is all around me since he fell asleep on the couch just yesterday, and I didn't have the heart to wake him up. So I just put the blanket over him and watched him sleep, wishing I could curl up next to him. Even more, I wished he would take my hand and lead me to my bed. But instead, I moved his hair away from his forehead and bent down to kiss him lightly and then I walked to bed. By the time I woke up this morning, he was gone, but he left me a little note on the counter like he always does.

Closing my eyes, I can't stop the tears, and my eyes are burning and getting heavy. Then I hear the soft knock on my door. I think it's my imagination, but then I hear it again. I get up and make my way to the door with only the light from the moon streaming in the window. I don't check to see who it is, which is stupid of me since not too long ago someone was in town chasing Casey's girl. I open the door, and I see him standing there with his hands gripping my doorframe and his head hanging. When he finally looks up, I see that his eyes are bloodshot. My heart breaks again when I look at the most beautiful man I've ever seen.

"Beau," I whisper in a plea.

"I'm sorry," he says, and the sob rips through me. "I'm so, so sorry."

Three

BEAU

"I'm so, so sorry." Those are the only words I say right now. I stand here, and my whole body is numb as I look at her still dressed. Her eyes and nose are both red, and her hand over her mouth stops the sob that rips through her. My hands drop from the doorframe, and I rush in, wrapping one arm around her waist. She wraps her arms around my neck and buries her face in my neck. All I can do is realize that with her in my arms, I feel like everything is going to be okay. Her tears soak my skin as I walk her farther into her house and close the door behind me.

Two hours ago, my life changed, and for the first time, I couldn't control it. I had no way of controlling how this was going to play out, and that made me struggle even more.

I sat in my office chair, watching the tiny droplets of amber liquid travel along the wall to the floor. My eyes remained fixated on the wall when the door opened , and I looked up to see Jacob walk in with Kallie behind him.

"What the fuck?" he asked, looking at me and then at the bottle. I didn't know what to say.

He came into the room and sat on the brown leather couch

against the wall. "Are you ready now?" I knew he was giving me time to cool off. I didn't even care that he sucker punched me because I would have done the same to him.

"Why?" I looked over at him and then Kallie, who sat next to him. She wiped her eyes with her thumb, not looking at me. "How?"

"I can't give you those answers," he told me, and all I could do was hang my head. "There is only one person who can give you that, and you know it."

"She lied to me." I wasn't even sure if I was asking him or telling him. All I knew was that it hurt. It hurt all through my bones.

"You have to give her a chance to explain," Kallie said quietly. "I didn't give Jacob a chance, and I lost eight years. Don't do that." I dropped my head back on the chair and closed my eyes. The only thing that played over and over again was the look in her eyes when I told her she wasn't worth it. Even mad, I knew that wasn't the truth. She was worth it all, and she deserved to have it all. "We can take you to her."

I blew out a long breath. "She's going to kick me in the balls and tell me to go fuck myself." I got up and had to hold onto the desk when the room started spinning.

"She's going to kick you in the balls whether you go there now or you go there tomorrow," Jacob said. Leaning forward, he folded his hands in front of him. "You don't want her to go to bed remembering the last words you said."

"Can you take me to her?" I asked.

And now, here I am, standing in the middle of her living room.

"Don't cry," I say, not moving for fear she'll let me go.

"I never wanted you to find out like this," she whispers and sniffles. I want to sit down and have her tell me the whole story. "I never ever wanted you to know."

"Stop crying, please," I say, and she slowly peels her arms from around my neck.

"Sit down," she says, and then she steps back. I watch her walk into her kitchen and go straight for her secret stash of whiskey. I know she doesn't like whiskey, but she bought it for when I come hang out.

"I don't want anything to drink," I say, putting up my hand. She looks so beautiful and tiny. Her brown hair perfectly curled even though I know she hates when it's all done up. She likes it straight and up on her head. Her blue eyes look darker in the dim light than if we were in the sun.

"It's not for you," she says, unscrewing the brown cap and grabbing a glass. She pours the amber liquid into the glass and takes the shot, wincing and coughing after. "I don't know how you drink this." I want to laugh, but all I can do is watch her. She takes another shot as I sit on the couch. Bringing the bottle and the glass with her over to the couch, she sits on the couch facing me and then sets the bottle down and the glass beside it. She pours more into the glass and looks at me. "Liquid courage."

"Before you start, I want you to know that I didn't mean it," I say, having to get it off my chest. Secretly, I want to tell her she is worth everything. She shakes her head, and I watch as the tears fall from her eyes, and it takes all my strength not to get up and go to her. To reach over and wipe her tears from her eyes while I tell her that nothing will change how I feel for her and nothing will ever come between us. But instead, I remain sitting, holding my breath as I wait for her to tell me the story. She looks up at me, and when I see the tears running down her face, I have this fear that my brother did something that I might have to kill him for. If he forced himself on her, I'll kill him with my bare hands.

"I think the best thing is to start at the beginning." She looks down and then up. "I've never told anyone this story." I wonder why she never told Jacob. I want to know why she kept this from me for so long. "I started working at the country club around the same time Liam came home for the summer." She takes the glass in her hand, and this time, she just takes a sip.

"He was his normal arrogant and obnoxious self." She is not wrong with her description of my brother. From as far back as I can remember, my brother was a ... Well, he's a bastard. He always had to win, and he wasn't opposed to cheating to ensure he won. I can count on one hand the times he won fair and square at anything, and then I'd need an army to count all the times he cheated to win. He wanted to be the perfect son in my father's eyes, so he would do whatever was necessary for Father's attention, whereas I couldn't give a fuck. I just did my thing.

"Well, one week in, I had fucked up an order, and this old member was on my ass. Your brother told him to relax, and he actually made it okay." I want to roll my eyes, but she beats me to it.

"I should have known something was up." She shakes her head, taking another sip. "I should have known, but you know me. He started coming into the club every day and being nice to me, so I thought he had changed."

"A leopard doesn't change his spots," I say, and she laughs bitterly.

"Isn't that the truth?" she says, finishing the whiskey and then pouring more in her glass. "He was there one night when I got off my shift, and he walked me to my car. He did that every night for a month." She takes a sip. "Each night, we would spend more time talking by my car, and by the second week, we just ended up sitting on the grass talking." I bite my tongue to keep from adding he lied, but she beat me to it. "He lied. He told me he loved me. It was the first time anyone had ever told me they loved me or held my hand or even hugged me. He was the first one to tell me that I was beautiful." Her eyes fill with tears.

She has to know how beautiful she is and how loved she is. She has to know I would do anything for her.

"He was probably just playing me from day one."

"He's my brother, and the only thing I'm sure of is that you were just a pawn in some game he was playing."

"Well, it figures I would lose my virginity to a man who would turn out to be the biggest waste of time. You were right about some things." She looks at the glass in her hands and then looks at me with a broken stare. "The apple doesn't fall far from the tree." She repeats the words, and my stomach burns.

"Don't say that," I snap, and she looks at me. "Don't say that. You are nothing like your mother." I try to be as respectful as I can toward her mother, but the bottom line is, that woman is a bitch. She literally kicked her daughter out of her house when she was sixteen. Well, she didn't kick Savannah out, but she decided she was going to move, leaving Savannah to find somewhere to live. Who does that?

"Needless to say, the joke was on me when two days later he walks into the country club with this blonde debutant on his arm." Her voice trails off, and she takes another sip. "Yup, his girlfriend was visiting." She shakes her head. "A girlfriend he never mentioned, and I knew nothing about. If I'd known ..." She looks me in the eyes. "If I'd known, I would have never ever gone there with him."

"I know," I reassure her.

"He sat in my section with her." She wipes away the tear from her cheek with the back of her hand. "It was so hard not to throw the glass of water in his face. It also made me feel like I was cheap ... God, he ..." She takes a gulp. "He got down on one knee in front of me and proposed to her. There in the middle of the country club, he proposed to her."

"Son of a bitch," I hiss while she refills her glass. This time, she takes the whole gulp. She must be getting used to it because she swallows without wincing. I wait to hear the rest of the story.

"I found out I was pregnant right away," she continues. "I don't know if you want to hear the rest."

"I want to hear it all," I say, then lean forward, folding my hands together. My stomach suddenly feels sick because I have a feeling I haven't even heard the bad parts yet.

"When I found out, I tried to reach out to your brother. I called, but he wouldn't answer. And then one day, I was stupid enough to seek him out." I can feel the worst part of the story coming. "I thought he would be at your father's office since he came home to be an intern."

She avoids my eyes when she says the next part. "I walked into the house, and your father was just coming into the hallway when he saw me. He looked at me like I was ..." She wipes the tears away. "He told me to follow him into the office, and then he closed the door behind me. At that point, I knew I should have left. I knew that nothing good would come from me being in that room. He walked behind the desk and sat down and asked me what I wanted. I stumbled with my words, before saying I was looking for Liam. It was like he knew. He told me that Liam was gone for the weekend with his fiancée, and that I should find someone else to hang around with." My hands form into fists when I think of what a bastard my father could be. Cold and calculating, he would knock down his own mother to get ahead.

"I told him what I had to discuss with Liam was private." She looks up now, and I see the broken girl who was there eight years ago. The girl who thought she was nothing and would walk with her head down to avoid eye contact. The girl she's fought every single day since then not to be. "I can still hear his bitter laughter in my head, and when he guessed I was pregnant, he stood and walked around the desk. I held my breath, not knowing what he was going to do, but then he put his hand in his pocket and took out two hundred dollar bills." My heart speeds up, and my blood starts to boil. "He threw them at me and told me to take out the trash." Watching her say the words, I know they cut her deep.

"I'll fucking kill him." The words fly out of my mouth, and I don't know who I'm going to hurt first—my father or my brother.

Four

SAVANNAH

"I'll fucking kill him," he hisses. My heart almost explodes in my chest when he flies off the couch. I sit here in shock as he paces in front of me. "I can't ..." he says and pulls his hair. "I can't even believe."

My heart has been in overdrive ever since I started telling my story. I had to take sips of the whiskey in order to continue because thinking back to that time in my life is not something I like to do. It was a dark period when I had no idea what I was doing nor did I realize the consequences of my actions to the people around me.

"Beau." I say his name softly, wanting to get the rest of the story out so I never have to say it again.

"There can't be more," he tells me, and the hurt fills his eyes as the tears fall. "They just wrote off their flesh and blood." He sits next to me, placing his hand on my knee. I know that it's just to comfort me, but I didn't know how much I needed his touch until then.

"I ignored your father and then finally got ahold of your brother." I swallow now and look at the empty glass and wonder how crazy it would be to pour another one. My head is already starting to spin, and I don't know how much more I can drink without blurting out everything.

Telling him that I love him isn't something I want to do on the same night I share my biggest regret. I don't regret Ethan for one single minute, and I never will. The only thing I regret is who the sperm donor was. I lean forward and put the glass down on the table, hoping he doesn't remove his hand from my knee. "I found him the week after. He was coming into the country club, and I told him I needed to speak to him." I close my eyes, ignoring the pain gripping my stomach as I think back to that day. "He looked at me like I was dirt." I avoid his eyes, not ready for him to see that it still affects me.

For my whole life, I've been looked at like I was dirt. Either that or a charity case. Not once has someone or anyone looked at me as just another person. I was always talked about in whispers. "She's the one who Mary Ellen feels sorry for." I would hear that one a lot when I walked into school, and some of the other moms would see me. The pointing was always evident. I tried to ignore it and tried not to let it bother me, but I would always go quiet and not make eye contact. "She's *her* daughter," they would say of my mother. God, that one would get me every single time. I would have to blink away the tears so fast that sometimes they would sneak out, and I would suddenly have "allergies." But my favorite has always been, "She's the one who ruined everything." That one has been at the top for the past eight years along with the finger-pointing, the rude stares, and the blatant hatred worn on their face.

"When I finally told him ..." My hands start to shake. "He told me it could be anyone's, and it can't be his since it was only one time."

"What a fucking moron," Beau hisses. Leaning back on the couch, he scratches his face with his hands and then looks at me. I have to stop talking for a second because all I want to do is lean back into his arms. I want him to wrap his arm around my shoulder like he does during scary movies. But instead, I take a deep breath and tell him the rest.

"I wasn't with anyone else," I say, looking down. "He was my first. He was my only." God, I can't believe I confessed that last part. He didn't have to know that, but since I'm already telling him my deepest, darkest secret, I might as well tell him the rest. The minute I say the words, I see the look on his face and the questions that are forming. I've been on dates, but they have never even gotten past first base. I tried, but the reality was, none of them were Beau.

"You don't have to." He looks at me, and I avoid his eyes.

"After he said that, I knew that I was going to be in this alone. I just ..." I put my hand to my stomach the same way I did eight years ago. "I went over it in my head for a week. I even went so far as to tell my mother."

"Oh, good God," Beau says and rolls his eyes. He isn't wrong.

"Yeah, that's a story for another day. Needless to say, she told me that I would ruin my life by having a baby." I have to get up now to say the rest of my story, the nerves running through me, but the minute I stand, the room spins, and I fall back onto the couch.

"No more whiskey," I say, and he smiles at me for the first time since he's gotten here. But I can't sit, so I try to get up again, and this time, I get my balance right.

"I scheduled an appointment and went to the doctor. I sat in that waiting room." I close my eyes, and I'm back in the bleak room with white walls and the blue plastic chairs. No pictures even hung on the wall. It was the most depressing room I've ever been in, and you have to think that there is no way it would ever be a happy place anyway. "I sat in the waiting room by myself, and I just kept telling myself that this was the only choice. It was the only choice." I wipe the tear off my face, but another follows right after. "They called my name, and I got up, but something just ..." I shake my head. "I couldn't do it. I just, he was the size of a pea, but I already loved him more than anything in the world."

I walk over to the fireplace and look at the picture sitting on the mantel. It's the first picture they took of Ethan when they placed him on my chest. I will never forget that feeling. It was an all-consuming love, a love I could never put into words. "That night was prom." My finger traces Ethan in the picture. I turn to look at him, and he sits there, looking like he wants to jump up and grab me, but he knows I have to get this out. "I didn't know what to do. I didn't know who to go to." I shake my head. "No," I say. "I'm lying. I wanted to come to you." I'm going to blame the whiskey for that slip. His mouth opens, but I don't give him a chance to say anything. "I wanted to run straight to you but ..." I shake my head. "I just couldn't tell you. I didn't want to see the look of disgust on your face."

He jumps up now, and before I even know what is happening, his hands are on my arms. "I would never ever do that to you," he says, his voice high, and he moves his face closer to me. He pulls me to his chest, and for the first time ever, I sob while someone holds me. For the first time, I have someone holding me up, and I am not standing by myself.

"I'm so sorry, Savannah." I wrap my arms around his waist. "It's over," he tells me with one hand holding my head.

Standing here in the middle of the living room, he holds me as I cry. This man who has been by my side since I can remember, this man who loves with his whole heart, this man who I would do anything for. "I'm sorry that I ruined your big night," I say into his soaked shirt. My ear rests on his chest, and I listen to his heart beating. "I never wanted you to find out like that." He just rubs my back. Neither of us says anything when his phone rings in his pocket. He ignores it, but then it rings again, and I step out of his arms.

"You should get that," I say and try to smile. "You're the mayor now."

He shakes his head and takes the phone out of his back pocket. "Fuck that," he says, declining the call. He looks at me. "It's my father."

"You should answer him," I say, and his phone beeps in his hand.

He looks down and then up at me. "Emergency family meeting. Tomorrow morning."

"Oh my God," I say, putting my hand to my stomach. "Do you think they know?"

"I have no idea," he says, tossing his phone on the couch. "Regardless of that, I'm going to tell him I know tomorrow," he says, and I suddenly get nervous because I didn't tell him everything. "What?" he asks me, putting his hands on his hips. "Don't tell me there is more."

"Well …" I look down and then look up. "There is only one more thing," I say but think to myself, *Well, two if I tell him I love him*.

"Should I sit down?" he asks, and I wonder if he should or not. "Savannah, you being quiet is not helping anything."

I shake my hands now to stop them and walk away from him. "Well …" I try to think of a way to tell him this next part. "I kind of …" I rub my face. "I blackmailed your father."

He looks at me in shock. "What?" He shakes his head. "What did you just say?"

"Well, when I couldn't go through with the abortion, and Jacob took responsibility for it, he came to see me." I look at him. "And he told me that he knew I was lying and all this shit." I get so aggravated. "And then he might have, you know, called me a whore." I roll my eyes now while Beau hisses. "Anyway, he got me mad, so I told him that I would tell the whole town, and I would sue Liam for paternity, and with that, I'd make sure he paid for the rest of his life."

"You didn't," he asks, almost in a whisper.

"Oh, I did, too." I fold my hands over my chest. "I had nothing to lose. The town hated me, Jacob secretly blamed me for Kallie leaving, and you ..." I shrug. "You stopped talking to me. I had nothing to lose."

"So what did he do?"

"He wrote me a check for three hundred thousand and made me sign an NDA and also made Liam sign a paper relinquishing his rights as father."

"Incredible." He rubs his face and sits down on the couch. "He basically sold his kid for three hundred thousand dollars."

"Enough for me to buy the bar and this house," I say, looking around, "and some of the furniture."

"My head is spinning," he says, leaning back on the couch. "This night isn't ending like I thought it would." I try not to let his words hurt me or wonder what he means by that. I know that he dates, and he goes out often. The girls he dates are not quiet about it either. I've gotten drunk many nights while a couple of them were sitting at the bar talking to their friends about him.

"I'm going to wash my face," I say and avoid his eyes. I walk to my bedroom and go straight to my master bathroom and turn on the water. I shouldn't have looked at myself in the mirror because when I do, I see that my eyes are puffy, my nose is red, and my hair looks ragged. After I wash my face, I slip out of the dress and hang it up, then put on my yoga pants and a tank top.

When I walk back out, I see he hasn't moved from the couch, and when I walk around the couch, I see that he's sleeping. I grab the cover that I was wrapped up in before and place it over him. He stirs for just a minute, and when I turn to walk away, he grabs my hand and pulls me down to him.

His eyes never open, but he puts his arm around me and pulls me to him. My head falls on his shoulder, and he kisses the side of my head. "I'm sorry," he mumbles. My eyes fly to his, and he wraps his other arm around me. He mumbles something else, and then he falls back asleep. I put my arm around his stomach, and my eyes slowly close.

Five

BEAU

Something tickles my face, and I reach out and brush it away, but then I feel a heaviness on me, so I slowly open my eyes. I'm on my back on a couch, and when I look down, all I see is brown hair. Savannah's sprawled over me, and my cock is happy about this. She moans, and when I look down, she hitches her leg up around my hips. I swear my cock is going to break down the zipper to get at her. Closing my eyes, I try to think about anything but her, but when she moans and then stretches, I almost toss her off me and jump up. We've fallen asleep on the couch together before, but I've never woken up with her in my arms.

"Morning," she mumbles. I look down at her, and she's blinking her eyes open and then closing them again. Yesterday was a day I would love to forget. Apart from the time I thought she slept with my best friend, this was the worst day of my life.

"Morning," I mumble. I wait for her to get up and take her hand off my waist. I also hold my breath, waiting for her to drag her leg off my hip. I'm hoping when she does that, she doesn't feel my cock.

25

"Are you stiff?" she asks, and I look down at her, my palms suddenly super sweaty. Her head moves from my chest as she looks up at me. "Is your neck sore from sleeping with no pillow?"

"Oh." I let out a sigh of relief that she isn't asking about my other stiff member. "No, it's fine."

When she gets up off me, her legs gently brush my cock, and my eyes fly to hers to see if she felt it. I start to come up with excuses in my head, but what excuse could I come up with?

"I'll make coffee," she mumbles, and I lie on the couch, watching her perfect ass walk away. I put my hand over my head and stare up at the ceiling that I helped paint last year. I then turn my head and see her standing in the kitchen just off the family room. She opens the cabinets and takes down two mugs, and I have to smile. Last year when we took Ethan to Disney, she bought me the Beast mug from *Beauty and the Beast*. I kept forgetting to grab it, so it's been here ever since. Every time she makes me coffee, it's in that mug. I sit up on the couch and rub my hands over my face and stand. My body screams as my muscles feel tight. Fuck, I guess sleeping on this couch did leave me stiff, and I groan.

"Did you want to take a shower?" she asks over her shoulder.

"Yeah," I say, walking to the kitchen, and the smell of fresh coffee fills the air.

"I still have your clothes from last time," she says, going to the fridge and getting her hazelnut creamer. "They are in my closet."

The last time I came over, it was right after one of my meetings, I was dressed in a suit and Ethan wanted to go to the park. Luckily, I had my gym bag in the car, so I changed and left my clothes here by accident. "I washed and ironed them."

She hands me the cup of coffee, and I sit down at the island. She stands on the other side and holds her own cup of coffee in her hand, taking a sip and then putting it down. She grabs her hair and ties it on top of her head, leaving her tanned neck open, and I know exactly where I would want to kiss her. "What time is your meeting?"

"Ten," I say. "But I'll get there when I get there. They can both fuck off."

"Um." She looks down, and I see that she is blinking fast, which means she is about to cry. I can't take her crying anymore. She's cried enough to last two lifetimes; it's time for her to smile. "I don't want to get in the middle."

"Savannah," I say her name, but she doesn't look up at me. "Look at me, sweetheart." Her head slowly comes up, and I see the same look she had last night. The turmoil, the hurt, the pain, all of the stress on her shoulders. "You did nothing wrong."

"I can't do it." She blinks and then swallows slowly. "I can't regret it. Ethan, he's ..."

"He's the best kid there is, and he's got the best father," I say, and she just nods. I get up, grabbing my coffee. "I'm going to head to the shower."

"Okay," she whispers. "I bought you new shower stuff." Say what you want about her, but she has to have the biggest heart, and she takes care of the people she cares about. We've been best friends forever, and in the past seven years, we've gotten even closer. I've been around for the colic and the teething. I've spent more nights on her couch than I can count, and we've eaten dinner together most nights of the week.

Walking down the hall to the door right next to Ethan's bedroom, I enter the bathroom and close the door behind me. I spend extra time in the shower, letting the hot water run down my neck, and when I get out, I grab a towel and then wrap it around my waist. As I open the door, I hold the towel at the side to make sure it doesn't slip down. I smell bacon as soon as I head to the kitchen, and when she sees me, her mouth falls open. "I forgot to grab my clothes." Walking to her room, I go into her small walk-in closet and spot the white button-down shirt hanging over the pair of blue pants right away. I walk back into the bathroom, then slip on my boxers and finish getting dressed.

When I walk back out, she's sitting at the island eating, and a plate is right next to her with food piled on it for me. "You didn't have to make breakfast," I say, sitting down next to her, and she looks over.

"I figured you would need your strength." She tries to joke, but it comes out with a sob, and I take her in my arms.

"Why are you crying?" I ask her as she lays her head on my shoulder.

"I don't want to lose you," she says so softly that if she wasn't whispering in my ear, I wouldn't have heard her.

"You won't lose me," I say. I don't add that she'll never lose me. *You won't ever lose me because I love you right down to the depth of my soul.* She pulls away from me and gets off her stool.

"You should eat." She grabs her still full plate and walks to the sink, throwing it out. "I'm going to get in the shower." I want to go after her, but how do I do that without telling her how I feel? I get up and grab my phone from the coffee table. I send Jacob a text.

Me: Family meeting at the mayor's office.

He answers right away.

Jacob: Do you need backup?
Me: Not sure, but you'll be the first one I call.
Jacob: I'll be here.

When she comes out of the bathroom wearing her jean

shorts and a white tank top, I'm just putting my dish in the dishwasher. "Can I borrow your car?" I ask. "I can come back after so you can go to work."

"That's okay. I can get a ride to the bar," she says. My stomach burns with nerves. "Will you call me?"

"As soon as I can," I say, and she hands me the keys to her truck. "Don't worry, nothing is going to touch you." Reassuring her, I lean in and kiss her cheek, but it's very close to her lips, which is where I really want to kiss her. When I walk out of the house, the sun is high in the sky, and the heat is starting to fill the air. I make my way over to my new office in Savannah's truck, and when I pull up, I see that my father and brother are already there. I get out of the truck and walk up the steps to the front door. When I walk into the house, the cool air hits me right away, and I look over at my new secretary. Well, the secretary I inherited from my father.

"Morning, Mayor," Bonnie says and smiles at me. She must be in her early thirties, and she looks like a debutante for sure. Southern to a T with her hair curled perfectly and her nails an acceptable length with a nude color on them. "Your father and brother are already in there. Would you like coffee?"

"No, thank you," I say as I walk to the office door and open it. Stepping into the room, I see that my brother is wearing khaki pants with a white polo and a khaki jacket. He even looks like a douche sitting there on the couch. I see a tumbler in his hand already, and I have no doubt it's not his first drink this morning.

He turns his head to look at me. "Nice of you to show up," he sneers and takes a sip of his drink. Looking toward my desk, I find my father sitting behind it. At one time, I wanted to be like my father because I thought he was the perfect father.

The three of us look exactly the same except my father's black hair has now turned white. He looks at me with narrowed eyes, and I see in front of him the paper that I had clutched in my hand last night. Then I look over at the wall but find the mess of the bottle from last night has been cleaned up.

"You're sitting in my chair," I say, and he just looks at me.

"That is the least of my worries today," my father says, pressing the button on the phone.

When Bonnie answers, he says, "We are having a meeting, and there are to be no interruptions," and releases the button.

"No interruptions." I laugh bitterly now. "What's the matter? You don't want to tell the whole town that your sorry excuse of a son isn't man enough to take responsibility for his actions?"

"What did you just say?" Liam says as he gets up and walks to me. I can smell the whiskey on him as if he bathed in it.

I go toe-to-toe with him. "How could you just walk away from your own flesh and blood?" I ask. "How could you?" Then I turn and look at my father. "And how could you live in a town and see him all the time and not want to get to know your own grandson?" I shake my head. "How the fuck can you do it?"

"Please," Liam says, rolling his eyes. "We don't even know for sure it's my kid." My hands flex into fists, but I try to keep my cool. "For all I know, she spreads her legs for everyone." I don't even think before I grab his shirt in my hands and yank him toward me. He's taller than I am, but he's lanky whereas I'm built like an ox thanks to the time I spend in the gym lifting weights.

"Let him go," my father says, getting up and coming over to us. "This is exactly what she wants," he hisses. I let go of my brother and turn to look at my father.

I hope he sees the hatred in my eyes. "You think she wants anything?" I ask him. "You think after you threw two hundred dollar bills in her face that she would want anything to do with you?" I laugh.

"Well, then I see she told you all about it," my father says, and he puts his hands in his pockets. "She signed an NDA."

"Who the fuck cares what she signed? She gave birth to your grandson. Does that not even register in your head?" I say, my voice getting louder. "How can you do that?"

"Oh, please," Liam says. "If you ask me, she got the better end of the deal." He walks back to his drink and takes it down in one gulp. "She wasn't even that good."

Yup, whatever control I had has snapped. I charge over to him, and my fist flies before he can register what is happening and falls back onto the couch. "You hit me!" His hand comes to his nose that is now pouring blood. "You broke my fucking nose!"

"Be happy I didn't break all your fucking teeth, you worthless piece of shit," I hiss, then turn to my father, who looks shocked by my behavior. I've always been the calm son. The son who did what his father said and never asked questions. "And, you." I look at my father, shaking my head. "You're even worse than he is."

"Tread lightly, son," he orders me. "I would hate to have to do something that you would regret."

"Fuck you," I tell my father, and he just glares at me. "You think you can stand in front of me and threaten me?"

"She is in default of her NDA agreement," my father says calmly, thinking he has an ace up his sleeve.

"Good. Fucking sue her then. Let the whole fucking town know that my drunk and sorry excuse of a brother fathered a good kid. That she blackmailed you"—I point at him—"into keeping her silence. I'm sure the town would love to hear all of the secrets that you have buried in your closet, Father," I say with disgust. Before I can say anything else, there is a knock on the door.

"Come in," I say, looking at my father. "This is my office after all."

When the door swings open, Jacob stands there, and I can see the rage on his face. "Savannah's bar was vandalized," he says, and I turn to look at my father, who stands there saying nothing.

Six

SAVANNAH

I knew something was off the minute I got out of Jacob's truck and saw the two potted plants that I keep beside the door tossed over. "What the heck?" I say, getting out of the truck and walking through the gravel parking lot. Only when I get close enough to the front of the door do I see the red spray paint.

TOWN WHORE

"What the fuck?" Jacob says from beside me. I look over at him, then I see what looks like a broken window at the end of the bar. I bought this bar seven years ago. It was half the size and in disrepair. When the owner asked for ten thousand dollars, I knew he didn't even make that in revenue that year. But I saw things he didn't, and I had a plan for the small twelve-by-twelve bar. He sold the land to me for an extra ten thousand and thought he was robbing me blind. But little did he know that five years later, I would be raking in close to half a million dollars a year, and that my country bar would be the place to be.

I take the keys out of my pocket and unlock the big blue door, gasping when I open it. "Oh my God," I say, stepping in.

All the bottles behind the bar and the glasses have been smashed on the floor. The stools that sit in front of the long bar are tossed over and all over each other. The wooden tables look like they've been thrown around. I take a step in, and the sound of glass crunches under my cowboy boots.

"Don't touch anything," Jacob says. He walks to the side, taking out his phone and calling Grady, his second in command. "Yeah, get the crew together and meet me at Savannah's bar." He listens and then looks around. "It's been trashed."

I can't stop the tears from rolling down my cheeks as I look around. I'm so angry that this still gets to me. I'm angry that someone trashed the place that I've worked my ass off to make successful, and I'm yet again the brunt of the hatred of this town. I built this bar up and expanded it five times since I bought it, bringing in something new each time. I walk over to the back where I have the pool tables and see that whoever did this also took their frustrations out on the tables and sliced the word whore in each table. "Was your alarm on?" Jacob asks, and I nod my head.

I walk over to the alarm system and see that it's off and no lights are on. "We set it every single night," I say, and he walks outside to check it. I walk over to the bar area, and I don't know why, but the sight makes me feel like I've been kicked in the stomach. All the bottles and glasses are shattered on the floor. I walk over to the side and see that my office door is still closed. I'm expecting to find that trashed, too, but my desk is perfectly neat, the way I left it, and the safe is still intact. Closing the door, I walk over and grab the broom to start sweeping up the glass. I ignore the pain in my chest, the tears running down my face, and the burning in my stomach. I ignore it all because this is what I deserve. It's what I've convinced myself I deserve for ruining everyone's life with my choices.

The front door opens, and Jacob enters with Grady behind him. "The wires were cut," he says, and I hear Grady hiss.

"What the fuck?" He looks around, then looks at me. "The guys should be here any minute. We'll get this place good as new."

"You have to call the insurance," Jacob tells me, and I just nod.

"I'll take pictures," Grady says, "for the report and the insurance agent." He takes out his phone and starts taking the pictures.

"Are you okay?" Jacob asks from beside me.

"Between last night and this?" I say. "It might just be the thing that makes me walk away."

"You don't mean that," he says. "After everything that this town put you through, you would walk away now?"

"There are only so many times I can be kicked and then stand back up," I say, and Grady comes over.

"I got off the phone with the alarm company. According to them, your alarm is still armed, and there has been no activity."

The front door opens, and I cringe when I see who comes in. Chase Patterson, the man who I went on one date with and the man who just kept showing up at my bar. He was new in town and had just started a construction company. If truth be told, I only went out with him because he asked me in front of Beau. It was right after Beau went out with Melody from the bank, and I had to listen to her go on and on about how big he was and how he didn't fit properly.

"Hey there," I say. He looks around, putting his hands to his mouth. He's dressed in blue Levi's, a white T-shirt with the logo of his construction company on the right side, and construction boots. "We aren't open for business." I try to make a joke, and he gives me a blank stare.

"Are you okay?" he asks, sounding concerned, and I suddenly feel bad for agreeing to go out on a date with him. For sure, I shouldn't have gone on that second date.

"Yeah, I'm fine," I say, looking around. "The rest of it is just superficial."

"What can I do to help?" he asks.

"Nothing really." I don't want to ask him for anything. "I just have to call the insurance, and then I can start to get things cleaned up."

"Okay," he says. "Give me a call if you need anything." I nod and smile at him. "Maybe I can take you out next week once you get everything settled."

I take a deep inhale. "You're a really nice guy," I start. He puts his hand up, but I ignore it and continue talking. "But I don't really have time to date."

"Well," he says with a smile, and I look at his brown eyes and blondish brown hair. "Let me know if you change your mind."

"I will," I say, and he turns and walks out. I look up at the ceiling and then look down.

"FYI," Jacob says, "it really sucks when you start with you're a really nice guy."

I turn to look at him. "I think it's better than 'sorry I just went out with you because the man who I loved was dating a girl, and she went on and on about how big his dick was.'"

Jacob looks at me, and his mouth opens. "He's not that big."

"Did you hear anything else I said in that sentence?" I ask, and he shakes his head.

"Speaking of Beau, I should go and make sure he's okay," he says. "Do you think you'll be okay while I go?"

"Yeah." I look around. "I'll be fine," I say, and he leaves. Walking back to my office, I sit behind my desk and grab my insurance folder to call in the claim. I answer all the agent's basic questions, and then she tells me that someone will contact me shortly. I hang up the phone and push away from the desk. There is one thing that I want to make sure is cleaned off. I find a bucket and fill it with water and a bit of soap, then grab a sponge and walk outside.

The humidity in the air is thick as I set down the pail of water and then walk to the back where I keep my ladders and stuff. Grabbing the ladder, I walk over to the side of the building and prop it against the wall. I bend over and grab the sponge, then squeeze it. Climbing the ladder, I hold on with one hand. I stop when the red comes into view, and I use the sponge to wipe it down. I don't know how long I'm actually on the ladder, but the side of the bar now looks pink. I'm about to head back down and rinse the sponge when I hear tires on the gravel parking lot. Looking over, I see Jacob's truck pull in followed by my truck and out jumps a very pissed off Beau.

"What the hell are you trying to do?" he yells, and I can't see his eyes because he's wearing his stupid aviator glasses which only make him look hotter. "Would you get the fuck down from there before you break your neck?"

I shake my head. "I'm fine," I say, climbing down the ladder and dropping the sponge into the water turning it pink.

"Your shirt," he says, pointing at my shirt. I look down and see that the front is all wet and see-through.

"Oh my God," I say, folding my arms over my breasts and turning around. "Stop looking."

"Go and see if you can change," he says, and I look over at Jacob, who just rolls his lips to keep from grinning. "And we can get something to eat."

"I'm really not hungry," I say, looking down, and he just looks at me. "What?"

"You are always hungry," he points out, and I roll my eyes at him. It's annoying that he knows me so well.

"Well, I'm not today," I say. Walking past him, I stop in front of Jacob. "Can you get Ethan today? I want to make sure that the inside is cleaned and all that before I leave."

"Yeah, no problem," Jacob says. "We were going to ask you if we can take him up north this weekend anyway."

"That's perfect," I say and walk away from them. Going inside, I finally drop my arms from across my chest. Heading to my office, I close the door and take the wet shirt off, putting on a black tank top with the bar's name across my chest. I walk out of the room, and I see Beau there in the middle of the room with his hand covering his mouth.

"This ..." he says. "This is." I blink my eyes, trying not to think about it.

"Yeah," I say and walk over to the broom, trying not to look at him.

"Savannah." He calls my name, and the way he says it just makes my heart fill up. "Look at me."

"No," I say. He's seen enough of my tears. I grab the broom and start to sweep, hoping that he walks away. But instead, I feel him coming closer. His hand stops the broom from sweeping, and then he places his finger under my chin. I try to fight it, but he doesn't let me, and I finally look up at him, and he sees the tears running down my cheeks. "Please."

He brushes the strands of hair falling out of my bun away from my forehead with his pinky. "Please what?"

"Please, I don't want to talk about this," I say, my lower lip trembling as I try to be strong. "I don't want to talk about it. I don't want to think about it. All I want to do is clean it up so I can put it behind me." His hand moves down to my cheek as he brushes the tear away, and I finally let it out. "I don't know how much longer I can do this." I admit my biggest fear to him. "I don't know how much longer I can stay in this town." I drop the broom. "At first, I stayed to show them that it didn't bother me, but now ..." I shrug. "But now, I don't think I have it in me."

"You can't let them win," he tells me quietly.

"But when am I going to win?" I ask. "When is it my turn to be happy? When do I get to walk down the street with my head held high and not get pointed and stared at?" My voice quivers. "When is it my turn to walk into a place and have people greet me with a smile instead of a sneer?" He takes me into his arms now, and for the second time in two days, he holds me as I cry my fears and shame away.

Seven

BEAU

I hold her in my arms as she cries, and nothing I can say will make her feel better.

When Jacob busted into my office and told me about the vandalism, I turned to my brother right away.

"If you did this ..." I pointed at him, and he held up one of his hands while the other pinched his nose.

"I wouldn't waste my time and energy on her," he said, and I looked over at my father, who just glared at me. I turned and started to walk out when my father called my name.

"You aren't leaving in the middle of a family meeting for ..." He looked at Jacob and then back at me. *"That woman."*

Jacob was the one I had to hold back this time. *"Let's be very clear here."* My voice came out in a low growl. *"That woman trumps both of you. So, to answer your question, yes, I am leaving because to me, she's family."* I turned but only for a minute before turning back. *"You need to get the fuck out of my office."* My father glared at me. *"Now."*

"You're unbelievable." Liam held a handkerchief to his nose. *"You wouldn't even be in this office without him."* He pointed at my father, and I rolled my eyes.

"You wouldn't be the worthless piece of shit that you are without him." I pointed at my father. "Now get the fuck out." I waited at the door, and my father reluctantly walked to the door, stopping to look at me.

"I would choose your side wisely," he said under his breath.

"See, that is where you and I differ. I choose my family's side," I said. Leaning in, I whispered, "And her having my nephew means she's family." I shut the door and looked at Bonnie. "I don't want anyone going into my office when I'm not here." She looked at me and then at my father, waiting. "If that will be a problem, I can find someone else to take your position." I didn't wait for her to answer. Instead, I turned and walked out of the house and down the steps.

"Dude," Jacob said from beside me. "I thought your father was going to ..." He stopped when I turned around.

"I don't care. What happened at Savannah's?" I asked, and he looked down.

"It's all trashed." His voice went low with the rest of it. "And some not nice words were painted on the side of the bar."

"Fuck," I hissed. "How fucking long is this going to go on for? It's been eight fucking years." I didn't wait for him to answer. Instead, I got my ass in her truck and made my way to her.

Now I'm standing in the middle of the bar, and my heart breaks for her. "Why don't you go wash your face, and we can go grab something to eat at my house?"

"Okay," she mumbles, and her voice just sounds defeated. She walks to the back of the bar where the bathroom is, and once she's out of earshot, I pick up the phone and call Tony, the town's contractor.

"Hey there, Mr. Mayor," Tony answers right away, laughing. "One day in the office and you're already on my balls." I have to laugh now. Tony has been in this town for over twenty years. He moved here when he was just twenty and out of school. He started his business slowly, and over the years, he's gotten all of the town's contracts. From the looks of every-thing that I've seen, he does his job, and he does it under budget, which is what you want.

"I'm not calling on official business," I say and then look to make sure that Savannah hasn't come back yet. "It's more of a personal favor."

"That sounds like a favor I want," he says. "It's always a good day when the higher-up owes you instead of the other way around."

I laugh now. "I need you guys to come out to Savannah's bar and fix it. Someone broke in last night and vandalized the place really good." I take a look around, and my stomach sinks again just as it did when I stepped in and assessed the situation.

"Um …" His voice goes low, and then he lets out a deep breath. "I can't."

My shoulders snap up, and my neck gets tingly. "What do you mean, you can't?"

"Listen, I don't want to be put in the middle," Tony says.

"In the middle of what?" I ask, and somehow what he tells me isn't a surprise.

"Got a call from your father about twenty minutes ago," he starts. His voice goes even lower, and I have to wonder if he doesn't want people to know he's on the phone with me. "If I so much as step foot on that property, my contract bid for the rec center is going to be passed to someone else."

"Motherfucker," I hiss. "Listen to me and listen to me good, Tony. My father has no say anymore. He has zero say in how I run my office."

"I didn't mean any disrespect."

"Your bid has already been approved for the rec center. It's been approved and has been recorded in the minutes at the last meeting." I shake my head.

"Minutes can be altered," he says. "Wouldn't be the first time."

"You have my word," I say, "that nothing will happen to your contract."

He huffs. "Fine," he says. "I'll bring a couple of guys with me."

"Thank you." I close my eyes. "I appreciate that. Also, I want you to bill me personally."

"You bet your ass I'm going to bill you personally and also as an emergency case. If the contract still stands, I'll adjust my invoice." His voice goes lower. "FYI, he's made other calls."

"What does that mean?" I ask.

"Let's just say, it's going to be hard for her to get anything to open that place again," he says. The bathroom door opens, and I see Savannah coming out with a brown paper in her hands.

"Thanks for letting me know," I say and hang up the phone. "Are you okay?"

"No." She shakes her head and looks at me, her blue eyes so bright you can get lost in them. "But it is what it is, and I'll deal with whatever I have to."

"There's my girl," I say, smiling at her. I grab her around her neck and bring her to me, kissing her forehead. The two of us have always been touchy-feely around each other, and I never make it seem that I love it more than I do. I just shrug it off and leave her after I either hold her hand or kiss her head. "Now what do you want to eat?"

She shakes her head. "Anything. I just don't want to see anyone."

"Got it," I say. We walk out of the bar, and she locks it and gets into the truck. When she pulls up in front of my house, I wait for her to turn off the truck before getting out, and she follows me up the front steps of the old Victorian house I inherited from my grandfather when he passed away ten years go. I've only just renovated it and made it more mine and less antique. I walk in, tossing my keys on the table in the foyer, and then head down the hallway past the stairs and into the kitchen.

"I forget how pretty it is in here," Savannah says, walking toward the back wall of windows as it faces out to two old willow trees with a hammock hanging between them. Something I put in for Savannah but never told her. She once told me when we were walking how her perfect date would be sitting in a hammock together and just listening to the birds or the crickets.

She turns around now and comes into the kitchen with me and opens the fridge. "Oh my God. What is that smell?" she asks, putting her hand in front of her nose.

"I have no idea," I say, and I cringe when I see all sort of food gone bad. "I don't usually eat here." She walks over to grab the garbage and starts tossing shit in the bin. "I usually crash at your house for dinner, or we go out."

"Yeah, we should definitely be eating here more." She shakes her head, and I want to tell her that she can come and eat here every single day if she wants to.

"The door is always open." I smile at her, and I want to bend my head and kiss her, but the doorbell rings. She looks at me, and I shake my head, turning and walking out of the kitchen and past the dining room and formal living room toward the big brown doors. I open the door and groan inwardly.

"Well, hello there, Mayor," Melody says, pushing her way in and leaning up to kiss my lips. It happens so fast that I don't have time to step back. I made the mistake of agreeing to go out with her on a date, and the minute I sat down, I knew that it was a one-and-done sort of date.

"Melody." I say her name and look at her. She's wearing a

tight red dress that has her breasts practically falling out of it. "I didn't know you were stopping by."

"Well, I tried to get to you at the party, but you disappeared, so I figured I'd drop by to congratulate you in person." She steps in closer, and I take a step back.

"It's really not a good time," I say.

"You've been saying that for weeks." She uses her finger to run down my chest. "I thought we had fun."

I want to tell her the last thing we had was fun. It was one dinner, and I kissed her on the cheek and then spent the night trying to wash the smell of her off me. Besides, she was like an octopus the whole night, and I felt like I was at a kung fu class. "Listen, Melody ..." I start to say, but she wraps her arms around my neck, and before I can peel them off me, I see Savannah standing off to the side. My head turns to her, and it makes Melody turn also. "Oh, hey, Savannah," she says, not taking her arms from around my neck. "I didn't know you were here."

"Yeah," she says, avoiding my eye contact and forcing a fake smile on her face. "I was just leaving," she says, walking toward the door. "I'll just leave you two be." She nods, and she is out of the house before I can even do or say anything.

"Well, now that we are alone ..." Melody says, and I can swear her hips thrust forward, making my cock duck for cover.

I slowly peel her arms away from my neck, and she looks at me confused. "Listen, Melody, I don't really have time for a relationship right now. I just became mayor, and I want to focus on that."

"But ..." she says, trying to think of something to say. "It doesn't have to be anything serious." She winks at me. "We could be friends." Her voice goes low. "With benefits."

"I couldn't do that," I say, and she crosses her arms over her chest, pushing her tits up even higher.

"I know about Teressa," she tells me, and I look at her, pinching my eyebrows together.

"Teressa, the woman who works at the bank?" I ask. She's the teller who always serves me.

"You don't have to pretend. I know that you guys have your dates, or shall we say rendezvous on Wednesday, and I—" I hold up my hand now.

"I have no idea what you're talking about, but there has never been anything with me and Teressa, nor has there been anything with any woman in this town." I don't mention that it's been a fucking long time since I've been with a woman. After I found out about Jacob and Savannah, I went after anyone I could get. I had sex just to have sex, hoping that I would get that connection with someone, but it all amounted to nothing. It always came back to the woman I wanted who I thought slept with my best friend.

"But," she says, and I shake my head.

"How about we forget that we had this conversation?" I try to make her feel better and less embarrassed about this whole thing. My phone starts ringing in my pocket, and I see that it's Jacob. "I really have to get this."

She looks down at the floor. "Of course, I'll get out of the way." She turns and walks to the door. "But the offer is on the table."

She turns and opens the door and walks out, and I let out the breath I was holding. The only thing I can think of doing is getting to Savannah when I answer the call.

Eight

SAVANNAH

I shouldn't have walked out of the house like a child having a tantrum, but I just couldn't stand there and watch it. I've seen it enough over the years from afar that I didn't want to see it in front of my face. Instead, I make my way over to the bar. Pulling up, I spot Tony and his construction van, holding his clipboard in his hand. He looks over when I get out of the truck.

"Hey there." I put my hand up in a wave, walking over to him.

"Hey, Savannah." He smiles big. He usually comes into the bar every weekday night at six to grab a beer before going home. Sometimes on Saturday, he comes in with his wife, but it's a rare thing.

"If you are here for your nightly beer." I smile at him. "You're fresh out of luck," I joke with him.

"I'm not here for that." He shakes his head. "I got a call from Beau." It shocks me that Beau would have called him already. "Decided to see if we could help."

I look at him shocked and speechless. "That is really kind of you." I look over at the bar. "But I can pay for it."

47

He nods. "Now that you're here, you can show me inside."

"Sure." I turn, making my way into the bar. After opening the door, I hear Tony whistle from beside me as he takes in the scene. The destruction still shocks me. "I tried to clean up some of it." I walk in and pick up a chair. "But"—I shrug—"I didn't get far."

"Wow." He looks around, taking it in. "They didn't miss anything."

"Nope." I shake my head while he writes things on his clipboard. I pick up a couple of chairs, then walk over to the bar and decide to sweep up all the bottles.

Thirty minutes later, Tony comes over while I finish sweeping the broken glass into a box. "I'm going to head out," he says. "We'll be here tomorrow bright and early."

"Okay." I smile at him. "I'll see what I can get done tonight, and I'll also be here tomorrow."

"See you then." He turns and walks out of the door. I squat down to clean up the remainder of the mess. I grab a notepad to take inventory of the glasses that are left. I'm about to put the pad down when the door swings open, and I look up, seeing Beau coming in with two bags in his hands. I try not to look surprised, but I'm sure that I fail miserably.

"What are you doing here?" I ask, setting the pad down on the bar top.

"I went by your house, and you weren't there," he says, walking in. "I figured you came back here, so I got you dinner." He lifts his arms.

"You didn't have to do that," I say, wondering what the fuck happened with Melody. Not that I care because he's free to do what he wants. But still.

"I know I didn't have to," he says, looking around for a place to put the food. He walks over and puts the bags down on the bar. Walking around the bar, he grabs a rag, wetting it and then wiping the bar down. He's always helped me close on the weekends and any other time he's in here. Most nights, he even helps bus the tables. "I wanted to." He tosses the rag into the sink and then turns to look at me.

"I got you your favorite," he says, taking a Styrofoam container out of the bag. "Meatloaf." He puts it on the counter. "Mashed potatoes." He takes out another one. "Fries." I look at him. "And slaw."

"You are too good to me." I shake my head, walking around the counter and picking up two stools for us to sit on. "Also thank you." I slide onto one stool, and he slides onto the stool next to me.

"Well, I promised you dinner." I look over at him. "And you ran out of the house like your tail was on fire."

I roll my eyes and try to pretend it didn't bother me. "I did not. Your girlfriend showed up. I wasn't going to stay around and be the third wheel."

Opening the container and grabbing a plastic fork, he takes a bite. "She is not my girlfriend," he says, grabbing his own fork. "She's just someone I went on a date with."

My stomach almost turns over, the meatloaf in my mouth suddenly tasting sour. "Whatever," I say, nudging my shoulder against him. "You don't have explain your dating situation to me."

"There is nothing to explain." He chews. "We went out on one date."

"Oh, come on," I joke with him. "You went on five dates with her in three weeks."

He looks over at me. "You've been keeping tabs on me?" His eyes light up just a touch, and a smile forms across his lips, but before I can say anything, the door opens, and we both look over our shoulder.

"Sorry," Chase says. "I didn't mean to interrupt. I just thought you might be hungry," he says, holding up a bag in his hand. I suddenly feel like the biggest bitch in the world for leading him on. I shouldn't have done it.

"Oh, that's so nice of you." I slip off my stool, going over to him. He is cute in a rugged type of way, and I tried really freaking hard to like him, but I just couldn't even get to that point with him. "Do you want to ...?" I point back at the bar where Beau now sits facing us as he glares.

"No." He shakes his head. "I should go. I have an early day tomorrow," he says, handing me the bag.

"You should take this." I motion to the bag. "There is already too much food here."

He grabs the bag back from my hand and nods at me. "Have a nice night, Savannah." He looks over my shoulder. "Beau," he says, nodding as he turns and walks out.

I wait for the door to slam and then the sound of his car door before I let out a huge deep breath. "That your boyfriend?" He points at the door with the fork in his hand.

"Shut up." I turn, walking back to the stool and slipping back on it. "He's as much my boyfriend as Melody is your girl-friend." Now he throws his head back and laughs out loud. I have the sudden urge to lean over and just kiss him. But instead, I look down at my food and take another bite. "It's going to be the first time since I bought this bar that I'm not open on a Saturday night."

"It's definitely going to be strange for a lot of people," he says while chewing. "It's the local watering hole."

I nod. "It is," I say proudly.

"You really did an amazing job of turning your dreams into reality." I look over at him. "I mean, remember when we cleaned out this place after you bought it?" He shakes his head. "You moved a crate from over there." He points at the corner of the bar. "And found a family of rats living there."

I shiver now, thinking about it. "It was a mother and all fifteen of her kids." He just laughs. "It was so gross," I say, eating another bite. "I couldn't have done this without you." I look over at him. "You were by my side the whole time. Cheering me on when I would get into my head and tell myself that I couldn't do it."

"If there is anything that I know." He looks over at me, grabbing a bottle of Coke and taking a drink. "It's that if you set your mind to it, you will do it."

"You really mean that?" I ask, looking back at my food before I get lost in his eyes.

"I do," he says. The sting of tears threatens to fall, and I blink them away. I pick at the food and finally give up trying to eat. Standing up, I put away everything.

Beau finishes his food and stands to start cleaning up in front of him. He puts everything in the bag and places it to the side. Then he walks over to the stage where the bands perform and begins to pick up some of the debris from there. "You don't have to do this."

"I know," he says, "but if I help, that means you can open sooner." He shrugs. "I don't know what I would do with my nights if I wasn't sitting on that stool."

With a laugh, I continue picking up the stools and wiping them off. "You always were in my way." I side-eye him. "Always coming behind the bar and trying to lure the ladies with your talk of pouring drinks."

He shakes his head. "I wasn't trying to lure anyone." He steps off the stage. "I was trying to help you."

I laugh, shaking my head. "You liar." Shrieking, I say, "You asked both Becky Johnson and Ashley Walker out while pretending to help me."

"Hey." He points at me, walking over. "They asked me out. I didn't want you to lose business, so I took them out on one date." He puts the box on the bar. "So technically, I was doing you a favor."

I roll my eyes and prop up the last stool. "That is such

bullshit." Walking over, I put the rag down next to the box with the trash and prop my hand on my hip. "I owe you a lot, Beau." My voice goes low when he steps toward me.

His hand reaches out to wipe my cheek right under my eye. "You owe me nothing, Savannah," he says. His voice goes a touch low, and we just look at each other. "You've already given me so much." My hands go to his hips, and I swear that my heart is going to beat out of my chest. "Besides, who else is going to help you fend off all the men?"

Nine

BEAU

Her blue eyes gloss over to a dark blue, the same blue as when she gets nervous. The same blue that I've fallen in love with. "Besides, who else is going to help you fend off all the men?"

She laughs, breaking the moment. I was so close to kissing her, and I thought this was going to be it. I was going to take the leap and just do it, but then she laughed and the moment was broken. Her hands on my hips now push me away, so my hand falls from her warm cheek. "Fend off what men?"

"All of them," I say, turning and grabbing the box with the debris that I picked up from the stage. "Literally all the single ones who wait by the bar to see if you will pick them."

She swings around now. "That's such hogwash." She bends down and picks up one of the chairs, only to have it fall on its side. I look down and see one of the legs are broken.

"You don't see it." I grab the broken chair and set it off to the side. "They stand there and watch you," I say, and she watches me while I pick up another chair to see if it's broken. "Sometimes when you twirl and dance to the music ..." I spot

53

a broken chair and set it down next to the other one. "They stand there and just watch you like you are the main event."

She stands there with her mouth hanging open. "That's not true."

I laugh now. "It's so true." Walking over to the bar and grabbing the wet rag, I toss it to her. "Wipe down the tables while you catch flies."

She glares at me now, walking to a table that's been flipped over. She puts it up right, then wipes it down. "I think you are just saying all these things because I teased you about your harem."

"My harem." I shake my head, putting all the good chairs to one side. "Harem or not …" I look over as she bends down and washes off a table. Her ass is perfect and round, and now I'm like one of those creeps checking her out. "I leave with only one girl every single time."

She looks over her shoulder at me. "That you do." She walks over to the jukebox and presses a couple of buttons. "Might as well sing while we work."

She heads to another table while "Slow Dance in a Parking Lot" comes on. "Dance with me?" I ask her, or maybe I am telling her. She looks over at me. "I like this song, and you can never dance when you are working."

She doesn't move. She just looks at me unsure on what to do. I reach out and grab her hand, pulling her to the dance floor. "We dance," she says to me when I slip my arm around her waist and pull her to me. "I mean, not all the time."

"We've danced four times," I say, and her eyes go big.

"Six," she counters, wrapping her arms around my neck. "Just last week, you walked behind the bar and pulled me to this dance floor."

I look down into her eyes. "I beat Teddy to it," I admit. "One of his friends dared him to come over and ask you to dance, so I beat him to it."

She throws her head back and laughs out loud. "You did not."

"I did, too." I smile, lifting one hand to push her hair away from her forehead. "He was just going to try to cop a feel," I fill her in, "and there was no way in fuck I was going to let that happen."

"Aren't you my knight in shining armor?" she says. We stop dancing and just stand in the middle of the dance floor. "Mr. Mayor," she jokes with me.

"I hate that title," I say, admitting that out loud for the first time in my life. "It's so old-school. Why can't I be Mayor Beau instead of Mr. Mayor?"

"You can be whatever you want." She raises her eyebrows. "You're Mr. Mayor."

"When my father told me he was retiring, something woke up inside me. I wanted to be the one who was in charge now. I wanted to be the one who made a difference. I wanted to be the one to bring new changes."

"Out with the old and in with the new." She moves her hands from my neck to my chest, laying her palms flat.

"Not everyone is going to like the new changes I want to bring." My voice goes low. "But I don't want to be just a little town anymore. I want to bring people here. I want them to come visit every single summer with their kids and have all these memories."

"What changes do you want?"

"I want to build a rec center. After-school programs, sports programs, community dances. Senior centers."

"That sounds amazing." She looks at me, and she has a tear in her eyes. "It sounds amazing, and I'm going to be the one beaming at you from the front row every single time you have a ribbon cutting."

I shake my head. "It's all talk for right now." My arms hold her closer than before, squishing her hands between us. "We have a meeting tomorrow, so let's hope that they are ready for a change."

"If anyone can convince them, you can." She smiles, and I start moving us in a circle. "Everyone loves you." I want to ask her if that means her, too. I want to know if she feels the same way. I want to tell her that everyone loves her, too, but I love her the most. I want to tell her all this, but I don't. I just look into her blue eyes as though I'm in a trance. My head moves down just a touch, and I swear I hear her breath hitch. The song stops, and it's now so quiet all you can hear is the two of us breathing. "You are going to do great things, Beau."

"You have that much faith in me?" I ask, and she smiles shyly and nods her head. I don't know if it's the dust or the fact that it's been a really shitty couple of days, but all I want to do is kiss her. My head moves closer to her. "Thank you," I whisper, and she just looks at me. "For being on my side," I say right before my lips land on hers. I don't know if she's shocked or not, but her mouth opens just enough for me to slip my tongue into her mouth. I swear this has to be the sweetest fucking kiss of my life. Her tongue touches mine, going around and around, and just when I want to take it deeper, I step away from her. I open my eyes just in time to see her eyes flutter open. She puts her fingers on her lips as if to make sure this really happened.

"You kissed me?" I don't know if she's asking me or she's telling me.

"Yeah," I say, ready to go in for another kiss but not wanting to push her. "I've been wanting to do that for a while," I tell her, and she just blinks, not sure how to handle what I just told her.

"I should get you home," I say, pretending I didn't just kiss her in the middle of her bar. "It's getting late, and I have emails to go through." She remains standing in the middle of the room, trying to mentally take everything in. "I have the bag of food. You get the lights." Turning, I clean up the food bags while she turns off the lights, and then we walk to the door. I watch her lock the door and then walk her to her truck.

"Thank you, Beau," she says softly as the light breeze sweeps through her hair. She gets up on her tippy toes and kisses my cheek. "Thanks for being you." Turning, she gets in the truck, and I watch her drive away.

Getting into my truck, I start to drive home but end up making my way to Savannah's house. I park in the driveway and ring her doorbell. She answers after a couple of minutes, and I can see that she just got out of the shower. "What are you doing here?" she asks, stepping aside so I can enter.

"I didn't want you to be all alone tonight," I answer her honestly, "so I thought I'd come keep you company."

The smile forms on her face so fast. "I am not admitting this more than once," she says, "but I was kind of scared to be home all alone."

"Why didn't you just tell me that?" I ask when she turns and walks into the house.

"Because then you would worry, and I don't want you to worry about me." She walks into the kitchen to the fridge. "You have enough to deal with." She takes out a water bottle.

"I'm going to go take a shower," I say. "Want to watch a movie before bed?"

"No." She shakes her head. "But I'll sit with you and probably fall asleep."

I laugh. "You do that anyway." Turning, I walk down the hallway to the bathroom I usually shower in. After turning on the water, I open the cabinet and grab my shorts that I keep here.

When I'm finished and walk back out there, I find her

already asleep on the couch. I don't bother turning on the television. I just cover her up and walk back to the spare room and fall into bed. The next morning, the alarm wakes me, and I find her still sleeping. I get dressed and leave her a note before going home and getting ready for the day.

I'm in the middle of drafting up an email when she texts me.

Savannah: You left, and I didn't even have to cook you breakfast. Thanks for yesterday. You always know what I need.

I smile and answer her back right away.

Me: You owe me breakfast, and I'll collect it soon. I don't know if I can get over to you today, already have a commitment.

Savannah: Have fun on your date.

I'm about to answer her when the knock on the door of my office has me looking up. "I have all the documents that you asked for," Bonnie says. "Also, the bridge club ladies are requesting you for their annual luncheon." I look at her. "They do it every year. Your father has always gone, even if it's only for a couple of hours."

"With all these teas, lunches, and dinners, it's a wonder he got anything done," I mumble, and she just smiles at me.

I go to lunch where I spend two hours doing nothing productive. Then I'm sucked into a meeting with a bridge club member's husband about some tradition that was done for over five hundred years, and when I finally walk into my house, my ass is dragging. I open my fridge to grab a water bottle, and I'm about to call Savannah and see where she is when my phone rings.

I walk back to the kitchen in search of my other car keys when the phone rings again, and I pick it up and see it's Jacob.

"Hey."

"Where are you?" he asks, and I can hear in his voice that he's frantic.

"I'm home," I answer, stopping what I'm doing. "What's wrong?"

"I just got off the phone with Savannah." His voice goes tight. "Someone just trashed her house."

Ten

SAVANNAH

"Don't touch anything!" Jacob says loudly. "Grady is going to be there in five minutes." I close my eyes and sit on the step in front of my house. "Did you call Beau?"

"No," I say softly. "He's on a date, and I don't want to disturb him," I say, ignoring the burning in my stomach and wondering if I can wake up and have a redo of this day. Actually, if I can have a redo of the past week, that would work also. I mean, not the whole week because I don't want to take back the kiss. The kiss that I've been waiting for all my life, the kiss to end all first kisses. To say that I was in shock is an understatement ... and then when he told me he's wanted to do that for a long time? My heart went pitter-patter while my stomach did the wave as I tried to think of how to respond. I should have just come right out and told him that I have also wanted to kiss him for a long time, but instead, I stood in the middle of the dance floor just touching my lips. "It's fine. Grady is going to be here, and we'll handle things."

"I'm so sorry I'm not there," he says softly. "If you want, we can come back. I know Ethan would understand."

"No," I snap. "This is going to be good for Ethan to enjoy the mountains. He doesn't need to be here for this shit."

"Okay, but if you change your mind ..." he says.

"Thank you, Jacob." My voice is still low, and I'm trying not to sound or feel defeated, but at some point, you just have to say fuck this shit and move on. It's becoming very clear to me that this is the line. Forget that my bar was trashed but now someone has broken the front windows of my house. I just got off the phone with the insurance agent, and he basically told me that I'm not covered with my bar since the alarm was tampered with, and I could have done it. "Not just for this but for—"

"No need to thank me. I'll call you when I get the report from Grady," he says and hangs up. I sit here on the step, looking out at the other houses around. I've been here for seven years, and none of my neighbors have ever smiled or waved at me. Let's not forget how they go out of their way to come out and wave at Ethan when he gets here. But me? Nada.

I hear a car approaching and see that it's Grady. He gets out of his truck, and I see a couple of people come out of their houses and stop to stare. He walks up the drive, smiling in his deputy's uniform and aviator glasses. "If you wanted to see me again, all you had to do was call," he jokes, and I shake my head.

"Guilty," I say, holding up my hands. "The jig is up. I did all this just to get you to come to my rescue," I joke with him and laugh as I stand.

"So what happened?" he asks, taking off his glasses and looking around.

"I was walking up the step when I got home, and my foot cracked on glass. When I looked up, I saw that the window over there"—I point at my big bay window—"was busted, and then when I got closer to the door, I noticed that the window on that side"—I point at the other side—"was smashed, too. I called Jacob, and he told me not to go in until you got here."

"He's right. Did you hear anything?" he asks, walking to the side of the house. "I'm going to go check the back." I nod my head and wipe the tear from my eye. When he returns, he says, "You have two more busted windows in the back."

"Great." I take a deep inhale and let it out slowly. "Just freaking great."

"Let's check out inside," Grady says. "I don't think anyone is inside, or they would have left already," he says, coming up the steps and waiting for me to open the door. I click open the door, and so far, everything looks the same except I see a brown brick right in the middle of the room where my bay window sits. Grady walks around me and picks it up and looks down at it, and he hisses.

I walk over to him and see that it has the word *bitch* painted in red.

"I've been called worse." I try not to let it get to me. I wonder what everyone would say if they knew I've had sex once in my whole life. We walk to the other room, and I see another brick. This time, I pick it up, and I see it has *whore* painted in red.

"Well, I'm sensing a theme." I shake my head, and my stomach sinks. The burning starts in my eyes and then moves down to my nose, and I wonder how I can pull off the whole "I have allergies" in the middle of the house. We walk into the kitchen, and I see both back windows with holes in them. One brick has *slut,* and the other one has nothing.

"I guess they ran out of words." When I try to laugh, a sob rips through me, surprising me. The brick falls out of my hand, making the loudest sound when it lands by my feet on the broken glass. I put a hand to my mouth, trying to keep the sound from echoing.

Grady walks over to me and takes me in his arms. I want to

tell him I'm fine, and it doesn't bother me, but the only thing that comes out is another sob.

"I'm so sorry," he says softly, and before I can say anything, I hear the front door open and Beau shouting my name.

He comes running into the kitchen and sees me in Grady's arms, and I think I see him glare but I'm not sure. "What the fuck is going on?" he asks, looking around and then he spots the bricks that Grady put on my counter. His eyes fly from the bricks to me, and I step out of Grady's arms. "Who did this?"

"I don't know," I say, walking to the side of the couch and grabbing a tissue. "I got here, and I saw the window."

"Why didn't you call me?" he asks. I shrug, but I don't make eye contact with him.

"Not much you can do," Grady answers. "I'm going to make a report and check to see if there is anything out of place in the bedrooms." I nod as he walks back to the bedrooms.

"Savannah." Beau calls my name, and I look at him. "Why didn't you call me?"

"Because I called Jacob," I say, and he just looks at me.

"Why?" he asks. I look at him and then quickly look away. It always hurts to look at him after he was on a date or whenever I hear the rumor mill going full force on his conquests.

"I figured you were busy," I say and walk to the fridge to get a bottle of water. Grady comes back from the bedrooms.

"It looks like everything is in its place, but I'm going to need you to confirm it." He looks at me. "Jacob said that he is going to send someone to board up the windows, but he doesn't want you spending the night here."

"I agree," Beau says, and I look at him. "Until the windows are replaced, you need to pack a bag."

"I'll be outside," Grady says, and he walks out.

"Fine. I guess I can stay at the motel in town," I say, pissed that I'm being run out of my home.

"Savannah." He calls my name when I look down,

blinking away tears. "You aren't staying at the motel in town." I bring the water bottle to my lips and take a sip. My mouth drier than the desert in the summer. "You can stay with me."

I'm about to tell him that I'll be fine and that I don't want to stay in his house. Standing here in the kitchen with him, I wonder if he was with someone just now and if I maybe interrupted his date. Knowing it is one thing but seeing it? Two different things. "I don't want to cramp your style," I say, leaning back on the counter and putting the water bottle on the counter. "I can call Jacob and see if I can crash on their couch."

"Cramp my style?" he asks, his eyebrows pinching together. "I don't even know what that means."

I've had a really shitty day, and whatever patience I have is gone. "It means that you have women who obviously like to stop by, and I don't want to be in the way."

"One," he says, walking toward me, "you never get in the way, and two ..." He stands right in front of me, and I really hope he doesn't touch me. "That's the first time anyone has come into my house." My heart speeds up, and I try to make sure that I have my poker face on. I'm not supposed to show him that it bothers me, and I hate it. He isn't supposed to know. "So pack your bag, Savannah."

"Fine," I say, rolling my eyes, and walk toward my bedroom. I ignore the loud thumping of my heart, and when I finally get into my bedroom, I sit on the bed and rub my hands over my face. Looking around the room, I see that nothing has actually been touched. My king-size bed is still made from this morning and the pictures of Ethan and me by the bed haven't moved. I open the drawer beside my bed and see the one picture I keep hidden. It's of Beau and me on New Year's Eve last year at the bar. He walked around the bar with five seconds to go, and when the countdown hit zero, he wrapped one arm around my waist and kissed me for a split second. The picture in the frame was taken at the exact moment before he kissed me. Both of us smiling from ear to ear, it's a picture I look at often but don't discuss. I close the drawer right when I hear footsteps coming toward my bedroom. I look up and see Beau fill my doorframe.

"Grady just left," he says. Leaning to the right, he folds his arms over his chest, making the muscles in his arms bulge. "How are you doing?"

"How am I doing?" I repeat his question and laugh sarcastically. "How am I doing? Well, let me see. The biggest secret of my whole life is out now. My bar got trashed, and my insurance is claiming that I did it because, well, every single normal person trashes their place of business. Destroying the only income that I have 'cause that's a great idea," I say angrily. I brush away the one tear that escapes my eye, not willing to give anyone else my tears. "Then someone or maybe the same person decides that I don't have enough shit going on right now, so they decide to break my windows with bricks." Another tear falls. "Fuck!" I shout and look up at the ceiling. "Why am I letting this get to me?"

He squats down in front of me and takes my hands in his. "You're human."

I shake my head. "Are you sure? I didn't see that written on any bricks. I did see the usual slut, bitch, whore. I wonder ...?" I look at him, and my voice goes low. "How would it feel to walk out of my house and have neighbors who smiled at me and waved. Or even asked me how my day was," I say, getting up. My hands fall from his as his eyes just look into mine with a look that is almost pity and sadness. "I bet it would be amazing." Turning, I walk into the bathroom and close the door behind me so he doesn't see me cry yet again.

Eleven

BEAU

I listen to the click of the bathroom door before I get up and sit on her bed. *What the fuck?* I knew that people were rough on her, and I knew that people were still assholes about everything that went down eight years ago, but she always just shrugged it off. Or at least made it seem like it didn't matter to her, but secretly, she was hiding all this hurt. I rub my hands over my face when the phone beeps in my pocket. I take it out and see a text from Jacob.

Jacob: We need to talk when I get back. Now that you're mayor, there are a couple of things you need to be aware of.

I put my head back, wondering what the fuck else is going on. I used to watch my father and think that this job was easy. Sure, he had to keep the people happy, but every time I saw him, he looked calmed and collected. Maybe I bit off too much. I hear the water stop, and then the door opens and she comes out. "I'll be ready in about ten," she says, walking to her closet.

"I'm going to make sure that someone is coming to board up the windows," I say, and she just nods. I walk out into the hot humid air and grab my phone when I see one of Savannah's neighbors outside watering his flowers. I walk over, and when he turns his head, I see him with his sunglasses and hat on, hose in his hand, and a cigar in his mouth. "Good afternoon, Harold. How are you doing today?"

He takes the cigar out of his mouth and smiles at me and nods. "Mr. Mayor."

"There was some vandalism at Savannah's house, and I was wondering if you saw anything," I ask, and he turns to look at his flowers. "Someone threw a couple of bricks through her window."

"Well, that's what happens when you date all these men." His words make my shoulders snap into place. "Could be anyone."

"Did you see anything?" I ask. His front door squeaks open, and I see his wife coming out, wiping her hands on her apron. "Afternoon, Shirley."

"Afternoon." She smiles. "Would you like some tea?" she asks. I smile at her and shake my head.

"I was just asking Harold if he saw anything out of the ordinary today?" I ask, and she just looks at me. "Someone threw a brick through Savannah's windows."

"We didn't see anything," she says. "Maybe if she wasn't so free with herself, these things wouldn't happen. She has a child, and it's not healthy to parade all these men in front of him. Different car in her driveway every other week. It's no wonder that this happened to her." My stomach sinks, and I have to walk away before I say something rude. "If you ask me, Jacob should just take her child away and be done with it. She is more and more like her mother."

"Shirley," Harold says, and she just shrugs.

"We both know that no men are paraded in front of Ethan," I say, making both of them look at me. "We also both know that the only people who come over to her house with

67

Ethan there is Jacob and me." I don't give them a chance to say anything. "You have a daughter. You wouldn't want anyone to—"

"We raised our daughter better than that," Shirley cuts me off. "Now if that is all, I'll get back to my baking. You have a wonderful day, Mr. Mayor." She turns and walks back into the house. Harold puts his cigar back into his mouth, and I know this conversation is over. I turn and walk back to Savannah's house, and the whole time my blood boils. I make it up one step, and the door opens, and she comes out with a small bag in her hand.

"What were you doing over there?" She looks at me and then over at Harold.

"I was asking them if they saw anything," I say, and she laughs.

"Last week, Shirley accused me of ruining the ozone layer with my truck." She shakes her head, walking down the steps. "The whole ozone layer is my fault because I have a truck." She stops in front of me. "Forget about the fact that they have a nineteen seventy Cadillac that sucks more gas than my truck."

"I didn't know ..." I start to say, my voice low. "How much you put up with."

She shrugs now, and when I look at her, I see that her shield is up, and her eyes are void of emotion. It's like she locked it down and only opens it when she's alone. "It is what it is. There is nothing I can say to change anyone's mind."

"But you aren't that person," I say, walking to the truck. "You aren't the person who people think you are."

She opens the back door to the truck and puts her bag in there. "I've never been the person who people think I am. Even before Ethan, I was labeled when I was fucking twelve and I got breasts. People assumed I would be like my mother. Flirt and sleep her way through the town. It didn't help that I got pregnant and stuck around." She closes the door now. "I

68

can't do anything to change anyone's perception of me, so as long as they are polite to Ethan and he's treated with kindness, I pick my battles."

I think of her selflessness. I think about how it would feel to know that you aren't wanted yet stay nonetheless. I think about the hurt she must feel, and I feel like a huge dick for not seeing it beforehand. "Has anyone ever told you how amazing you are?" I say, walking to her and standing in front of her. "Has anyone ever told you that?" My hand cups her cheek, and my thumb moves back and forth. "That you're pretty amazing."

She looks down now, and I can see that she's embarrassed by this and not used to it. "I wouldn't go that far," she says. Her stomach grumbles, and she laughs.

"When was the last time you ate?" I ask, and she shrugs.

"Two days ago," she mumbles and then turns around to the driver's side of her truck. "It'll be fine."

"Two days ago?" I shout. "Two days ago?" I repeat, and she gets up and into her truck. "You go to my house," I say through the open window on the passenger side. I reach in my pocket and hand her my key to the house. "I'm going to the diner and pick up food," I say, and she leans over and grabs the key.

"What if one of your women shows up?" she asks, and I just glare at her.

"I don't have women, and that was the first time anyone has stepped foot into my house." She raises her eyebrows. "Not counting you."

"Yeah, yeah, yeah," she jokes and starts the car. "You do know that I'm a bartender, right?" she says, and I just look at her. "You do know that I'm almost a shrink."

"What's your point?" I ask her.

"My point is that people talk. Women, especially, so you may not have women in your house, but you have women," she says, putting the truck in reverse. "And all those women are waiting with bated breath to see who you'll pick." She looks away from me and backs out.

"I pick you," I say to the empty space in front of me as I watch her drive away. I walk to my truck and make my way over to the diner. The bell rings over the door when I walk in, looking around at the tables that are full. Most of the people look at the door and smile at me when I walk in. Mr. Lewis comes out of the back kitchen and smiles at me. I walk over to the counter and sit on one of the red stools in front. "Hey there, Mr. Lewis."

"Mr. Mayor." He smiles big. "What can I get for you?"

"I'll have two cheeseburgers fully loaded," I say, looking up at the menu board that hasn't changed in over ten maybe even twenty years. "Some fries and rings with that also."

"Will do," he says, turning and walking back into the kitchen. The door opens again, and I look over my shoulder to see that it's Grady. He stops at a couple of tables on his way to the counter and takes the stool next to me.

"Hey," he says. Mr. Lewis comes back out, and Grady places his order. "Did Jacob call you?"

"No." My thumbs move on the counter as Delores comes out and puts two Cokes down in front of us with a smile. "Why?"

"I'm going to grab a couple of guys and go over to Savannah's to put some wood up tonight," he says, and I look at him confused.

"Why would you be doing that?" I ask. He avoids my eyes, and I know deep down that this has to do with my father. I can feel it in my bones.

"Seems everyone is busy," he tells me, taking the Coke and bringing it to his lips, "with no spare time."

"Is that so?" I ask. He just nods and looks over at me. "Interesting."

"I think so, too," he says.

"Do you need help?" I ask, and he shakes his head. "I can drop off the food and then come back."

"Nah," he says, shaking his head. "It's all good. I have two guys coming in to help me."

Mr. Lewis comes out with a bag in his hand. "Here you go." He hands it to me. "I'll put it on your tab."

"Thank you," I say. "Add Grady's also."

"Now that, Mr. Mayor ..." Grady starts, and he hides his smirk when he says the next line. "They could count that as a bribe."

"Fuck you." I shake my head, laughing. "Let me know when it's done." He nods, and I walk out of the diner. When I pull up to my house, something inside me shifts when I see her truck parked in the driveway, and I park right behind her.

Opening the door, I don't hear any noise. "Hello?" I shout, but when I make it into the kitchen, I can't find her anywhere. My heart starts to speed up, and I jog up the steps and go to the spare bedroom. I find her bag on the bed, but that is it. I walk to my bedroom and see that she isn't in there, and when I jog back down the steps, I look out and see that she is lying in the hammock. Opening the back door, I walk down the steps and head across the grass. She sways side to side, and her eyes are closed. The sound of a branch breaking under my foot makes her eyes flutter open.

"Hey," I say softly. "Were you sleeping?"

"No," she says, "but I was resting my eyes." I watch her, taking in how beautiful she is, and with the sun going down, her eyes are a darker blue. "It's so relaxing."

"Come and eat," I say. "Then you can come back once you're fed."

She gets off the hammock. "Fine." We walk into the house side by side, and she devours her burger, fries, and half the onion rings. "God, that was good." She gets up and cleans up, then looks at me.

"Do you think I can take a bath?" I just nod and don't say anything because the fact that she's going to be under my roof naked and in a bubble bath makes my cock so hard I almost groan out in pain. "Great," she says and walks away, going upstairs.

I clean up the kitchen and try not to think about the fact that she's upstairs. I try not to think about the fact that I want to see her naked, and that I've been thinking about it more and more recently. I try not to think about the fact that I want her here more and more. I try to also talk myself down off the ledge. It takes Grady an hour to text me that they've finished at Savannah's house and then another text from Tony letting me know that it'll take him three days to get everything replaced and back to normal. Grabbing my laptop, I scan my emails now and make a list of things to follow up on.

Only when I look over and see it's dark outside do I realize it's past ten o'clock. I shut down my computer and then walk upstairs. The light is on in the spare room, but when I walk over, nothing could prepare me for what I see. She lies in the middle of the big bed in the fetal position. Her eyes are red and puffy because she has been crying.

"What happened?" I ask, my heart stopping in my chest. I walk to the bed and sit beside her.

"Nothing," she says, her voice so soft you can barely hear it. "Absolutely nothing."

I reach out and push her hair away from her face. "Then why the tears?"

"My whole life, all I wanted was to be better. I saw the way they would look at my mother, and all I could do was say I was going to be better than that," she says, the tears so big they roll over her eyes. "I should have left." Her voice sounds so broken. "I should have taken the money I had and left."

I lie down in bed with her on top of the blankets and take her in my arms. "I'm glad you didn't. I don't know what I would do without you," I say, but she doesn't answer. Instead, she cries in my arms.

I don't know how long we are both sleeping, but when I hear the sound of glass breaking, my eyes open, and then I hear a car peel off. "What is that?" she mumbles. I get off the bed and walk over to the window that overlooks the front lawn and both of our cars. "What is it?" I hear from beside me, and then she must see what I see. "Oh my God."

I walk to the side table where I placed my phone and call Grady, who answers after one ring. "Mayor."

"Hey, no rush," I start to say and look over to Savannah who stands there with her hand over her mouth, "but someone just smashed my car windows."

Twelve

SAVANNAH

"I have no idea. I heard the sound of windows breaking and then a car speeding away." Beau stands there on his phone, and the only thing I can do is look down at his windows. "Yeah, tomorrow is fine."

He hangs up the phone, and he rubs his hands over his face. "I'm sorry," I say softly. "This is all my fault."

He looks over at me, and his hair is all rustled from sleep, his shirt untucked and wrinkled. "How is any of this your fault?" he asks, putting his hands on his waist. "It could be all the women who are after me," he tries to joke. "I did send what's-her-name away, and now your truck is in my driveway."

I sit on the bed. "Everyone knows we are best friends, and you would never date me." I try to make the words not matter.

"Why you do think I would never date you?" he asks, and I avoid his eyes. "If anything, you're the only one I would date." My eyes fly to his. "I mean, let's face it, we are best friends," he says. "I'm with you more than anyone else. Also, that kiss was out of this world."

My stomach dips just a bit when he mentions the kiss. The

kiss that I've wanted more of ever since. "Even your Tuesday girl?" I joke with him, and he glares at me.

"What is it with this fucking Tuesday girl?" He throws his hands in the air. "I haven't fucked anyone on a Tuesday in a while, let alone every Tuesday." He walks to the door. "I'm going to take a shower."

"So feisty," I joke, and he looks over his shoulder. "Maybe you should be having sex if you are this uptight." Though the thought of him having sex with other women makes me physically sick. He sticks up his finger, flipping me off, and walks toward his bedroom. I hear the door close and then the water turns on. I put my hand to my stomach, and I get up, walking downstairs to get some water. I walk back up the stairs and walk back into the bedroom. I'm about to slip into bed when my phone starts to ring. I immediately jump up, my heart hammering as thoughts of Ethan being sick make my heart beat even faster.

I pick up the phone, seeing that it's an unknown number. "Hello?" I say and then don't hear anything. "Hello?" I say again, and I hear the phone beep and then look at the screen, seeing that it's off. The phone rings again, and I answer now right away, and it's the same thing.

"Are you hungry?" Looking toward the door, I see Beau's out of the shower and standing in the doorway wearing shorts. Looking at him with my mouth hanging down, I look away and wonder why this bothers me now when I see him like that all the time. Maybe because I'm in his house. "What's wrong?"

"Nothing," I say. "Someone called me twice times and hung up. I thought it was Jacob, but it's an unknown number."

"Maybe it's a wrong number," Beau says, coming closer to me. The scent of his body wash overwhelms me, and my hands tremble.

"Maybe." I look at him. "This guy met this girl, and she gave him the wrong number or vice versa."

"So he's calling her in the middle of the night?" He laughs now.

"Booty call," I joke with him. "It's almost dawn."

"Yeah, let's go make breakfast," he says, and I walk past him toward the door.

"The last time you said that, you stood there holding a cup of coffee the whole time, pretending to take notes." I remind him of the time we went away to a cabin up north with Ethan, and he didn't do any cooking.

"I told you this," he says from behind me while I walk down the stairs. "My job is to get the food, and your job is to cook the food."

"In what universe?" I ask, walking to the kitchen.

"Earth," he says, laughing, and I look at him.

"You make coffee." I point at him, and he nods.

"That I can do," he says, opening up a cupboard and making the coffee. I grab bacon and sausage out of the fridge and start them both when my phone rings again.

"I'll get it," he says and picks up the phone. "Unknown number." He slides his finger and puts it to his ear. "Hello?" I watch him say hello again and then put the phone down.

"This woman or man is in desperate need of something if they are going to call me three times." I shake my head, and he laughs. When he walks past me, he puts his hands on my hips, and my whole body shivers when he lets me go. I try not to think of where he touched me, but my hips are still warm from his touch.

"Here you go," he says, handing me a mug of coffee made just the way I like it. "It already smells great," he says, and we hear a soft knock on the door. "That must be Grady."

He walks to the door, and I hear Grady's voice while I flip

the bacon and start preparing the pancakes. "Morning," he says, and I just smile at him.

"Would you like some coffee?" I ask as he sits at the island.

"I'd love some," he says, taking out a pad and paper. I turn and lean up to grab a mug and then make Grady a cup.

"Here you go." I hear Beau coming into the kitchen, and he hands me a white robe. I look at him and then look at Grady who just rolls his lips and looks down at the paper in front of him.

"What is that?" I ask him and look down at my outfit. It's shorts and a tank top. I'm even wearing a bra.

Beau comes closer and says, "It's a robe," under his breath as he puts it around my shoulders. "In case you get splashed by the food." I look at him.

"So cooking with a robe that is twice or maybe even three times my size is better than burning myself?"

"Yes." He grabs his coffee and turns around to go sit next to Grady. "What do I need to tell you?"

I listen to him give his side of what happened while I put the robe on and roll the sleeves. I finish breakfast at the same time as Grady finishes taking the report. He joins us for breakfast, and I clean up as soon as they are both done. I'm closing the dishwasher when my phone rings again, and this time, I see it's Jacob.

"Hello," I say, looking over and seeing that it's just after seven a.m.

"Hey," he says, and I can hear music in the background. "Just letting you know that we are on our way back."

"What? I thought you were going for a couple of days. Is everything okay?" My heart starts to pick up speed.

"Kallie isn't feeling so hot," he says. "She was throwing up all night, and then I think Ethan is catching it also."

"Oh, no," I say, sitting down. "Well, call me when you get home, and I'll come and get Ethan from you."

"Are you sure?" he asks, and I hear Ethan in the back shouting that he's going to throw up. "I'll call you back."

I hang up the phone the same time Beau comes downstairs, and he's dressed in black dress pants and a white button-down shirt. The cuffs are rolled up to his elbows, showing off the silver watch his grandfather gave him at graduation. "Who was on the phone?" he asks, running his hands through his hair. I wonder if it feels as soft and silky as it looks. He keeps it longer on the top so he can just brush it over.

"Jacob," I say. "He's on his way home. Kallie and Ethan are throwing up."

He grimaces. "Gross."

I laugh. "Oh, trust me, I know all about you and your queasy stomach." He walks over and takes out a to-go cup. "Remember when Ethan was a baby, and you thought it was a good idea to throw him in the air?"

"Oh my God." He puts his hand to his stomach. "He threw up right in my mouth." I throw my head back and laugh, thinking about it.

"It took you two seconds to hand him over to me, and then you threw up in my flowers." I can picture it like it was yesterday.

"Be happy I didn't throw up on you," he says and closes the lid for his coffee. "I have a meeting with the sanitation department in ten minutes," he says to me. "Do you want to come to the office for lunch?"

I stretch. "Might as well get it over with."

"What does that mean?" He takes a sip of his coffee.

"It means that the news of the bar is probably all over town," I start. "Then the news of my windows was probably all over town even before Grady showed up. Shirley is the town's gazette."

He shakes his head. "Fuck 'em." Pushing off, he comes

around the counter and stands right next to me. "See you for lunch," he says softly. I watch as he leans in, and I wonder if he is going to kiss me. I close my eyes, then I feel his lips right beside my lips. "Call me if you need anything." My eyes flutter open, and I just nod. There is nothing more that I trust myself to say. Also, my tongue is in my throat, and I feel that any words that might come out are going to be slurs. After I watch him walk out of the house, I get up and walk to the door, seeing his red taillights drive off. I walk upstairs and pull out a pair of white jeans and a pink top. I'm just walking down the stairs when my phone rings, and I see it's my mother. I roll my eyes, knowing that she already heard the news, and she lives two towns over.

"Hello, Mother," I answer, putting the phone on speaker while I make the bed.

"Don't hello me, Savannah," she says, and I hear her blow out. She's already smoking. I shake my head. "Why didn't you call me?"

I roll my eyes. "Why would I call you, Mother?"

"Because I'm your mother," she huffs out, and I want to laugh. She is more like the annoying big sister. There was nothing motherly about my relationship with her.

"And what were you going to do?" I say.

"Do you know how embarrassing it is to find out news from Mary Ellen?" She blows out again. I sit on the bed and close my eyes. "That my own flesh and blood didn't tell me but—"

"I get it, Mother," I say. "I should have called you for you to do nothing and then to tell me that you told me so."

"I wouldn't have said that," she huffs out. "I also heard about the party."

I close my eyes. Of course, she did. "Shocking," I say sarcastically. "Who filled you in on that, Mother? Couldn't have been Mary Ellen." I know that whoever was in that room at the party would not have called my mother. "So when did *he* call you?"

"I saw him yesterday," she says, and my stomach sinks. "He was in the area."

"I bet," I mumble. He was in the area a lot when we were living in a tiny trailer on the other side of the town, too.

Of course he would sneak over at night and then leave before the sun came up. I remember the first time I caught him walking out of my mother's room with his shirt over his arm and carrying his shoes. He looked at me and sneered and then turned back to look at my mother who was walking out in her purple satin kimono tied lightly around her waist and her hair all disheveled. She nodded at him, and he walked out, then she took one look at me and said that what happened in our house was private and to keep it as such. I was nine. I didn't understand it then, and when I was twelve, I asked her if she even liked Mary Ellen. She gasped and said that she was her best friend. When I asked how she could do this to her, all she said was, "Everyone has needs, Savannah."

"It doesn't matter that he was here. What matters is that you make sure it doesn't get out to anyone else," she hisses out now. "You signed that paper. Don't forget," she reminds me.

"Oh, I know, Mother. I remember signing it. I also remember you assuring him that I wouldn't tell a soul," I finally snap. "I also remember when he forced you to move, thinking that I would go with you."

"He didn't force me, Savannah," she says, blowing out again. "I decided that it would be a good time to start over." I shake my head.

"I guess it helps that he pays for your apartment now, and that you don't have to work anymore," I remind her. "That helped you decide for sure."

"I worked my whole life!" she shouts. "You think it was easy what I did? I had no choice. I was a mother."

I snap, "A mother?" I shake my head. "Clearly, I am remembering it very different."

"Of course you are," she sneers, and I can see her rolling her eyes. "I did the best that I could."

"You did the bare minimum, Mother. If that." I close my eyes, feeling like a bitch for telling her how shitty she was. "You never once read to me or did homework with me. You barely knew what grade I was in."

"Oh, please. I kept a roof over your head and food in the fridge." I laugh at that. "I did the best I could with what I had."

"No," I finally say. "You did what you needed to do to keep up the appearances for the town."

"Why, you ungrateful bitch," she says, and I laugh.

"And that's the end of that," I say. "Listen, you tell that horrible excuse of a man that if he or his son is behind the shit that is happening to me, then I'm going to tell the whole fucking town my secret." That's a lie because there is no way I would do that to Ethan and Jacob. "Tell him that if I find out they were responsible for any of it, I'm going to stand in the middle of town square and sing like a fucking canary."

"I would not advise you to do that." My mother's voice goes low.

"Of course you wouldn't, Mother. You've never advised me to do anything besides spread my legs and keep my mouth shut." I hang up when she gasps out, and I rub the tears away. I don't know why I expected it to be different. I don't know why I thought for once she would be on my side. I keep hoping that one of these days she'll stick up for me, but I know deep down in my gut that it will never happen.

Beau: We were just invited over to Casey's house for a barbecue. Be ready in five.

81

I want to tell him that I don't want to go. I want to tell him that I shouldn't go, but he doesn't give me a choice

Beau: If you aren't ready and are coming up with excuses, I'll just tell you now that I'll toss you over my shoulder.

"Great," I say to myself. "Just freaking great."

Thirteen

BEAU

"Hello," I answer the phone as soon as it rings.

"Mr. Mayor." Casey laughs out loud, making fun of me, and the only thing I can do is moan.

"What do you want now?" I ask. "I told you that I'm not doing anymore real estate shit for you."

"That isn't why I'm calling. I was calling to invite you over tonight for a barbecue."

"Really?" I ask him. "What's the occasion?"

"It's just a little get-together," he says. "Now that Olivia has decided to stay, I wanted to get all my favorite people together."

"Look at you." I joke with him now, chuckling a little bit. "Being all in a relationship."

"I know." He lets out a deep breath. "Never thought I would see the day, but when you meet the one."

"Shit, are you telling me that you are hanging up the bachelor title?" I ask.

"There is no one else that I want to be with," he says. "So I'm trying to do what I can to make her fall in love with this place and never want to leave." Olivia is all city girl whereas

Casey is as country as you get. But the two of them together just fit. I'm happy for him. He's gone through a lot.

"Well, count me in," I say, pulling up to the mayor's house.

"You can check with Savannah and see if she wants to come. Jacob and Kallie will be bringing Ethan, who are feeling okay now."

"Yeah, I'll tell her. Now that the bar is closed, she has the time."

"I heard about that." He blows out. "Let me know if you need anything."

"Will do." I get out of the car. "See you tonight." I hang up at the exact moment that I open the door, and I'm greeted by a huge smile from Bonnie. *Here I go*, I think to myself.

"Morning," she says, walking around her desk and handing me a coffee cup. I grab it from her. "You have your schedule on your desk," she tells me as she follows me into the office. "Your first meeting starts in ten."

"Thank you." I toss my keys on the desk and look over the schedule. "Busy day with meetings."

"It sure is. It's a good time for everyone to meet you and for you to fill them in on how you'll be running things."

I nod at her and sit down. "Thank you, Bonnie." She nods and walks out, closing the door behind her. The only thing I do before I start the meeting is text Savannah about the plans tonight.

The day flies by the time I get up and walk out of the third meeting of the day with everyone else who attended the meeting. When I shake the head guy's hand, I have to think about his name, and when I can't come up with it, I just smile. "Let me know if you need me for anything." He nods, and I turn to walk to Bonnie. "Any messages?"

She smiles at me. "No, but your mom did call and told you that she expects you for dinner tonight."

"Yeah," I say, shaking my head. "That's not going to happen," I mumble while I walk into my new office. I sit behind the desk, leaving the door open. Taking out the budget folder that I was looking at in the meeting, I see a couple of things that I didn't understand. The logical thing would be to ask my father, but I'd rather eat nails. I'm looking at the numbers when I hear a knock and look up, seeing Jacob.

"You're back?" I lean back in the chair, and he nods, coming in and closing the door behind him. He sits in one of the chairs in front of the desk and leans his head back and groans.

"I didn't think I would make it," he mumbles. "By the time we got to the house, they were both puking out the windows."

"Yuck," I say, shaking my head. "Where are they now?"

"I dropped Kallie at her parents' house, and Ethan is at your house," he says, and I nod my head. I don't acknowledge the way my stomach flipped at the thought of them in my house. I grab my phone and send Savannah a text, asking her if she wants me to bring her lunch instead of meeting me. "Grady told me about your car." I toss my phone down and nod. "You think it's the same person as Savannah?"

"Doubt it," I admit finally. "My guess is it's my brother." He just looks at me. "Do you think my brother also did that shit to Savannah?" I ask, my stomach sinking. "You really think he's that much of a prick?" I ask, and his face says it all. "Fuck."

"Anyway," he says. I watch him, and I know he's nervous about something, but I can't imagine what it is. "The reason I wanted to meet with you is to go over the mayor's role." I cross my arms over my chest and listen to him. "It's no surprise that you are not your father," he starts. "And he had his own way of doing things." He looks me in the eye when he says the next part. "Not ethical either."

"What the fuck does that mean?" I ask, not sure I want the answers.

"It means he did things his way, and you either were with him or you weren't. And if you weren't, it sucked for you because you wouldn't get anything." He comes right out and says what I was thinking. "He was always the one cashing in on favors."

"I called Tony while I was at the bar," I say. "He said my father made it clear that she was off-limits. He thought it would lose the contract."

"Wouldn't be the first time," he tells me, and I just look at him. "Let's just say it's good to have a good guy sitting behind that desk."

"What else am I missing?" I ask, and he takes a deep inhale.

"Your father was not a liked man," he says. "He did things shady as fuck, but he made sure he covered his tracks."

I shake my head and hang my head. "This is the man I wanted to look up to and be like," I say.

"You surpassed him a long time ago," he tells me. "That said, we are on the same page, and we both want what is best for the town."

"I agree," I say, and he gets up. "Now if you will excuse me, I'm going home to shower and then get my girl." He stops halfway to the door. "You going to keep Savannah with you?"

"Yeah," I say.

"You going to tell her that you love her anytime this decade?" he asks, and I shake my head.

"I don't want to ruin what we have," I say. He puts his hands on his hips, and I raise my hands. "I know, I know, but ..." I shake my head. "I will take her any way I can, and if it's only through friendship, then that is what I'm going to do."

"She might need you more than just a friend," he says as he walks out of the office, slamming the door behind him.

I rub my hand on my face, and I'm about to call her when there is another knock on the door. This time, it opens just a bit, and my mother sticks her head in. "Knock, knock, knock," she says with a smile as she enters. I get up to greet her. Of course she is dressed perfectly in a skirt and a matching top with a sweater tied at the neck. Her pearls hang perfectly around her neck. Her blond hair curled to perfect and even her makeup is perfect. That is my mother, perfect all the time. "There he is. My son, the mayor."

She comes over and hugs me. "So nice of you to come out," I say, and she nods at me. "Come sit down." I point at the couch. "Bonnie, can you get us something to drink, please?" I ask. Bonnie gets up, smiling.

"You look tired," my mother says when I walk back to the couch. "I heard about Savannah."

"Yeah," I say, sitting down.

"It's terrible," she says, putting her hand crossed in front of her while she folds her legs to the side. "Your father told me this morning when he got back home."

"Back home?" I ask her. "Where did he go?"

"He had some sort of meeting somewhere." She brushes it off. "A business venture. Now that he's not mayor, he needs something to keep him busy." Bonnie comes in with a tray of tea before I can answer.

"Thank you, dear." My mother smiles at her. "My favorite cranberry tea."

"I stock it up just for you," Bonnie says and walks out of the room.

"She's nice," my mother says, looking at me. "I said I wasn't going to say anything." My mother pours herself some water in the cup. "But now that you're mayor, it's time for you to start planting roots."

I close my eyes. "Are you saying that I need to have a kid?"

"I didn't say that exactly," she says, putting her cup down

delicately. "I'm saying that now that you're mayor, you need a wife and then a child." My mother is the most traditional woman I've ever met. Church every Sunday and cooks every meal for my father. She waits on him hand and foot and never talks back to him.

"I think I'm okay, Mom," I say.

"Your brother," she says, shaking her head. "He isn't even close to giving me a grandchild." I swallow now, not saying a word. "I think they are having problems."

"Well, he probably should lay off the booze a bit more," I say, and she just looks at me.

"He's under a lot of stress." My mother's making excuses for him, and I have to shake my head. She was very good with that when we were growing up. She made an excuse about everything when it came to my brother and father. I was the only one who took it like a man and admitted when I was wrong. She called me the wild child for doing this.

"He is barely working," I remind my mother.

"He consults on a lot of stuff," my mother says, and I laugh. "It's not funny, Beau. You should think about hiring him to help out here."

"Doing what?" I ask. "Drinking?"

"You know what I mean. He can help take some pressure off your shoulders."

"Mom, having him here would put even more on my shoulders." I try to let her down quietly and with as much respect as I can. When, in fact, I want to tell her that he can find a rock and hide under it for all I care.

"Anyway." She changes the subject. "I'm making a huge dinner tonight," she tells me. "I've invited a couple of friends and their eligible daughters to come over."

"Mom ..." I shake my head. "Not going to happen. Besides, I have a barbecue at Casey's with Savannah and Ethan."

"Honey." She picks up her cup and puts it to her lips. "I know that Savannah is like a sister to you and all that." I cringe when she says that because the things I want to do to Savannah are nothing that you should do to your sister. "But this is a chance for you to meet eligible women to date and get to know."

"Again," I say, "I'm not interested in any of them. I know most of them, and I'm happy the way I am. I don't have a lot of time to donate to a relationship right now."

"Love isn't going to knock on your door, Beau," she says, shaking her head. "You have to put yourself out there."

"I'll think about it," I say, knowing it's the only thing I can say to make her stop bugging me. "Now, what are your plans for the weekend?"

"Well," she starts, "I was hoping that your father would take me to the beach, but he has another thing that he has to attend this weekend. So I'm going to go to the beach with a couple of the women from my bridge club."

I look back at my mother. "I'm sorry, Mom, but I have a meeting to get to."

She gets up, making sure her skirt is perfect and not wrinkled. "Of course, dear." She smiles and then leans up to kiss my cheek. "Think about tonight for me." I don't bother telling her that it is never going to happen. The only thing I do is grab my keys and make my way over to pick up Savannah.

Fourteen

SAVANNAH

I have changed my outfit no less than fifteen times. I switch out the jeans for shorts and then think that's too much. Going back over and over again, I finally settle on black jeans and a pink crochet top that falls off the shoulder. I think about changing it when the front door opens, and I hear Beau.

"I'm here!" he shouts.

"I'm in the guest bedroom!" I shout back and then look at myself again. He fills the doorway a couple of minutes later, and I look at him. "Is this too much?"

He looks me up and down, giving me a chance to finally see that he's wearing blue pants with a white button-down linen top, the sleeves rolled up to his elbows showing off his tanned arms and his watch. "You look beautiful." He smiles, and my stomach flutters. I wonder if there will ever be a day when he doesn't make me feel like a love-sick teenager waiting for my crush to finally see me.

I look down at my outfit again. "Not too much skin?" I point at the shoulder that is showing.

"No." He shakes his head. "Stop overthinking it."

"Easy for you to say." I shake out my hands, walking over

to put on my wedges. "This is." I look at him, there was a time when the Barnes' family hated me, heck, there are probably a couple of them who still do. I sit on my bed, trying to still my heart. The whole day has made me a nervous wreck. "I broke five glasses today."

I look at him, and he comes to sit next to me. "If you don't want to go, we don't have to."

I shake my head. "Casey is one of your best friends. I wouldn't do that to you." He puts his arm around my shoulders and brings me closer to him, which just makes my heart speed up. The smell of his musk makes me want to just put my head down on his shoulder. "I mean, unless you'll go without me."

"Nope," he says, his thumb rubbing my arm. "Besides, what am I going to tell Ethan when he asks where you are?"

"That I'm at home watching Netflix." I smile when he glares. "Fine." I get up now. "Let's go before I change my mind." I hold out my hand, and he takes it, getting up.

He holds my hand as we walk out of the house. After locking the door behind him, he opens the truck door for me and smiles, grabbing my face. "Relax." I sink into his touch. "If at any time you feel that you don't want to be there, all you have to do is tell me, and we'll leave."

"Okay," I whisper. He leans his head in, and I think he's going to kiss me on my lips. I don't move for fear he might back away, and when he comes closer, I hold my breath. I wait for it, but instead of kissing me on the lips, he kisses me right beside my lips. Then he steps away from the door and closes it. I watch him walk around the truck and then get in.

"Shit," I say out loud. He looks over at me while he starts the truck. "I don't have anything to bring."

"It's a barbecue," he tells me. "You think Charlotte hasn't been cooking up a storm all day."

"I guess you're right." I shrug, and he pulls away from his

house and I look out, trying not to have a panic attack. The drive goes a lot faster than I thought it would. I thought it wouldbe longer, or at least I hoped it would. We pull into the driveway, and I notice more cars than our usual get-togethers. There are about twenty trucks parked all different ways. We park right behind Jacob's sheriff truck.

"How many people did he invite?" Beau says, turning and grabbing the door handle. He opens the door, and I follow him out. The sound of country music fills the air along with the sound of people talking.

Beau waits for me, grabbing my hand. "Don't be nervous," he says, and with my hand in his, we walk around the house toward the backyard. There are a couple of people who I recognize from the bar who also work for Casey.

"Hey there," one of them says to me, bending his head and raising his cowboy hat. "How you doing, Savannah?"

I swear I can hear a growl from beside me. "I'm doing fine. Thank you, Trent." I nod at him.

"See," Beau says when we walk a couple of steps. "He was coming on to you." I stop walking and look at him.

"Trent?" I ask, and he just nods. "He's nineteen." He's about to say something when we finally walk into the yard. There are two grills that are going, and people are standing around talking to each other. A couple of people turn to look at us. Some stop talking, and some just ignore us.

"Savannah." I hear my name being called and look over to see Billy, Casey and Kallie's father, coming toward us. "Mayor." He nods at Beau.

"Mr. Barnes," Beau says. "I'm going to be passing a bill that says if you have picked me up when I was drunk and underage, you can call me by my name."

I throw my head back and laugh at this and so does Billy. "Good to see you two." He turns to me. "Would you like some sweet tea?" He hands me one of the glasses from his hand. I don't want to be rude, so I accept it and take a sip.

"This is good." The sweetness of the tea hits my tongue right away, but then there is a burning. "What's in this?" I ask, looking at the glass in my hand.

"Just my special recipe," he says, and I take another shot. "It's good."

He just smiles and walks away. "You go easy on that sweet tea," Beau says while we walk more into the yard. "I can just imagine what his special ingredient in the tea is."

I roll my eyes, and I'm about to say something to him when I hear Ethan yell my name. "Mom." I look over and see him running over. "Hey, Uncle Beau," he says when he gets close enough.

"How you feeling, baby?" I ask, hugging him and kissing his head.

"I'm not a baby, Mom," he groans. I want to stick my tongue out at him and tell him tough, but instead, I drink a bit more sweet tea. "Come and see what I made." He pulls me with him and my hand that was holding Beau's is now hanging by my side. I stop and look over at him.

"I'll come find you," he tells me with a smile. "It's going to be fine," he says softly.

I follow Ethan through the backyard, and we come to a table that is under a tent. "Gramma," he says, and I look over at Charlotte, who is preparing something on the plate. "Can I show Mom the pie I made?"

"Of course you can," she says, wiping her hands on the white apron around her waist. "So good to see you, dear," she says, grabbing my arms and kissing my cheek. My heart speeds up, and my hands start to get clammy. "You look pretty," she says, and my tongue gets heavy while a lump forms in my throat. I take another gulp of the tea instead, and Ethan shows me the apple pie that he made with Charlotte. "He even put an E on it so he would know it was his."

"I did it all by myself," he says so proud. "I'm going to go play."

"Not too far," I say. "I think it might be time to eat soon." He just turns and runs away.

"You did a good job," Charlotte says from beside me. "He's amazing."

"Thank you," I say, and she turns and walks away. I walk to a seat and sit down, almost as if I'm hiding.

Billy finds me with my empty glass of sweet tea. "I got you another glass," he says, taking my empty one.

"Thank you," I say, and he walks away. I sit in the chair all by myself and just people watch. I scan the crowd for Beau and find him talking to Casey and Jacob with a beer in his hand. I finish another glass of tea when I hear someone call my name and look over to see that it's Kallie.

"I've been looking for you," she says, sitting down on the empty chair beside me. She's wearing a tank top and jean shorts, and has left her blond hair loose. "It's a nice night out."

"It is," I say. I go to take another sip of the tea and find it's empty. "How are you feeling?"

"Better," she tells me. "It was harsh. I think it's the chicken we ate from the rest stop." Billy comes over and hands us both some sweet tea. "Dad," Kallie starts. "You are going to have us rolling out of here."

"I'm celebrating," Billy says. "My son finally got his head out of his ass and found himself a gem."

I can't help the laugh that comes out of my mouth. Casey is or was the most eligible bachelor in the town. Well, it was a toss-up between him and Beau. Jacob made it clear to everyone that he was not interested in the least, so no one really bothered with him. "Well, I, for one, am going to miss him bringing in the women." I smile at Billy. "He was good for business."

"I bet he was," he says, turning and walking over to fill empty glasses of tea.

"There you guys are." I hear another female voice and look over at Olivia. "I have been dodging your father and his sweet tea the whole night."

I nod at her. "Ms. Tequila." I giggle, and my cheeks suddenly feel flushed.

Kallie now laughs from beside me. "She has had a touch too much sweet tea." I shake my head.

"Nah, this is only my third." I gulp some tea. "It's good. The burning stops after one, so I don't think there is anything in this one."

"Oh, fuck," Olivia says, and I look at her. She is wearing a pink summer dress with matching wedges. Her hair is loose and curled. "Who is going to tell Beau?"

"Not me," Kallie says, and I look at them.

"What aren't we telling Beau?" I ask, suddenly confused, then looking for Beau and spotting him with another fucking debutante.

"How many debutantes can one town have without it being overkill?" I ask and only then realize that I've said the words out loud and not just thought them. Kallie and Olivia both laugh now. "Seriously, though, and why are they all single?"

"They are waiting for the top prize," Olivia says, and I drink some more tea.

"He is a top prize," I say, mumbling to myself, but Kallie and Olivia share a look. My neck starts to get hot. "I don't mean he's the top prize," I stumble.

"We need to get her some food," Olivia says, getting up. "And no more sweet tea," she tells me, and I think I pout. She walks to the barbecue and passes Beau at the same time, and he smiles at her. She must say something to him as he looks over when she points at me. He nods to the debutante and then walks over to the grill to grab some food and then walks over to me.

"He's hot," I say again in my head, but it comes out, and Kallie just laughs.

"I would not say anything unless you want him to know everything," she tells me, getting up. "Also, is it okay if we take Ethan home? I promised him I would try to make chocolate chip pancakes without burning the chocolate." I nod at her. "I'll bring him over to you after lunch if that's okay?"

"Yes," I say. She gets up and walks toward Beau, saying something to him and laughing. He just glares at me as he walks to me.

"How much tea have you had to drink?" he asks me, almost barking.

"None of your business," I say, drinking another sip. "Go speak to your debutantes."

"What?" He sits down in the chair that Kallie was just in. "I got you a burger."

"Thank you," I say, taking it from him. "What's got your panties in a twist?"

"My panties are not in a twist," he says. Leaning back in the chair, he puts his arm around my chair, holding the beer bottle in his hand.

I take a bite of the burger and moan. "This is so good," I say, moaning out again when I take another bite.

"For fuck's sake." I hear Beau beside me. He sits forward, putting his elbows on his knees. "Can you stop doing that?"

"What?" I say with my mouth full. "Eating?"

"No," he grumbles. "The moaning. Can you eat without moaning?" He closes his eyes, and I have no idea what the hell he is doing, but I can see his lips moving.

"Are you praying?" I lean in and ask him.

"You could say that," he says and takes a pull of his beer. I turn back, taking another bite of my burger and ignoring the fact that I want to kiss him more than I want my next breath.

Fifteen

BEAU

"This burger is so good," she moans, and I swear my cock is going to fall off or get suffocated from being restrained. Standing next to the barbecue with Casey and Jacob, I have been watching her the whole time, making sure she was okay and she didn't feel out of place.

"I'm going to the bathroom," she says, getting up and turning to put her paper plate on the chair. "Oh my God," she says when she moves right and falls literally in my lap. She throws her head back and laughs now. "Holy shit, my head is spinning." She puts her arm around my shoulder. I look down at her, seeing that her cheeks are flushed and her blue eyes clear. "You're hot," she says, giggling, then puts her hand in front of her mouth. "Shh." She puts her finger against her lips. "Don't tell anyone."

Her ass is right on my cock, and my arms are around her waist. "You aren't so bad yourself." I push the hair away from her face. "Always beautiful," I say without thinking, and her eyes get just a touch darker.

"I hate the debutantes," she whispers in my ear, her cheek rubbing against mine. I wait for her to say something else, but instead, she gets up off my lap, and my hands go to her hips. "I'm good," she says and wobbles just a bit. Kallie comes over to help.

"Do you want me to take her to the bathroom?" she asks.

"I have to pee," Savannah says, trying to whisper, but it comes out in almost a shout. Kallie rolls her lips and just nods. "I'll be back, Mr. Beau Hunk," she says, giggling, and Kallie's eyes open wide.

They walk away from me, my eyes following her as she walks inside Casey's house. Casey walks over now. "Where's your woman?" he asks, and I motion with my head that she's inside.

"She really is the one for you?" he asks, and I just take a pull of the beer, the warm beer that suddenly tastes like ass.

"She's my best friend." My stomach burns.

I look over at Casey. "One of these days, she's going to stop waiting on you to make a move," he says. "Then what are you going to do?"

"She isn't waiting for me to make a move," I say. "She doesn't look at me like that."

"Idiot," he says, and the back door opens with Kallie coming out.

I get up, walking to her. "Where is she?" I ask.

"She is sitting inside drinking water with my father," she says, and I walk inside and see that she is sitting at the island with a bottle of water in her hand.

"Hey there." She smiles at me when she turns her head. "I was coming out to find you."

"Were you?" I ask, slipping on the stool beside her.

"I was," she says softly, our shoulders touching. Billy walks out of the kitchen, leaving the both of us. "It's a lot less awkward than I thought it would be."

"I told you that it would be okay." I nudge her shoulder

with mine, and she gets off the stool. I turn, putting my back to the counter.

My legs are open, my feet wide, and she walks between them and puts her hands on my shoulders. She's never done this before. "You are always right," she says, stepping closer to me. My hands go to her hips. "We should have a bet." Tease me, yes, touch me, yes, joke with me, yes, but flirt with me, never.

"Oh, yeah?" I say, my mouth getting dry. "What would you bet?" I ask her.

"I can't tell you that." She giggles. "But you would have won, and I would have lost." She shrugs her shoulders. "In the end, I would have won anyway."

I'm about to ask her what she means and bring her even closer to me. I'm about to do things to her I have only dreamed, but the door opens, and Ethan comes in. "I'm leaving, Mom," he says, not even batting an eye at our intimate position.

"What time is it?" she asks, and he shrugs.

"It's already after eight," I say, and her eyes go wide. "We should get going also."

"We should," she says, and I get up, my hands not moving from her hips, she turns in my arms now and I hold one hip tight to make sure she doesn't stumble. We walk out with Ethan and say goodbye to everyone. Billy hugs her with the promise that he will be coming by the bar when it opens to give her the secret sweet tea recipe.

She nods at him, smiling. I slip my fingers with hers, and she holds me as we walk to the truck. "That sweet tea was good," she says, giggling.

"How much sweet tea did you have?" I ask, opening the door for her.

"Two," she says and then laughs, putting her hands to her mouth. "Ten." She then puts a finger to her lips, telling me to shh. She turns in the seat, and I fasten her seat belt. "I call you Beau Hunk," she whispers, laughing. "Get it?" I roll my lips. "'Cause your name is Beau, and you're a hunk."

"I get it," I say. "Watch your hand," I say, turning and shutting the door, then walking around and getting in. I start the truck, and she turns over to me when I back out of the driveway and put the truck in drive.

"Those girls need to get off your dick," she says, and I almost burst out laughing. "Like we get it, you want his dick, but you need to get off it. I mean, I want his dick, but I'm not on it all the time." She shakes her head, and my mouth hangs open. "It makes them seem desperate." She looks over at me. "Doesn't it?"

"I agree," I say, and she just looks out the window, not saying another word. We pull up to my house, and she tries to unbuckle her seat belt, but nothing is working, so I lean over and unclip it. "Wait for me," I say, getting out of the truck and walking around to open her door. She grabs my hands, and we walk up the steps. The sounds of crickets all around. I unlock the door, opening it for her. She steps into the entry, giving me just enough room to walk in. I close the door behind me, and I turn to her. She stands there in the almost dark entryway. "Are you okay?" I ask with my back to the door.

She steps forward, closing the distance between us until our chests are almost touching. My hands go to her hips automatically. "We really should have bet," she says in almost a whisper.

"What would you have bet?" I ask, my heart speeding up, my fingers gripping her hips just a touch tighter.

"I would have bet you." Her hands now come up and she plays with the collar to my linen shirt, she comes in just a touch more. "A kiss," she says it so soft and low I'm not sure I heard her. She leans her body into me, her chest now crushing mine. "One kiss," she says. "If you would have won, you would have gotten one kiss." She looks down now at my neck. "But I would be the one winning."

"Savannah." I say her name almost in a whisper, and I'm not even sure I should do this. But her here with me is more than I can fight. I've been dreaming about this for my whole life. "Savannah." I say her name again, maybe warning her that I'm about to snap.

"Beau." She whispers my name, and her face gets so close to mine that all I see is her. Then she licks her lips, and it's the last straw. I finally take what I've dreamed about.

My hands come up from her hips to her cheeks. "Baby," I say softly, my lips almost touching hers. I kiss her lightly, and she leans in. Her hands leave the collar of my shirt to roam to my hair.

"Kiss me," she says, and here in the dark, I kiss her. My heart speeds up, and my palms get clammy, but my lips touch hers, and it's all over. My tongue slides with hers, tasting the sweetness of the tea. The kiss isn't soft; it's a kiss of passion. Her hands go through my hair and wrap around my neck, pulling me close to her as she falls into me, our mouths fighting with each other.

"Beau." She says my name breathlessly, coming back and kissing me again. Turning her head to the side, she slides her tongue with mine again and moans. This is the kiss that I've been waiting for, and it's worth it. It's everything. My hands go from her cheeks to her hair, and I pull back just a touch to see her. Her eyes open almost as if she's in a daze.

"Your kisses ..." She runs her fingers through my hair. "Your kisses make everything better." She brings her lips back to mine again, but this time, it's not soft. This time, she moans into my mouth and arches her back. Her hands now slip from my hair to my shoulders, and she runs them down my back and puts them on my hips. She turns her head to the other side, deepening the kiss as her hands slip under my shirt and slowly make their way up. She lets go of my lips.

"Can we take off your shirt?" she asks. "I've dreamed about this for so long, touching you the way I want to." I'm standing here almost stunned at her drunken confession. She turns now and slips her hands out. "Actually, this would be better in bed." Her hand finds mine, and she pulls me to the stairs.

She stands on the first step and turns around. "I miss your lips." She smiles and dips her head so I can kiss her. She nips my bottom lips, and my cock is ready. I put one arm around her waist and pick her up, wrapping her legs around my hips as I carry her upstairs. Her tongue licks mine, and the kiss is out of this world. It is so needy. When I stop beside the bed, she slips off me, and she is face-to-face with my chest. She leans in and kisses me right in the middle of my chest, then she pushes my shirt up.

"Want to know a secret?" she whispers, and I see that her eyes are glimmering in the dimly lit room. "I would watch you in the lake and wonder what you would taste like." She kisses her way around my abs. "I would wonder how you would fit in me." She cups my covered cock, and I have to move her hand away before I come in my pants. I rip the shirt off me and toss it on the end of the bed.

"You know what I wondered?" I tell her, pushing her hair away from her face. "I wondered how you would taste." I lean down and nip her bottom lip now. "If you sat on my face, what you would taste like." Her mouth hangs open, giving me the right moment to slip my tongue in. My hands leave her face and move down to her shoulders, and then I cup her tits. Her head falls back as she moans out. "I wondered if you would fit in my hand like you do now." Her eyes close as I pinch her nipples.

She lies down in front of me with her feet hanging off the

bed. "Come lie down with me." She holds out her hands for me, and I lie down next to her.

"I've waited a long time for this," she mumbles, pulling me to her for a kiss. My tongue slides with hers, and my hand slips under her shirt. Her hands go to my cock, and she is more brazen this time, slipping the button open.

"Please don't stop," she whispers when I move my kiss from her lips to her neck.

"There is no way I could stop this even if I wanted to," I tell her as she pulls my zipper down. The sound of our heavy breathing fills the room as her fingers slip under the waistband of my boxers. I look at her as she slips her hand around my cock. Closing my eyes, I hang my head for just a second as she grips me in her hand.

"Fuck," I hiss, and then my hand goes down to her jeans. I don't even have to unbutton them; I can slip my hand right into her jeans. I don't stop at her thong; I just slip under it, and I'm met with her landing strip and then her slick slit.

"Oh, God." She arches her back, and her hand stops moving as she opens her legs wider. I slip a finger inside her. "Fuck," she says, and her hand moves over my cock. I finger fuck her with two fingers now as she jerks me off. The restraint of her jeans makes it hard to slip another finger in.

"Don't stop," she tells me, and I capture her mouth in mine. Our kiss is frantic as we both move our hands in unison. I feel her pussy squeezing the shit out of my fingers. She lets go of my lips to call out my name, and I bury my face in her neck as I follow her off the edge. We both lie here, our chests rising and falling.

"If I don't remember this in the morning, I really hope that my dreams remember it." Her hand slips out of my pants now, and she lies there. I slowly slip out of her, and then I look over to see that she is sleeping. I shake my head and move out of her grasp.

"I really hope that you remember this in the morning, too," I say to her sleeping body. I turn and walk to my room, falling on the covers. My hand goes to my chest as I press down on my heart that is beating so fast. I waited to be with her for so long, but I never thought it would be like that. I never thought that it would be a kiss that would make me not only want to kiss her tomorrow but to kiss her forever. I fall asleep to the memory of us together with her name on my lips.

When I get up the next morning, I smell bacon, and I know that she is already up. I walk down to the kitchen. "Morning," I say, seeing if she turns and looks at me differently. She turns with a huge smile on her face.

"Morning," she says. "I woke up with the biggest headache," she says. Walking to the coffee machine, she makes me a cup and then hands it to me. "I am never drinking sweet tea again." I stand here in the middle of my kitchen, not sure if I should tell her what happened. Do I bring it up, or is she embarrassed by it? "I also need to get the recipe."

I sit down and drink the coffee faster than I should, and the burning hits me all the way down. "Well, I'm sure Billy will give you the recipe."

"Do you have a busy day?" she asks, and I nod. "I'll make your plate and then go take a shower." She prepares my breakfast, not saying anything about the kiss. I look at her, and she avoids my eyes.

"Why don't you come down to the office for lunch?" I say, ignoring the awkwardness. "Bring Ethan."

"Okay," she says, walking away with her cup of coffee. I get dressed, and when I walk out of my room and go to her room, she is sleeping on the bed. I walk out of the house with my heart heavy, and my head going in all types of direction.

I pretend to pay attention when I have another meeting, but I'm not even listening. I'm sitting in the chair, looking out the window when the phone buzzes and Bonnie's voice fills the room. "Beau," she says my name. "Tony is here for you."

I get up and walk out of the office. "Tony," I say, turning to see him sitting in one of the chairs. "What can I do for you?"

"You ..." He gets up and grabs the folder that is on the chair next to him. "Can sign this paper." He opens it and hands me the paper that is a bill. "It's for the work that is being done and will be getting done." I turn to walk into my office while I check to make sure he's gotten everything there.

"You need to include the windows at her house," I say, and his eyebrows shoot up. "Yeah, don't ask."

"What the fuck is wrong with people?" he asks, and I grab a pen. "She works her ass off. She stays out of all the drama. She's a good person." I look down and sign the paper. "By the way," he continues, and I look up, "I got a not so nice phone call from the senior last night."

I shake my head. "He has no control over anything," I say and then make a mental note to call my father. "Trust me, you're all good." I hand him back his folder, and I'm about to say something else when I hear the sounds of the sirens, and I walk out of the office. Grady pulls up at the curb, then puts his car in park and gets out, running up the steps.

"What is happening?" Bonnie asks from her desk, and the only thing I can do is look at Grady and wonder if something happened to my mother or my father. Maybe even Liam. The last thing I'm expecting is what comes out of his mouth.

"Beau," he huffs, his chest rising and falling. "You need to come with me."

"What happened?" I ask. He looks at me, and I see the turmoil in his eyes, almost like he doesn't want to say the next words.

"It's Savannah," he says. My heart stops in my chest, and I feel my body turn to stone. "Someone ran her off the road."

Sixteen

SAVANNAH

"Don't move!" Jacob yells when I try to turn around to see if Ethan is okay. My heart is hammering in my chest. My hands shake so hard I can't pick them up. I look around, seeing grass everywhere.

"Is he okay?" I ask, sobbing out. "Jacob, is he okay?" I try to look in the back, but I can't move my neck.

"He's fine," he says, and I look to the side and see that Jacob is climbing out of the ditch with Ethan in his arms. "He's all good." He hands Ethan off to the paramedic that has just arrived, and then he comes back down into the ditch for me. "Okay," he says, opening the door. "Are you hurt anywhere?"

I look down and lift my hand, and Jacob grabs a hold of it to stop it from shaking. "My neck." I move my neck, and he winces.

"Seat belt gash," he says, and I look over to see if I can see Ethan.

"I'm sorry," I say. "I'm so sorry. I tried to avoid it. Ethan."

"Hey," he says to me, and I move my eyes to his. "He's fine."

"I couldn't get to him," I say between sobs. "After I crashed, I tried to get to him, but the air bag ..." I close my eyes. "It disoriented me."

"Jacob." Someone calls him, and when he looks over his shoulder, I see a fireman coming down the ditch.

"Blake," Jacob calls him. "You got here fast." He moves to the side. "Did Grady call you?"

"Yeah, I got the call and came right out." He sticks his head in. "How are you?" he asks.

"I'm okay," I say. "Forget about me. Check on my son."

"Ethan is doing okay," Blake tells me. "He's actually very worried about you." He unclips the seat belt, and I wince. "You're lucky you were wearing that."

"Yeah," I mumble, and I lick my lips that are dry. "I'm not sure how you consider me lucky," I try to joke out.

"I'm going to put this neck brace on you," Blake says. "To make sure that you don't move." I nod my head.

"Um, Blake." I call his name, and he looks at me. "I'm not trying to rush you and all that, but I'm starting to get a bit claustrophobic, and I really need you to get me out of here."

He laughs. "It's the adrenaline going through you." He puts one hand under my legs, and before I know it, I'm being lifted from the truck. He walks up the ditch and puts me down on the stretcher that is there.

I hear sirens in the distance, and I look over to make sure that I can see Ethan who is now sitting with a paramedic as she checks him out. Kallie comes running over and looks at me. We share a look, and she nods her head and walks over to Ethan who jumps into her arms. She listens to him say something and then points over at where I am, and he wipes the tears from his face.

"Savannah!" I hear Beau yell my name from somewhere, and then I see him run through a couple of people. He wears a look of worry on his face as he sees Ethan first and hugs Kallie and him, and then she must tell him where I am because he looks over. He rushes over, and Jacob has to stop him. "Let me go!"

"Go easy. They are checking her over," Jacob says, and Beau walks to me. I feel my lower lip tremble when I see him, and I suddenly need him to hug me. I need him to take me in his arms and tell me that this is going to be okay. I just need him.

"Baby." He calls me the name so quietly I almost don't hear him, but then he steps in front of me, and I see the tears in his eyes. "I need you to tell me you're okay."

I look at him. "I'm okay," I whisper, and then he grabs my hand and brings it to his lips.

"What happened?" he asks, then turns to look over at Jacob and Grady.

"I was coming to see you for lunch. I was going to stay home with Ethan, but he took a shower and said he felt better." I start the story. "This truck was following close behind me, and I kept speeding up just a touch to get away from him, but the more I sped up, the more he was right there." I swallow now. "Then he bumped me. At first, I didn't know what happened, and I wasn't sure, but then he bumped me again. The third time, he tried to pass me, and once he was beside me, he just kept coming closer and closer, and the road got smaller and smaller. The last thing I remember is looking back to make sure Ethan was okay."

"Do you remember what color the truck was?" Grady asks.

"Silver, I think." I close my eyes and try to remember. "Or a dark gray."

"Did you see who was driving?" he asks, and I shake my head.

"No, the windows were dark and tinted. I saw a silhouette but nothing else," I say.

Then the paramedic cuts in. "She's good to go."

Jacob nods. "We are going to meet you at the hospital," he says and then looks at Beau. "You go with her. I got Ethan."

Beau just nods as they load me up into the ambulance. Only when the door is closed and he sits beside me does he let out a breath. "Are you okay?" I ask, and he shakes his head.

"I died a thousand times on my way here," he says softly. "The only thing that went through my head was getting to you."

"I'm sorry I made you worry," I say, and he leans in now, and he kisses my forehead. "And I'm sorry that I ruined your day."

"I'm sorry that I wasn't with you," he says, pressing his forehead to mine. "I'm sorry that you went through that without me." He takes my face in his hands and kisses me softly on the lips. "I am so sorry I wasn't there to protect you." He kisses me again, and I don't say anything only because I can't. I just close my eyes while he wraps his arms around my shoulders, and I finally feel safe.

It's a whirlwind once I get to the hospital, and only after two hours am I able to see Ethan, who comes run into the room and jumps on my bed. "Mom!" I take him in my arms, closing my eyes and smelling him. "Are you okay?"

"I'm okay, baby," I say, holding his arms and making sure that he's okay. I smooth down his brown hair and hold his small face in my hands, rubbing my thumbs over his cheeks. "Are you hurt anywhere?"

"Just my elbow," he says, picking up his elbow and showing me the bandage. "The nurse said I was really brave."

I blink the tears away. "You are very brave."

"Uncle Beau called me a ladies' man and said I was a natural flirt," he says, and I smile and look over at Beau who looks up.

"We need to go over the rules again," Beau says, coming to

the bed. "There are things we tell your mom. If I finish the sentence with bro code, that means it's for guys only."

I look at Ethan who opens his mouth and then smiles. "I forgot."

I laugh now, suddenly feeling okay. "I think I'm going to be able to leave soon," I tell Beau. I lean back in the bed, and Ethan lies beside me. "Where is Jacob?"

"He's in the waiting room with Kallie. He is going over the video surveillance that Casey sent in. Apparently, Casey wired half the town with cameras when the stuff went down with Olivia."

I close my eyes, but when the door opens and the nurse comes back in, my eyes flutter open. "Okay." She smiles. "You are cleared to go. If you get a headache later, it could be a concussion, so please come back in. You'll definitely be sore tomorrow."

"I can sort of feel that now." I try to sit up, and every single muscle in my body screams.

"Is there anything she can take?" Beau asks the nurse. "Can she nap when we get home, or is it best to keep her up?" He doesn't wait for the nurse to answer him before asking another question. "And if she does fall asleep, should I wake her hourly?" The nurse rolls her lips to keep from laughing. "How long before I bring her in if she does have a headache? Is it right away or do I time it?"

The nurse puts her hand on his arm. "I will get you a paper with instructions and all questions should be answered on that." She looks at me. "I can just imagine when you get pregnant. This man is going to crawl out of his skin."

My eyes fly to Beau, and I don't know if he realized what she said or not. "Oh, he's my best friend." It slips out before I can take it back. What else was I supposed to say? He's the man I want to be with. He's the one I've been dreaming about since forever.

The nurse looks at me and then at Beau. "Well, then, you've got a great friend," she says and walks out of the room.

"Let's go," I say to Ethan who gets up and hops off the bed.

"Uncle Beau." He calls him. "You were freaking out right now."

"I was not." He looks at Ethan and shakes his head. "I was just worried." Ethan laughs now. "I am."

"Sure," he teases and waits for me to get off the bed. I try not to show how much pain I'm in when I get up, but Beau must catch the winces.

"Do you want a wheelchair?" he asks, and I scoff at him.

"I do not, thank you very much," I say, walking slowly out of the room toward the waiting room. Ethan walks ahead of us.

"How much pain are you in?" Beau asks quietly beside me.

"Not that much," I lie, and before he can say anything, Jacob and Kallie spring out of their chairs and come over to us.

"What did they say?" Kallie asks worried, and I have to give it to her, she is a better person than I am. I lied and broke them up, ruined their relationship without so much as thinking twice about it. But she stands here asking me if I'm okay, and she loves my son as much as I do, and for that, I can never ever repay her.

"Not much. I'm going to be sore tomorrow." I repeat what the nurse said.

"Okay, why don't we get going?" Jacob says. "You guys can ride me with, and Kallie will go pick up some food and meet us back at Beau's."

"Why can't we go home?" Ethan asks, and I look down at him.

"I told you. There was a fly in the house and then while I was chasing it, a spider fell on me and I panicked and threw a ball at it, but I missed, and it went out the window." I look at Beau who rolls his lips, and Jacob has to put his hand in front of his mouth to cover his smile. Kallie just looks at me with her mouth hanging open.

"I was put on the spot, okay? That's the best I could do," I mumble to them, and then Kallie looks at Ethan.

"How about you come with me to pick up the food, and we can meet them later?" she asks Ethan, and when he looks at me and then at Kallie, she leans in and whispers something in his ear.

"Is that okay, Mom?" he asks, and I just nod my head.

"Only if you promise to bring me back some pizza," I say. "With pineapple."

"That's so gross, Mom," he says, taking Kallie's hand. "We have to get it for her since she's sick," he says to Kallie, and they walk away.

"Can we do all the questions once I get to a couch?" I ask them, knowing that more questions are coming.

"Let's go," Jacob says. I walk as fast as I can to the truck, but my body feels like it was run over by a Mack truck. I close my eyes in the truck, and when we get to Beau's house, he doesn't even let me walk. Instead, he carries me inside, and I don't even have the energy to fight with him.

He walks to the couch and places me down in the corner and then looks over at Jacob. "Grab me a water bottle," he says.

"And some whiskey!" I shout at him, and then Beau glares at me. Jacob comes back with the water, and he sits down on the couch facing us. I love this family room. When we were picking out the couches, I didn't want to get up because it was perfect for this room. "Thank you," I say, grabbing the water and then looking at them. "Okay, what are you two thinking about?"

"The bar, the bricks in the house, the phone calls," Beau starts. "It's all related."

"What phone calls?" Jacob asks, and I roll my eyes.

"It's nothing," I say the same time Beau talks.

"Started last night, calling and hanging up." I drink another sip of water, really wishing it was something more.

Jacob gets his phone out, and he starts typing. "I just texted Casey to start tracing your phone."

"Oh my God," I groan. "It's fine. It's all fine."

"It's not fine!" Beau shouts. "None of this is fine. And it all started as soon as I found out that ..."

"Don't say it." I point at him. "Don't you say it."

"It could be my brother," Beau says, his voice almost breaking. "Or better yet, my father."

"Your father wouldn't get his hands dirty," Jacob says. "But he would order it."

"You guys, I think you are overthinking this," I tell them, not ready to believe that he would actually harm me. I mean, destroy my life, yes, but harm Ethan and me? He wouldn't ... or would he?

"She needs protection," Jacob says.

"She needs more than that," Beau says, and I look at him. "They won't touch you if you're mine," he says, and I don't even know if I heard him right or not. "The only way this is going to stop is for us to get married."

Seventeen

BEAU

"Married." I don't even realize the words coming out of my mouth until I hear Savannah gasp. This day started shitty with my car windows getting busted, and then my heart stopped when I was in the car with Grady. The whole time we drove to the scene, I was making deals with God about everything. I would tell her how I feel if she was okay. I would take care of her and protect her. Once we arrived at the scene, I was stuck; my legs didn't move. The sight of two ambulances with their lights on, the fire truck, and then I saw her truck in the ditch with the front end smashed, and it just was like a knife to my stomach.

"Married?" Savannah whispers.

"Holy shit." I hear Jacob, and he leans back into the couch, waiting to see what else I will say.

"My brother is an asshole," I start, sitting down. "My father is a fucking coward, but ..." I hold up my hands. "No one will mess with you if you have my name."

"Married," she says again, and I don't know if she is asking me a question or simply just in shock. "To you?" I try not to let it hurt that this idea is probably her worst nightmare.

115

"To me," I say, swallowing down. "Think about it."

"It's not the stupidest idea he's ever had," Jacob says. "It will finally get the town to stop fucking talking about you."

"Oh, yeah," Savannah says, turning and wincing when she gets up. "This is going to get them to stop talking about me. Poor Beau, he had no choice but to marry her."

"They are not going to say that," I say, and I hope she isn't right. "Listen, for as long as they remember, we've been friends. We could say that seeing you in the accident jolted something inside me, and I professed my love for you," I say, trying to convince her without her knowing that this is exactly why I'm doing this. I want her as mine. I want to take care of her and protect her.

She sits back down. "This is a nightmare," she says, rubbing her hands over her face. "What about Ethan?"

"What about him?" I ask. "I love him like he is my own, regardless of anything." My voice goes low, and she reaches over to grab my hand.

"I know that," she says, "but don't you think this will confuse him?"

"I don't think so," Jacob finally says. "It's not like he's a stranger. It's Beau."

"This is crazy," she says. Her phone rings, and I look up to Jacob who looks at me as we share a look.

"Who is it?" I ask, and she grabs the phone.

"It's Chase," she says, and my stomach burns. "He probably heard about the accident," she says as she answers the phone. She gets up and walks out of the room to go talk to him.

"Nice," Jacob says when he hears her voice coming from the other room.

I rub my hands over my face. "It's like the words were coming out, and there was no way I could stop them," I say, looking over my shoulder to make sure she can't hear me.

"You're right, though," Jacob says. "This smells like your father."

"I know," I admit. "But would he actually hurt Ethan?" Jacob just looks at me. "It's his flesh and blood."

Jacob leans in a bit. "Listen, I hate to be the one to tell you this, but your father is the shadiest fucking person I know." I watch him. "He's done shit being mayor that is unethical and morally wrong. I was just waiting for him to cross a line, but he's smart."

"It could be Liam," I say. "He is dumb as fuck, but now that I found out and the secret is out of the bag ..."

"I caught him," Jacob says. "After she left your office during the party, I caught him trying to manhandle her."

"That fucking ..." I start to say, and Savannah walks back into the room. "What did Chase want?" I ask her.

"He heard about my house and about the accident, and he wanted to make sure I was okay and to offer me a place to stay."

I scoff. "Yeah, right." She looks at me and folds her arms over her chest. "You wouldn't stay there with Ethan, and you know it."

"I wouldn't stay there because I don't want to stay there," she says. "And I don't want to play games with his feelings."

"Well, now that you're engaged," Jacob says, "that shouldn't be a problem."

She's about to say something when the front door opens, and we all hear Ethan yell, "Mom!"

"In here!" Jacob shouts, and Ethan comes into the room with a bouquet in his hands.

"What is that?" Savannah asks as he walks over to her.

"This is to make you feel better," he says. She sits down on the couch in front of him. "I know you feel bad about the accident and because you broke the windows in the house."

"This is ..." she starts to say, and the tears come out.

Scooting next to her, I put my hands around her shoulders and pull her to me. She looks up at me. "He bought me flowers."

I nod. "Yeah, he did."

"And pineapple pizza," Ethan cuts in. "Kallie said we had to, but we also got a meat lovers." He smiles. "And Ms. Charlotte sent over cake."

"Really?" Savannah says almost like it's the most unfathomable thing in the world.

"My mother bakes when she gets nervous," Kallie says, walking to the couch and sitting next to Jacob. "So when I called her about Ethan and the accident, she went a bit overboard and made sure that she made him his favorite everything."

"She did," Ethan says. "Apple pie."

"You have to share that," Jacob says, and he just moans. I get up and hold my hand out for Savannah, who actually takes it. Kallie and Jacob get up also and walk to the kitchen with Ethan following them.

She waits for Ethan to be out of earshot before she puts a hand to her mouth and sobs. I take her in my arms, crushing the flowers between us. "Shh," I say softly, and she wraps one arm around my waist. "It's okay."

"They could have hurt him," she whispers. "Didn't even cross their mind that he was in the truck with me." I don't know what to say; the only thing I can think of is to hold her.

"I'll get to the bottom of this," I say. "And if I find out that it's them, I'll make them pay."

"Don't," she whispers. "You don't know what they're capable of."

"No," I say, and I make sure she is looking at me when I say the rest. "They don't know what I'm capable of."

"Are you two coming?" Jacob asks, and we both look up at

him. "See, you already look like lovebirds," he jokes, and I shake my head.

"Did you mean it?" she asks softly. "When you said we should get married?"

I try to get my words right, knowing I have one shot to actually convince her. "I would do anything for you," I say. "I would do anything for Ethan." I look in her eyes now, and I'm ready to get lost in them. "I would do whatever I have to do to protect you." I'm hoping she can read my eyes.

"Mom!" Ethan yells for her to come and get her pizza.

"We should get in there," I say to her, and she nods. "I don't think anyone would eat your pizza, but the meat lovers one ..." She throws her head back and winces, putting one hand on her neck.

"That pizza is awesome, and you know it." She smiles, and my whole chest feels like it's going to expand. She walks away from me and stops, then turns back. "I'm sorry I'm dragging you into this mess." The smile is now gone from her face. "I'm sorry that my nightmare has just become yours, too." She walks out, and I answer her again under my breath.

"Your nightmare is my dream come true." I stand here in the living room that she picked out. She doesn't even realize that this whole house is everything she's picked out. I wanted her to have her dream home. I wanted to give her that, and now I'm going to have my chance.

"Hey," Jacob says, coming into the room. "Are you coming?"

"She thinks marrying her is a nightmare," I say, my chest getting tight again.

"You need to tell her how you feel," Jacob says, grabbing my shoulder with his hand and squeezing it. "Take it from me. The minute you say the words to her, this whole weight will be lifted off you."

I shake my head. "You heard her. Marrying me is her nightmare."

"That's because she doesn't know how you feel," he says, and I just look down. "You have to tell her." He turns and walks out of the room, and I follow him this time. I try to get involved with the chatter around the table, but the only thing that I can think of is what I blurted out.

Jacob and Kallie leave as soon as the apple pie is eaten. "Come on, buddy," I tell Ethan. "I'll set the shower for you so Mom can rest." He nods and walks toward the stairs. "Do you want me to carry you upstairs?"

"No," she says, "I can walk." I wait for her and walk up the stairs with her. "Are you sure you're okay?"

"You know that I've helped him shower before," I remind her. "Four nights a week."

"Yeah, I know. Cool Uncle Beau lets me set my own water." She mimics Ethan. "Cool Uncle Beau doesn't stand in the bathroom and make sure I'm okay."

I laugh now. "Go lie down." Turning, I walk to the bathroom and hear the water running, so I stick my head in. "You okay?"

"Yeah, Uncle Beau," he says, so I turn to go and get his bed ready. Another thing that I did was make a room for him at my house. For the times that I would watch him while Savannah was at work or Jacob was working overnight and Cristine, Jacob's mom, couldn't watch him. I grab a pair of pjs that he left here the last time and walk back to the shower. "Buddy, I put your pjs here for you." I lay them on the counter. "Remember to brush your teeth."

"Okay, Uncle Beau," he says and opens the door. "Do you have any of your body wash?" he asks, and I look at him. "This is bubble gum, and I'm a growing boy." I roll my lips and nod at him.

"I'll get you some," I say, shaking my head and walking to

my bathroom to get him mine. I don't see her standing there when I walk out of my bedroom. "Are you okay?"

"What are you doing?" she asks, pointing at the soap in my hand.

"Well, Ethan is a growing boy," I say. "And he doesn't want bubble gum soap anymore."

"So he asked you for yours?" She smiles, and I see tears in her eyes. "He really loves you."

"Well, I love him just as much," I say.

"If things turn bad between us." She wipes a tear away, and I walk to her. "He ..."

"He will never lose me," I say. "Never. Neither of you will ever lose me."

"Okay," she whispers, and my heart speeds up faster and faster.

I look at her. "Okay?" My voice almost cracks.

She looks down at the floor, and I can tell that she's nervous because she is wringing her hands, and her voice comes out almost in a whisper. "I'll marry you."

Eighteen

SAVANNAH

I don't even know I'm saying the words even though they are coming out of my mouth. Marry him. "I'll marry you," I repeat it again so I can hear it again. His eyes open wide as if he's in shock that I would agree to marry him. When he doesn't say anything, my heart starts to speed up and my legs start to shake. Maybe he changed his mind. "I mean, if the offer is still on the table," I say nervously while I wring my hands in front of me.

"Yeah." He looks down, and when he looks up, a smile covers his face. "The offer is still on the table."

My whole body finally releases the tension that it was holding. I'm about to say something else when he steps into me, closer than he was before. So close our chests almost touch. "We're getting married," I say, trying to break the tension that has somehow built between us. My chest rises and falls when he steps in just a touch more.

I look at him. "We're getting married," I repeat, and he leans in just a little bit more. I can taste the kiss; I can feel his heat on me. It's finally going to happen.

"Beau!" Ethan yells his name, making us both take a step back.

"I should bring him this." He holds up the body wash. "I think we should tell him before we tell anyone else."

"I agree." Nodding my head, he turns to walk back to the bathroom but stops five steps in and turns around, looking at me.

"Married." He smiles, but he doesn't give me a chance to say anything before he goes into the bathroom. I put out my hand to hold the wall, my knees suddenly buckling under me.

"What the fuck did you do?" I ask myself. "How could you drag him into this?" I walk back to the bedroom and sit on the bed, wiping a tear away from my eye. Forget the fact that I want to marry him. Forget the fact that it's going to be a sham of a wedding, and I always said I was never going to get married. Okay, fine, I said it because there was no one but Beau who I wanted to be married to.

He stands there in the doorway, watching me. "It's not that bad." He tries to joke, but the look on his face says that he's not joking at all. His eyes almost look angry. He's probably pissed that he has to marry me, putting an end to all the extra activities he does.

"Um," I say. "I know that it's going to be a marriage of convenience at this point." I try to swallow, but it feels like I have a lump in my throat. "But the other women ..."

"What other women?" He folds his arms over his chest.

I roll my eyes now. "You don't have to pretend, Beau." My thumb taps my index finger. "I'm a bartender. Do you know that means I'm almost a shrink? I serve people alcohol, and with that, they tell me their problems, or their secrets, depending on who it is."

"Okay," he says, not getting where I'm going.

"You're ..." I point at him. "Well, you're active with

women." His eyebrows pinch together. "I've heard it in detail."

"You heard in detail that I was active with women?" He asks the most awkward question he's ever asked me.

"I mean, I've heard a couple of stories." My legs starts to move up and down, and he sees it. "I never ask. I wouldn't do that. It's your private business."

"From who?" he asks, crossing his ankles.

I look out the window now, blinking away the stinging of tears that are threatening to come out. I'm about to answer him when the bathroom door opens, and Ethan comes out, walking to us with a towel wrapped around his waist. "Mom." He calls my name, walking past Beau, not even realizing that he just saved me. "Smell me." He puts his neck next to my nose. "I smell like Uncle Beau." I smile at him. "Can you buy me this from now on?"

"Aren't you a bit too young for that?" I look at him, and he smirks.

"Mom, I'm going to be ten soon," he says.

"In two years, buddy," I remind him, and he looks defeated.

"Why don't you go get dressed?" Beau says. "Your mom and I want to talk to you about something."

"Okay." He turns, walking out of the room.

"We are going to have maybe two minutes before he's dressed," Beau says. "So we are going to have to table this discussion."

"I would rather not continue it," I say, and he shakes his head.

"That isn't an option." I know just by his tone it isn't a suggestion. "Things need to be said." He walks away now.

My stomach rumbles, and I have to put my hand to it. "This should be fun."

Ethan comes out of his room in less than two minutes,

wearing his Spiderman pjs with a white T-shirt. "I'm ready," he announces, so I get up and walk to the door.

"I'm downstairs!" Beau shouts up. Ethan and I both walk down the stairs and find him in the family room. A bottle of whiskey sits on the counter, and I look over at him, seeing that he has a glass in front of him. *This is a mistake*, I think to myself. There has to be another way to do things. There has to be something else that we can do if just the thought of being with me and only me has him drinking. I walk to the couch, and I'm about to sit down when Beau looks at me. "Come sit next to me." I walk over to him and sit next to him.

"Is this a family meeting?" Ethan asks, and I just look at him. "I hear some of my friends say that they have family meetings. Is this what it is?"

"Yes," Beau answers at the same time as I answer, "Kinda."

"Ethan." Beau leans forward. "Your mom and I have decided to get married."

"Okay," he says, looking at me and then at Beau, repeating it twice more.

"To each other," I fill him in, just in case he wasn't getting it.

His face fills with the biggest smile of his life. "I knew you guys loved each other." He claps his hands.

Beau and I share a side look. "I love your mother very much." His voice is soft and sincere. I know he loves me; he just doesn't love me like I love him. He looks over at me. "And, well, I'm lucky that she feels the same." He puts his hand on my knee, my eyes flying down to his hand.

"Is that why you always watch her?" Ethan asks. "And why you mumble things to yourself when she walks away?"

I look over at Beau. "Everyone loves differently," I say.

"Cool," Ethan says. "Where are we going to live?"

"Um ..." I'm about to tell him that we will still live at our house, but then it'll be hard to explain how a man and wife don't live together.

"I like it here," Ethan says. "We can bring our stuff here."

"You can," Beau says.

"Cool," he says again. "Can I go watch television until bedtime?" he asks, and we both nod our heads. When he walks out of the room, Beau finishes the rest of his whiskey.

"Well, that wasn't as bad as I thought it would be," he says, hissing after taking four gulps of whiskey.

"Could have been a lot worse." I close my eyes and lean back.

"Do you want to move in here?" he asks, and my eyes open now. "We can always live at your house. I just figured this is a bit bigger than your place."

"Just a touch." I laugh. "When are we going to do this?"

He's about to answer me when his phone rings and so does mine. "It's my father," he says.

I look at my phone. "It's my mother."

"Well, this is the perfect opportunity," he says, and my heart starts to speed up. "No time like the present."

"I think I'm going to vomit," I admit. He looks down and swipes to the right to answer the call.

"Hello," he says, and I can hear his father's voice rumbling out. He just listens. "I'll be by the house tomorrow. Will you be there?" His father continues talking. "Good, I'll be there at eight." He hangs up. "Your turn." He points at my phone that is ringing in my hand again.

"Hello." I answer my mother.

"Good God," she huffs out. "Took you long enough to answer." I roll my eyes and glare over at Beau who snickers. "Mary Ellen just called to inform me about your accident."

"Good news travels fast, I see," I say sarcastically.

"That isn't funny," she hisses. "I told you that you were being reckless."

"I don't think me getting run off the road by a crazy driver is me being reckless, Mother." I close my eyes, feeling that my head is going to start to throb any minute now.

"I warned you that you were pushing Clint," she whispers, and I look over to see if Beau could hear anything she just said. "I told you it wouldn't end well." I swallow now, my body starting to shake. Beau spots it, and his face looks frantic. "It was a warning."

"A warning?" I repeat the words in a whisper. "A warning."

"You're just lucky," she says, and I cut her off.

"I was with Ethan." My voice trembles, or maybe I think it does. "He could have been hurt."

"And you would have no one to blame but yourself." I look at the phone now. This is my mother, the person who is supposed to protect me, the person who is supposed to pick me over everything else.

"Mother." My voice comes out in what sounds like a hiss and a shout. "Are you fucking kidding me?" I look over at Beau, and I know he's going to have questions. "What if something happened to Ethan?" My tears come now, and I don't even move to wipe them off. "What if he got hurt or worse?" I don't say the words, and I refuse to think the thought.

"Well, he's fine," she says.

"That's it," I say. "I'm done." I look at Beau who sits there with clenched fists. "It's over, Mother."

"Finally," she huffs. "You said something smart for a change. I told him you would see the light."

"Oh, no, Mother, I'm not talking about that." I shake my head. "I'm talking about this. Me and you, our relationship." I throw my hand up. "Or whatever you want to call it."

"Savannah." She laughs. "I'm your mother."

"I think that is where you are wrong," I tell her. "A mother protects her child. A mother lives for their child. A mother will put her life before her child, each and every single time and not just when it's convenient for them."

"I gave you everything, you ungrateful little shit!" she shouts. "Everything. I had to move away because you got yourself knocked up, and instead of doing the right thing, you had the bastard."

"Goodbye, Mother," I say, hanging the phone up. It rings again, and this time, I decline the call. The sob rips through me, and Beau leans over and grabs me into his arms.

"It's okay," he whispers. "It's going to be okay."

I bury my face in his chest as his hands rub my back. "You were right," I finally say between sobs. "You were all right." I lean out of his arms, and I look at him. "It was your father."

Nineteen

BEAU

I'm not sure I hear her when she says the words between her sobs. "What did you say?"

I ask her again.

"It was him." She gets up now and has to pace, something she does when she's nervous. "I never thought he would do something like that." She shakes her hands. "Ethan." A sob rips through her, and she bends, putting her hands on her knees. "Me, okay, but him?"

My blood is boiling. "I need you to go upstairs and stay with Ethan." When I get up, she looks at me. "I need to go speak with my father." I walk over to her. "Can you do that?"

"I don't want you to go," she says, and I've always wanted to hear her say those words. "Don't go."

"It's going to be okay," I say. "I promise you that I'm going to be right back."

"But ..." She clings to my arms. "What if he ...?"

"I promise you that I am coming right back," I say, and she just nods. I want to kiss her before I leave. But I don't want to rush this kiss. No, I want all the time in the world to kiss her for however long she lets me. Hopefully forever.

I turn and walk out of the house, calling Jacob. "Hey." He answers on the second ring. "Is everything okay?"

"No," I say, getting into the car and wanting to punch the steering wheel. "I'm going to talk to my father. Savannah thinks it was him."

"Fuck," he hisses.

"Do you think you can find proof it was him?" I ask him, and he huffs.

"You're my best friend," he says, "but I've been trying to pin something on your father for the past fucking six years. His hands are always squeaky clean."

"Fuck." I shake my head. "I'll let you know how it goes."

"Do you think it's a good idea going over there when you're this heated?" He's always the voice of reason.

"Probably not," I say, making my way over to my parents' house. "But I need to tell them that I'm marrying Savannah."

He laughs now. "She finally caved."

I breath out now. "Yeah." My stomach burns, thinking that to her this is her nightmare.

"I'm here." I look over, seeing the lights on in my parents' house, and forget that my mother was having a dinner. "I'll call you later."

"I'll be on standby," he says and hangs up. I walk up the steps and open the door, hearing the sound of music from somewhere in the house along with people chattering. I walk to the dining room, and it's no surprise that there must be forty people here. My mother is always one for hosting. She looks up and sees me, her face lighting up with a smile.

"Beau," she says, getting up from her place and walking over to me. "Glad you could make it." She kisses my cheeks and whispers, "You couldn't dress better?"

"I'm not here for dinner," I say, looking around the room and smiling and nodding at whoever is looking at me. I spot my father sitting at the head of the table. He leans back in his chair, his linen suit perfectly tailored to him. I look a lot like him, but that is where it stops. "Father," I say, "I was wondering if I could have a word with you."

"Now isn't a good time, son." He smirks. "We have company."

I look at him. "I have no problem saying what I want to say in front of everyone if that is what you want." He must see that I'm livid, and he just laughs.

"It's hard passing the reins over." He puts his linen napkin from his lap on the table. "If y'all will excuse me, my son needs me. He's a chip off the old block always working to make the town perfect."

"Really, Beau?" my mother says between clenched teeth, a smile on her face. "You are ruining my dinner."

"I'll be back, dear." He kisses my mother's cheek, and she just nods. My father leads the way to his home office. He opens the door and waits for me to walk in before closing the door behind me.

"Now, what has ruffled your feathers, boy?" he asks, walking toward his liquor cabinet. Taking his crystal tumbler in his hand, he pours a whiskey.

"Was it you?" I ask, and he just looks at me. "Were you responsible for Savannah's accident?"

He looks at me and then turns back to his drink. "I don't know what you're talking about."

"I'm asking if you were the one who made sure Savannah's truck was forced off the road." I watch him. He smirks to himself, picking up the glass and bringing it to his lips.

"Son." Just the way he says it makes my skin crawl. "It's not my fault that woman has made enemies." He takes a gulp of his whiskey. "It's just sad that her son was mixed up in it."

"You mean your grandson." His eyes fly up, and he looks at me, glaring.

"Watch your tone." Any other time, I would have just

walked out of the room, but not this time. Not after everything that I found out.

"I'm going to marry her." I watch his face. "I asked her to marry me, and she accepted."

"Your brother's sloppy seconds," he says, and I step toward him.

"You should choose your words wisely, Father. I would hate for someone to hear the secret that you've gone to great lengths to keep." I advance more now. "You'll also show my future wife respect."

"You have got to be out of your mind if you think you are going to marry her." He shakes his head. "There is no way. You are a self-respecting mayor. You come from the best family that there is. You have generations upon generations of blue blood."

"And?" I look at him.

"You can't marry that woman." He slams his glass down, and his voice gets a touch louder. "She's a woman you fuck, not marry."

"That's two," I say, putting up my fingers. "You insult her one more time, and I'm going to forget you're my father when I slam my fist through your face."

"You'd better watch yourself." He glares at me as someone knocks on the door. "What is it, Mary Ellen?"

The door opens, and my mother comes in. "Listen, you two," she says. "I will not have our good name dragged through the mud. People will think you are in here fighting with each other."

I look at my mother. "I was informing Father that I'm getting married."

My mother puts her hands together. "Oh, that is wonderful."

"To Savannah," my father tells her, and the smile on my mother's face drops.

"Beau." The way she says my name is almost in pity. "That's not going to happen."

"Really, Mother?" I put my hands on my head. "And why is that?"

"Well, she has a child," she starts.

"Mom, are you saying I have to marry a virgin? Because I can tell you right now, your debutante girls are not virgins," I say, and she shakes her head.

"It's not just that. She has a child." My mother wrings her hands. "But it's just not suitable."

I look up. "I'm not here for your permission," I tell them. "Either of you. I'm here just to let you know that I'm marrying her, and she's mine." I look at my father now. "And with being mine, that means I will do what I need to do in order to protect her. Even if it's from my family."

My mother now sniffles. "This is crazy."

"I love her," I say out loud, and my mother just stands there with her mouth open in shock.

"What has love got anything to do with it?" my father asks. "She's a little slut. You see her. She's probably slept with half the town already, and you're the idiot who is going to marry her."

My mother gasps. "That's three." I turn and walk to the door. "Also, that's your last warning." I look at my mother. "I take it you aren't going to offer me your mother's engagement ring?"

"It's a family heirloom," she says.

"Yeah, that's what I thought," I say, then look at my father. "I meant what I said. She's mine now. You fuck with her, and you are fucking with me." He stands there with his shoulders square and his back straight. "You should also know I can play just as dirty as you, old man." I grab the doorknob. "What was it you said? Chip off the old block?"

"You'll regret this," he says.

"I would hate to think that you just threatened me." I wait for my father to say something else.

"Of course not," my mother says. "He would never hurt you. You're his son."

I laugh bitterly. "Have a nice evening." I walk out of my parents' house and make my way back to my house. The whole time, my body shakes with rage and my hands have a white-knuckle grip on the steering wheel. When I pull up, I see that the house is pitch black, and I wonder if she left. Opening the door, I see that a little light is coming from the family room, so I walk back to the room, and I see that she is pacing the floor. She looks like she's been crying.

"Where is Ethan?" I ask, and she looks over at me, putting a hand to her chest.

"Jesus, you scared the crap out of me," she says. "He's in bed." She comes to me now. "Are you okay?"

Holding up my hand, I walk over to my whiskey and pour two fingers in a glass. Then I take it down in two huge gulps, and it burns all the way down to my stomach. "It was him," I say the three words that I never thought I would say. Maybe I was naïve about it, or maybe I was just hopeful that he would be a decent human. I don't know what it was but admitting it just ... I pour another two fingers and look over at her.

She stands there, and I take her in. She put on one of my sweaters that is way too big for her. Tears roll down her cheeks as she clutches at her stomach. Her whole body shakes, and I rush to catch her right before she falls. I put one hand around her waist and another on the back of her head. She clings to me, her hands gripping my shirt while her tears soak through to my skin.

"He's not going to hurt you," I whisper to her. "I promise you that he will not hurt you." She just sobs in my arms. "I got you, baby," I say.

"I have to leave," she says. The four words I never want to hear. "It's not safe for Ethan or for you."

"You aren't going anywhere," I say. "Not now, not ever. This is your home."

"I can build another home," she says, looking up at me, and my hand goes to her cheek. "I can buy another bar." Her voice goes lower now. "But I can't buy another you."

"I told them I was going to marry you," I say, omitting the nasty things my father said. "Tomorrow, we have to go get you a ring."

"You really are going to go through with this?" she asks, confused. "This is a mess, and you don't need this. You just got elected mayor."

"We," I say, rubbing my thumb across her cheek. "We are going to go through with this."

"I don't think it's a good idea," she says, and all I can do is pull her to me and hold her. I hold her in the family room for as long as she lets me.

"How about we talk about it in the morning?" she suggests, and I just nod. "I'm going to go to bed."

"I'll be right up," I say. "I'm going to lock up down here." She walks out of the room, and I turn off the lights after I put the glass in the sink. When I walk upstairs and peek in on her, she is already asleep. I take another shower, trying to let the tension go, but when I slide into bed, all I can do is look up at the ceiling.

The phone on the side table buzzes, and I reach for it, seeing it's Jacob. I sit up now, knowing that nothing good is going to come at two a.m. in the morning. "Hello?"

"Is Savannah with you?" he shouts, and I get up now.

"She's sleeping," I say and hear shouting in the background, then a car door slam. "Where are you?"

"I'm on my way to the bar," he says, and I wait for the other shoe to drop. "Someone just set fire to Savannah's bar."

Twenty

SAVANNAH

I hear the buzzing coming from somewhere, but I think it's a dream until it starts again. This time, my eyes fly open, and I jump up, seeing the unknown number on the screen. "Hello?" I grumble.

"You need to get gone, bitch." The sound of the male voice is muffled.

"Who is this?" I ask, but the phone beeps, letting you know the person has disconnected. I'm about to put the phone down when I hear Beau's voice. "She's sleeping." I slip out of bed, walking in the hallway. After he walked out of the house to go to his parents' house, I ran to the bathroom and threw up whatever was in my stomach. Ethan came down to find me over the toilet bowl. The worry in his face made me feel even worse than I did before. I got up and rinsed off my face, assuring him that I was okay. "What do you mean, it's on fire?"

My whole body feels the dread, my body preparing for the worst, yet not really believing that it could be coming. "Fuck," he hisses. "Where is she now?"

I stand here in the doorway to his bedroom, and he sits on

the side of his bed. He's in white basketball shorts and no shirt with his head down as he listens to whoever is on the phone. "Okay, I'll get her up." He tosses the phone to the side and rubs his face.

"What's the matter?" I ask softly, and his head snaps up.

"Why are you up?" He doesn't bother answering my question.

"I got a call from the unknown number." I shrug. "This time, he spoke." He flies off the bed and comes to me.

"What did he say?" he asks at the same time we hear a soft knock. "Fuck, that's Kallie."

"What's going on?" I look at him while he walks past me, going downstairs to open the door.

"Hey." I hear Kallie, and then I walk down the steps, and the two of them just look up at me. Kallie has tears in her eyes.

"What happened?" I ask again, and this time, my heart starts to speed up because they both look like someone died. "I'm starting to freak out."

"There's a fire." Beau starts to say something, and it's like my everything is going on around me, but I'm not there. I see their lips moving, but all I can do is listen to the galloping of my heart.

"Beau." I hear Kallie say his name. "I think she's going down."

He rushes to me, but my ass hits the step before he can get to me. There is screaming somewhere, a bloodcurdling scream. "Ethan," Kallie says his name, and I turn to see him standing at the top of the stairs with tears running down his face. Kallie runs past us to gather him in her arms. "It's okay, buddy," she tells him.

"Baby," Beau says, "you need to look at me." I blink, turning to see him, noticing that I'm now sitting in his lap.

"Why?" is the only thing I can say. "Why?" I whisper again

and again. He gets up and walks back up the steps, going to his room.

"I have to change, and then we can go," he says, putting me down. My hands fall in my lap limp, my whole body is limp. He rushes to the closet, coming out dressed in jeans, when the buzzing starts again. Looking down, I see it's Beau's phone with Jacob's name flashing across the screen. "Yeah," he answers. "We're leaving now." He looks at me. "How bad?"

He doesn't say anything else; he just puts his shoes on, then gets my shoes on, and I'm carried out to his truck. I don't see anything, and I don't register anything until he turns the corner, and the sight of orange flames fill the sky. I gasp, seeing that a fire truck is already on the scene, and the water is going. "Oh my God," I say, watching the flames getting higher and higher. Beau stops the truck, and I get out. My hand holds the door as I take in the sound of wood crackling. I start to walk toward my bar when I'm pulled back by Beau.

"You can't go too close," he says, and I stand here hopeless, watching everything that I have ever worked for go up in flames. The sound of the windows breaking makes me jump a bit. "We need to find Jacob."

"It's gone." My eyes fixate on the sight of the bar. I remember when I bought it; I thought I owned the world that day. I sat in my studio apartment, looking over the deed to the bar. There was nothing that you could have said to erase the smile on my face that day. I owned something. Something was finally mine, and I was going to show everybody that I could do this. I would make them eat their crow when I owned the most successful bar that ever was. It took blood, sweat, and tears, but I did it. There were more tears and sweat, but I did it. I put my bar on the map, and people would come from two counties over just to be at my bar on a Friday and Saturday night. I provided for my son and for myself, which is the only thing I ever wanted. "It's gone." I repeat when I see a part of the roof has collapsed. "It's going to be all gone."

Beau stands behind me with his arms around my shoulders. We stand here just watching the fire spread until the whole roof collapses. It almost sounds like a tree falling in the forest when it takes down other trees around it. "Jesus." I hear Jacob's voice beside me, and when I look over, I see him clearly in the dark night with the fire lighting up the sky. "I just spoke with Blake," he says. "He says it could take a couple of hours before the fire is out."

"Do you want to go?" Beau asks, and all I can do is shake my head. The three of us stand here and watch as my bar burns down to the ground. Little flakes of ash float through the air like snow. I wipe the tears away with soot on my hands. The whole time, Beau holds me, his hold never loosening, and it's a good thing because I don't think I would be able to stand. Every time another piece of the bar collapses, he kisses the side of my head.

The dark of the night eventually turns an amber color when the sun comes up. I don't know how long we stand here, but when I see Blake coming my way, the look of devastation and tiredness is all over his face. Smudges of black soot are on his face. "I'm so sorry, Savannah." I can't say anything. I just look at the pile of rumble that is left. "We tried to save it."

"I know," I say, my heart broken. "It's not your fault."

"We are going to go through it later when all the fire is out and get you a report as soon as we can," he says with his helmet under his arm.

"What do you think it could be?" Jacob asks, and he looks down.

"It can be a whole list of things." He tries to be as diplomatic as he can be. "Let's not speculate."

He turns and walks back to his team as they all look at me.

"We all know that this was intentional." My voice comes

out clear as day. "Right before you called, I got a call." I turn in Beau's arms, but he doesn't let me go. Instead, his arms move lower, and he holds me around my waist now. "From an unknown caller. I thought it was another crank call, but this time, he spoke. Told me I needed to be gone."

"Who did?" Jacob asks while I shrug.

"His voice was muffled, but it was a male," I tell them, looking back at the bar. "Guess they made sure I would get gone."

"We should get you home," Beau says. "Ethan is worried sick about you."

I go through the movements of walking away from the bar. I get in the car, looking out the window the whole time. "I shouldn't have threatened him," I say. "You shouldn't have gone over there."

"If this is my father's doing," Beau says, "he's going to pay for it."

I laugh bitterly. "He's never paid for a single fucking thing he's done in his whole life." I shake my head. "Last year, Herman," I mention the guy who owned the gas station, "he disagreed with your father at a town hall meeting. He wanted to see the budget because he didn't understand a couple of things. Two weeks later, he was out of business. No suppliers would sell anything to him. He tried to keep it going, but when you can't get gas there, it kind of defeats the purpose of having a gas station."

"What?" he asks, shocked.

"You really didn't know?" I look over at him. "Like at all?" He just shakes his head. "Dude," I say, looking down at my hands and seeing they are almost black from the ashes.

We pull up, and as soon as we shut off the truck, the front door is thrown open, and Ethan comes down running, tears streaked down his face. "What the fuck am I doing all this for?" I mumble as I get out of the truck and catch him in my arms.

"Mom." I pick him up now, something that he's stopped making me do since he's 'a growing boy'.

"Are you okay?"

"Yeah, buddy," I say and walk toward the door where Kallie stands.

"I couldn't get him back to bed. He just kept asking questions," she says, and I smile at her. "Ethan, why don't we cook a huge breakfast for everyone while your mom and Beau go and shower?"

I look over and see that Beau has ashes all in his hair and streaks of it on his face, too. "That sounds like a great idea."

"Are you hungry?" Ethan asks, and I lie, nodding my head. "Can we make pancakes?" Ethan turns to ask Kallie, who would give this kid the whole world if he asked for it.

"That sounds good," she says and holds out her hand for him. He squirms out of my arms, then walks up the steps and into the house with Kallie.

I turn, sitting on the steps. "It dawned on me that I only opened that bar to show people I could do it," I tell Beau who stands in front of me. "I wanted the people who spoke of me with disdain to look at me and say wow, she's doing it or, better yet, look at how far she's come."

"We'll rebuild it," he says without missing a beat.

"I used to go into the bar, and I wasn't Savannah the home wrecker or Savannah the one who had a child out of wedlock or ever Savannah 'that one.' I was Savannah, owner. No one felt sorry for that Savannah, and no one said a bad word about that Savannah. I was everyone's best friend when I was pouring them a drink. They joked with me and told me secrets. It was as if I was never that first Savannah."

"You are the bravest woman I know," he says, squatting

down in front of me and grabbing my hands to bring them to his lips. I take one of my hands and put it on his cheek.

"Has anyone ever told you how amazing you are?" I ask, then smile as the tears come. "Of course they did. You're Beau."

We both look at the street when we hear a car door slam. Jacob gets out of his truck and walks to the stairs, and he sits down on the last step. "I'm so fucking done."

"You and me both," I say.

"Well, you guys have a couple of hours before we need to be ready," Beau says, and we both look at him. "We're getting married," he tells me. "Today at three."

Twenty-One

BEAU

"We are getting married." She doesn't know if I'm asking her or telling her, so I just nod.

"Today?"

"Today," I say and look at Jacob who stares at me with the same look of surprise that's on Savannah's face.

When we pulled up to her bar, and I saw the flames, I knew there would be no saving it. I also knew that the bar was a piece of her, and now it would be gone forever. I also knew that this would be another reason for her to want to leave, so I had to act fast in order to make her stay because losing her was not an option at this point. "Don't you need a license or something?" Savannah looks at me and then at Jacob.

"I'm the mayor," I say. "I know who to call."

"But ..." she says. "But it's not worth it anymore."

"Why do you say that?" I ask, and she throws her hands up.

"There is nothing else they can take from me." She stands up, and I stand with her. "Literally, they have taken everything I have."

"So you are just going to let them win?" I ask, putting my hands on my hips.

"I've lost every single time." Her voice goes low. "Might as well lose this round, too."

"You have seven hours," I say after I look at my watch. "Come hell or high water, we're getting married today."

"You're serious?" She finally sees that I'm not joking. "You really want to get married today?"

"I do." I smile. "See that? I'm practicing."

She opens her mouth to say something, but nothing comes out, and when she thinks of something else, she opens her mouth again, but literally nothing comes out. "You're going to catch flies if you keep your mouth open much longer," I say, and she glares at me.

"I don't even have a dress," she says.

"Lies," I say. "You went shopping last week and bought two dresses for my party, and well, you only wore one."

She glares at me. "You're annoying when you try to sound like you know everything."

I throw my head back and laugh. "Go eat and then go shower."

"This is crazy." She throws her hands up.

"I don't say this often," Jacob says from beside me, "but she's right."

I turn to glare at him. "Today at three, you're the best man." I grab his shoulder.

"Ohh," he says. "I've never been the best man before."

"You two," she huffs up the steps, "are not thinking straight."

"I've never been more sure in my whole life," I say while I look in her eyes. She doesn't say anything else as she walks into the house and slams the door shut behind her.

"I don't know much about weddings," Jacob says, "but

pissing off the bride on the day of the wedding is not a good thing." The front door opens, and Kallie comes out now.

"What did you do to Savannah?" she asks, folding her arms over her chest. "She stormed in and stomped up the steps." I smile. "It sounded just like Ethan did last week when I said he couldn't play video games on a school night."

"We're getting married," I say, and I can't explain how happy I feel right this minute.

Jacob holds up his hand when he sees that Kallie is going to ask something. "In case you were wondering when, it's today at three."

"What?" she shrieks. "Today?"

"Today," I repeat. "Oh, do you think she would want to get married at sunset instead?"

"I think she would want to get married when she has a dress and flowers," Kallie says. "And maybe her hair done."

"I don't care what she wears," I say, and Kallie rolls her eyes.

"We're aware," Kallie says, "but this is a wedding."

"Can we at least push it back a couple of hours?" Kallie says. "Get maybe a couple of people to help decorate or something?"

"You would do that?" I ask, not sure she would have even wanted to come.

"Listen, she isn't my best friend," she starts and looks at Jacob, "but she's Ethan's mom and seeing Ethan happy is something that everyone has in common."

"I agree," Jacob says. "Plus, this is a big deal."

I don't disagree with him. It is a huge deal. Her as my wife is everything that I've ever dreamed of. "Okay, whatever you want. Three, five, seven, don't care as long as by tonight, we are married."

"Talk about shotgun wedding," Kallie says, turning around and walking into the house.

"Are you going to tell her?" Jacob looks at me, and I just look at him. That is such a loaded question, and I don't know how or what it means. "Are you going to tell her that you love her?"

"I was going to ease into that," I say.

"Usually, you ease into the I love you and then you get married." He laughs. "But I'm not even going to lie, this is exactly like you two."

"What does that mean?" I ask, and he just shakes his head.

"Both of you in love with each other, but both of you too chicken shit to admit it." His words are like a kick to my stomach.

"She doesn't love me," I say. "You heard her yourself; marrying me is a nightmare."

"How can you be so smart yet so dumb?" he asks, and I'm about to answer him when the door opens, and Ethan comes running out.

"We're going to have a wedding," he says, jumping up and down and clapping his hands at the same time. I call it his excited dance. "Kallie just said that I have to walk Mom down the aisle since no one in the world loves her more than me."

"Yeah." I nod at him.

"She says I have to put on my Sunday best," he groans and gives it the thumbs down.

"What are you guys doing standing around?" Kallie says from the door. "We have a wedding to plan."

"Dear God," Jacob says. "She just used her 'I mean business' voice."

"That's not good," Ethan says now. "That means no one will have fun."

I smile at all of them, walking inside to take a shower. When I get out, I'm ushered out of the house and put in the truck. "You can't see the bride on your wedding day," Jacob says.

"I saw her an hour ago," I point out.

"Listen to me, and listen to me good." He leans in and points at my face. "This shit that you just pulled has everyone teetering on a fine line of crazy. My mother called me and she has all the flowers settled," Jacob says. "Olivia—don't even ask how—found someone who is going to send over a one-of-a-kind wedding dress from some designer on a television show. Charlotte and Billy are gathering whoever they can to cook the food. Casey has someone coming in with decorations, and I'm not even going to tell you everyone in town who is stepping up for her."

"Does she know?" I ask, and he just shakes his head.

"Kallie said it's best if we surprise her, and again, she used a voice I've never heard before," Jacob says. "Now, I'm in charge of getting you and Ethan a suit, which, by the way, Ethan is against, so good luck with that."

"We'll match." I look at Ethan who sits in the back and just glares at me. "How about you wear the suit for the wedding, and then you can change as soon as we are married?"

"Fine," he groans, "but I don't like it."

"Noted," I say.

"I want to get married in my backyard," I tell Jacob who just nods.

"That was already decided. That is the only thing Savannah wanted was to get married at either her house or your house." I smile when I think about her making that decision.

We drive a town over to get our suits, and we all agree on a cream linen suit. Well, we don't. Kallie said that it had to be cream or gray. When we get back in town, I drop Jacob and Ethan off with a promise to pick them up in an hour. I walk into my office and see that Bonnie isn't at her desk. I look around and still don't see her, and when I try to walk into my office, the door is locked. I knock on the door, and all I hear is rustling, and then the door opens and Bonnie comes out, her hair all over the place as she adjusts her blouse.

"I'm so sorry," she says, avoiding my eyes. "I thought you would be gone all day." She walks past me, and I open the door to see my father tucking in his shirt.

"Are you fucking kidding me right now?" I shake my head. "Bonnie, you're fired."

She looks at me with her mouth open and then looks behind me to see if my father will say anything. And being the awesome gentleman that he is, he doesn't say a word.

"But ..." she huffs. "He ..."

I put my hand up. "I'm really not interested in the story." Walking into my office, I say, "Just so we're clear, this isn't your office anymore." He glares at me. "Why?"

"Why what, Beau?" He looks at me.

"You're married. I mean, in case you forgot, to my mother," I say. "Everyone talks, you know. You hear whispers, but I would always say it can't be. My father would never do that to my mother. He loves her. And then I just ignored it because how can you fight for something that is a lie?"

"I do love her." He puts his hands in his pockets. "But I have certain needs, and those things you don't bring into your house."

I shake my head. "You're disgusting," I say. "If I hear the whispers, don't you think Mom does, too?"

"Your mother knows her place," he says. "She is the one I'm married to. What I do on my private time in the privacy of my space is mine."

"Get out." I shake my head and walk to the desk, grabbing the phone number of the judge who is going to marry us. I walk to the door now.

"You think you're better than me. You'll be just like me," he says almost proud of himself. "It runs in the family."

"Then I must be adopted," I say, "because there is no way I would do that to someone I love."

"Ask your future wife about what is expected of her. I'm sure her mother has taught her well," he says, and my stomach lurches.

"You think I don't know you are sleeping with her mother." I shake my head. "You think you're so slick, but you're not. I was sixteen, and I was supposed to be at Jacob's house that weekend, but I didn't feel well, and I came home early."

"I didn't know," he says, and I shake my head.

"Don't pretend you care now," I say, walking out of the room. "I'm having the locks changed."

He starts yelling, but I ignore him as I get into the truck. I have one more stop before picking up Ethan and Jacob.

We walk into my house, and I have to stop in my tracks because it has been transformed. Tea lights are hung in the trees everywhere. The willow tree in the back is almost lit up, and candles make a path to where a white canopy is set up.

"You have ten minutes," Kallie says, and I nod, going to the bathroom to change. When I walk out, I'm wearing the suit that I bought that day, and Charlotte is there with a flower, pinning it to my jacket.

"You look so handsome," she says, kissing my cheek. "I'll see you out there," she says, and Jacob comes now.

"Are you ready?" he asks, and I just smile.

My whole chest fills up when I answer him. "I've never been more ready for anything in my whole life."

Twenty-Two

SAVANNAH

"It's time." I hear Cristine, Jacob's mom, say as she comes in and looks at me with a smile. "You look ..." She puts her hands on her chest. "So beautiful." She smiles and walks out of the room, leaving me with Kallie and Olivia.

My hands shake when I put my hand on my stomach and look back into the mirror. As I look at my reflection, I didn't expect to even be married in a wedding dress with such short notice. But it happened. When I walked into the room four hours ago, I had a white top and white jeans in my hands. I knew that it wasn't what I wanted to be married in, but it was sprung on me at the last minute.

I was in a daze, my mind in a fog as I played this moment over and over in my head. I was marrying my fairy-tale prince, but he just didn't know it. The white lace dress fits me as if it was made for me. The cap sleeves sit on my shoulders, going down into a modest V. I run my hands to my hips where it fits tight all the way to the bottom, getting loose toward the knees. I turn to look at the open back and small lace train. "Do you think this is okay?" I ask the two girls who came in and made me feel like Cinderella.

"This dress." Olivia walks next to me, dressed to the nines in a light pink chiffon dress. "Was made for you." She smiles, and I turn to look at her.

"I don't have a lot of friends," I say, and tears sting my eyes. Kallie comes over and hands me a linen handkerchief. I grab it, looking at her lilac dress that is tight all the way down and has a sweetheart neckline. Her hair is tied up in the back. "I mean, I don't have any friends really except for Beau." I smile, bringing the handkerchief to my eyes. "He's my best friend."

"And in about five minutes, you'll be standing with him," Olivia says. She is the one who got me the dress without even batting an eye. She got on the phone, and in ten minutes, she checked off wedding dress from the list. Kallie came in and had my makeup and hair booked. She wanted me to wear my hair up, but I love when Beau pushes the hair away from my face. I love when he picks up my hair at the ends and twirls it through his fingers. Basically, I will do whatever I need to make him happy and to get him to touch me.

I inhale and then slowly exhale. "I think I'm going to vomit." I look at them, and they both laugh.

"If you throw up on that dress, it will be a bad omen," Olivia tries to joke, but her face is anything but joking. "This dress is not even for sale yet. It's next season."

"What?" I look down at the beautiful dress. "How much is this?"

"You don't want to know," Kallie says. "You also don't want to vomit on it."

"Now I think I'm going to be sick for other reasons," I mumble, but then there is a knock on the door. It opens, and Ethan comes in wearing a little linen suit.

"Oh my God," Kallie says, walking to him. "Aren't you just the handsomest thing ever?" She hugs him, and my heart is about to explode. She loves him like he is hers, and as a mother, that is all you can hope for when you co-parent.

"I look like Beau," he says with a huge smile on his face. "He's also nervous, and he just almost threw up."

My neck gets suddenly hot, and I have to sit down. "Oh my God, he is so sick about marrying me that he is getting sick about it." I look at the girls who just look at me.

"No," Ethan says. "He thinks you're going to run. Dad had to calm him down. Then he started to sweat, and Uncle Casey had to get him a towel."

I'm about to ask him so many more questions when there is another knock on the door. This time, it's Jacob, who sticks his head in. "Hey," he says, looking at us, and then smiling when he sees Kallie. "Not to rush you or anything, but if you don't get down there, Beau is going to come into this room, and he says this is where you will get married."

"Over my dead body," Kallie says. "We busted our ass for this." She points at Olivia. "You go out there." She looks at Jacob. "You go tell him that she's coming and to calm his tits." She looks at Ethan. "You go get your mother's flowers. And you." She points at me. "You need to get up and go get your man."

Jacob comes into the room now and goes to her. "I love when you're bossy," he says, and Ethan laughs.

"That isn't what you said in the car when she called you with a list of things to do." He shakes his head while Kallie rolls her lips, and Ethan laughs.

"After this, we need to have a talk," he says to his son. "About the things we say in front of girls and the things we hide. Now before Uncle Beau has a heart attack, let's get down there."

I get up now, my knees a little bit wobbly, but I stand straight. "Let's get out there," I say to them. Olivia walks out first and then Kallie follows, leaving Jacob, Ethan, and me.

"You look beautiful," Jacob says. "I'm happy for you."

"Yeah," I say, but swallow *if only this was for real*. Ethan walks out of the room now. "I just feel like I'm tricking him."

He shakes his head. "Beau wouldn't be doing this if he didn't want to." Ethan comes back with my bouquet of wildflowers. "See you out there." He walks out, and Ethan looks at me.

"You look pretty, Mom." He smiles, and I nod. Walking out of the door, I see rose petals on the floor. I walk to the back door, trying to get my hands to stop shaking.

We get to the back door, and I see the backyard totally transformed. Tea lights are hung everywhere, bowls of water with flowers and candles in them line the path to the altar, I try to take it all in, but my eyes fall on Beau and nothing matters anymore. He stands under the big willow tree, looking around and wiping his forehead, and when he spots me, his eyes light up and a smile fills his face. He is dressed in a beige linen suit exactly like Ethan. Wildflowers are secured to his jacket lapel, and his black hair is perfectly combed over. I lift my dress, stepping out on to the patio, and I can hear the music now. The sound of music drifts from somewhere, but I only have eyes for Beau. As I walk down the steps with Ethan, Beau and I lock eyes on each other, and when I finally make my way to him. He hugs Ethan and then comes over and hugs me.

"You look beautiful," he says, making my heart speed up and my stomach flutter.

Beau grabs my hand and brings it to his lips, and we step under the canopy of flowers that I just realized is there. "Dearly beloved," the preacher begins, and I look over at him by the side and see that he is nervous as he breathes in and out. I squeeze his hand, hoping that he can feel how nervous I am also.

"Please look at each other and hold hands." I hand my

flowers to Ethan, who stands by my side, then turn and put my hands in Beau's, and he looks me in the eye while the preacher speaks. "Beau, do you take this woman to be your wife, to live together in matrimony, to love her, to honor her, to comfort her, and to keep her in sickness and in health, forsaking all others, for as long as you both shall live?"

Beau squeezes my hands and smiles while he says, "I do."

"Savannah." I look over at the preacher when he says my name for just a second, and then my eyes go back to Beau. My heart has not stopped hammering since I walked down the aisle. "Do you take this man to be your husband, to live together in matrimony, to love him, to honor him, to comfort him, and to keep him in sickness and in health, forsaking all others, for as long as you both shall live?"

Looking down, I feel my heart slow, and a peace surrounds me. "I do," I say with all my heart.

"We will have your exchange of rings," the preacher says, and I now freak out. "If you would take Savannah's left hand."

"I didn't get a ring." I lean in, and he just smiles at me.

"I've got it covered," he says, and I shake my head. He turns to Jacob, who is his best man, and he hands him the rings. "I didn't have a chance to give you an engagement ring," Beau whispers.

I want to tell him I don't care and that it doesn't matter if he takes a twig and rolls it like a ring. All I care about is him being my husband. "Beau, place the ring on Savannah's finger and repeat the following, 'I give you this ring as a token and pledge of our constant faith and abiding love.'"

He takes the rings from Jacob and places it at the tip of my finger. "Savannah, I give you this ring ..." His voice is so soft as he slips on the rings. "As a token and pledge of our constant faith and abiding love." I look down, and my mouth drops open when I spot my diamond wedding band and on top of it my engagement ring. Which is huge, too huge. The princess diamond with diamonds on the side, and it looks like the figure eight.

"Savannah," the preacher says, and I just listen to him say the words. Jacob leans over and hands me the golden wedding band, and I just look at Beau.

"What's the matter?" he whispers.

"Nothing." I shake my head and hold his hand in mine. I place the ring at the tip of his finger, and my arm starts to shake. Not because I'm nervous or because I'm scared. Apart from having Ethan, I have never been this happy in my whole life. "Beau," I say, "I give you this ring as a token and pledge of our constant faith and abiding love." Then I slide it down his finger.

The preacher smiles at us. I don't hear what else he says because the only thing that registers to me is, "I now pronounce you husband and wife. You may kiss the bride."

Beau doesn't even second-guess or go easy. Instead, he takes my face in his hands, and his mouth crashes down on mine. I forget that there are even people watching.

Twenty-Three

BEAU

My wife. I want to jump up and fist bump her, but instead, I claim her mouth. She isn't going to forget this time. My hands slip from her face and wrap around her waist, my tongue slipping in and then out. I can kiss her all day long, every day, and now I can do it for the rest of our lives. I just need to make her fall in love with me.

The sound of cheering makes her laugh, and she puts her face in my neck to hide. "Now that's how you kiss a woman." I hear Olivia and look over to see Casey glare at her. She smiles at him, leaning forward and wrapping her arms around his neck.

"Wife," I say softly. "It's time to walk down the aisle."

Savannah looks at me, and I have to say she has never looked more beautiful in her whole life. "Oh my God," she says while Ethan hands her the flowers he had to hold.

"Come here," I say, and he walks over to me. I hold his hand with mine and then hold Savannah's, and I wait for the preacher to finish.

"Ladies and gentlemen, I introduce Mr. and Mrs. Beau

Huntington and Ethan." I raise both my hands as everyone cheers, and the three of us walk down the aisle.

I stop once we get to the step. Ethan drops my hand and hops over to Kallie. I put my hand around Savannah's waist and bring her to me. "Married," I say softly and press my lips to hers. Her breath hitches, but she doesn't stop it.

"Gross. Now all they are going to do is kiss like you guys." I hear Ethan say, and then it is followed with laughter.

"I think we are grossing him out," Savannah says once I let go of her lips, her hand coming up and holding my cheek.

"He should get used to it," I say, her eyes going a softer blue. "Besides, the last time we kissed, I obviously didn't make that much of an impression if you didn't remember it." I see her eyes moving side to side as she looks at me.

"I remembered," she says almost in a whisper. "I just didn't know if you did."

"The thing is, Savannah," I say, pushing her hair back, seeing her neck and suddenly wanting to lean forward and just kiss her softly. "With you, I remember everything."

She's about to say something else when people now come up to us to congratulate us. "Congratulations." Jacob is the first to me, hugging me. "No running away from you now," he whispers in my ear.

"Nope," I say, feeling a little bit of a sting knowing that had she not been backed against the wall, she probably would have never married me.

"Let me see," Kallie says from beside us. "Let's see the ring."

"It's ..." Savannah says, looking down at her finger and then looking up at me again with tears in her eyes. "It's beautiful and too much."

"Holy crap," Kallie says, then hits my shoulder. "You did good, Beau."

"Let me see this," Olivia says, taking Savannah's hand and

looking over at me. "Princess cut." She whistles. "What is this, four or five carats?" I look down at my hand still around Savannah's waist.

"Four," I say, trying to avoid Savannah's eyes.

"With the eternity band," Olivia now says. "That, right there, is the dream. Look at the side," Olivia says, turning it.

"It's the infinity symbol," I say and look down at her finger with my ring on it. "Means forever."

"Beau," Savannah whispers, and my eyes go from her ring to her eyes. "It's ..." She brings the ring closer to her. "It's too much."

"It's forever," I say, grabbing her hand and kissing it.

"Let's eat." I hear Charlotte and Cristine.

"What is that?" Savannah points at the far yard where more lights are strung.

"It's our reception," I say, grabbing her hands.

"We need a picture," Kallie says to us. "Pose over there under the canopy of flowers."

I grab Savannah's hand and link our fingers together. "How do we pose?" she asks when we get under the canopy.

I wrap my arms around her waist. "We pose like we are a couple in love," I say, and she stops talking. "Smile and pretend that today is the best day of your life."

I hear the clicks and see the flashes of the phones, and then I lean in. I'm about to kiss her when she puts her hands on my chest. "But what if it is?" she says with a soft smile. "After having Ethan, today is the best day of my life." That's the last thing she says before I bend to kiss her. This time, I don't stop, and my tongue slips with hers. One of my hands goes to her face, and I move my head to the side, taking the kiss deeper. I kiss her until we are both breathless. "I think they got the picture," she says.

"You guys need to get a room," Casey says, making everyone laugh. "Good thing we got you that wedding gift."

Savannah looks at me, and I shrug. "No clue."

"Well, we didn't know what to get you two." Casey comes over to us now. "You know, since you gave us five hours' notice. So ..." He looks at Olivia. "We did the only thing we could. We are giving you my cabin in the woods for the weekend."

"You leave tomorrow," Olivia says, all excited. "It's a one bedroom in the middle of nowhere. There isn't even a Wi-Fi signal." She folds her arms over her chest, side-eyeing him.

"I bought it so I can get away," he says, putting his arm around her shoulder.

"Humanity," Olivia says. "It's perfect for newlyweds."

"Um," Savannah starts, mumbling, "we can't."

"Trust me, you can and you will," Kallie says. "We already fixed it up with Ethan."

"Well, then," I say, and she looks at me. "Looks like we have a honeymoon."

"I guess so," she says, and Billy comes over with two glasses of champagne.

"Here you guys are. It's time for the toast, Jacob." Billy looks over at Jacob, who nods and walks toward the two tables set up around a wooden dance floor.

"Is that a dance floor?" Savannah leans in and asks, and all I can do is nod. I take her hand in mine and walk over, sitting down in a chair, and she sits next to me. "These are real plates." She looks down. "Who had time to do this?"

"I think it was Kallie and Olivia," I say, and she gets tears in her eyes. One slips out and starts to roll down her face. "No tears on our wedding day." I lean in now and kiss her on the lips, something that I have been dreaming about forever.

"It's just a little bit," she starts to say. "I don't deserve all this."

I take her cheek in my hand. "You deserve everything." I'm about to kiss her again when I hear the sound of clinking glasses and look up to see Jacob standing in the middle of the dance floor with his own glass of champagne.

"If I can have everyone's attention," he says, and we both look over at Jacob. "Time for the best man's speech." He looks at us. "Usually, you are given time to prepare a speech, but it's just like these two to just YOLO everything." Everyone laughs, and I look around to see a handful of people who have attended, and I also note the people who attended are the only ones I would want at my wedding. There will be no drama; there will be no one trying to one-up. Or no one making sure we follow all the rules at a wedding. It's perfect, and it's us. "Savannah and Beau, you are my two oldest and dearest friends, and I couldn't be happier for you like I am now." He holds up his glass of champagne. "To your happily ever after."

Everyone picks up their glass and holds them with a smile. "To happily ever after." I clink my glass with Savannah and take a sip.

"We need to say something," I say, and she looks like a deer caught in a headlight. "Okay, fine, I'll say something. You stand beside me looking beautiful," I say, and we get up, walking to the dance floor.

"If I can have everyone's attention," I say, and they stop, looking over at us. "Before the food comes out, and the party starts. I ..." I slip my hand into Savannah's. "We just want to thank you all for coming this evening on such short notice." Everyone laughs. "Ethan"—I turn to look at him—"thank you for allowing me to marry your mom." He smiles and nods at me.

"You're welcome, Uncle Beau," he says loudly, making everyone laugh.

"Kallie and Olivia, who pulled off this amazing wedding in the short time. For Charlotte and Cristine for organizing all the food." I look over, and they all just look at us with love. "And to each and every one of you who showed up today to be a part of this day. And to my wife." I look over at her. "Thank you for making me the luckiest guy around."

Everyone cheers, and Savannah looks down almost as if she's shy. "Time for the first dance," Casey says, going over to the small DJ booth they have set up.

"We are going to dance?" Savannah asks from beside me, looking around. "What song?"

"I have no idea," I say, finishing my champagne and walking to the table to put down the empty glass. She follows me, downing the champagne. "We've danced before."

"But not in a wedding dress and suit and all this," she says nervously, looking around.

"Relax," I say softly, "It'll be okay. Just pretend it's only you and me. Just look at me." I turn and lead her to the dance floor.

I put one hand around her waist and pull her to me. When I hold up my other hand, she puts her hand in it, and I bring it to my chest. "The music hasn't started yet." She looks at me and then smiles. "Shouldn't we wait for the music?" It's right then that the music comes on, and I throw my head back and laugh when the first beat comes out. "What song is this?"

""Die a Happy Man,"" I say, leaning in and kissing her. Then I sing the words to her.

Twenty-Four

SAVANNAH

Can someone's face crack from smiling too much? I wonder to myself after all the guests have left our wedding reception. Married. I'm married to Beau. I look down at my left hand and take in my massive ring, my heart filling so big I think it might burst. "If you don't like it, we can exchange it." I hear his voice and look up at Beau.

His jacket is tossed somewhere. "No, it's just a little bit too much?"

He shrugs his shoulders, walking to the little makeshift bar that they set up. I look around, and it is just the way I thought my wedding reception would be. I mean, when I thought about it, which wasn't often, I wanted this, and I wanted him. He hands me a bottle of beer and sits down on one of the chairs. "Did you have fun?" He takes a long pull of his beer.

"I did," I say, taking my own pull of my beer. "I remembered," I say. "The kiss. I remember every single part of it." He looks over at me. "I just wanted you to know."

He smiles now. "Good to know. We'll have a lot to compare it to."

162

My stomach literally does the wave. "Is that so?" I take another pull.

"Yeah," he says, and he looks at me as he finishes his beer. "Let's go to bed." He stretches his hand out, and I just watch him with I'm sure what is shock on my face or maybe even fear. "Not like that, Savannah. I mean, let's go to sleep, so we can leave for the cabin early in the morning."

I grab his hand, picking up my dress a bit and walking to the house. "What are we going to do for two days?"

"Sleep," he says. "Talk." Then he looks down. "There are things that I need to tell you." My heart suddenly rushes fast. "Nothing to worry about. Just some things that should be said now that we are married." I swallow.

"I like that idea," I say, thinking it's time to finally tell him how long I've been in love with him.

"Good," he says. Turning off the lights, we make our way upstairs, and I don't know if I should go to the spare bedroom or not. I mean, I know that he said he wants to sleep, but does he want to sleep in the same bed as me? *This is stupid*, I think to myself. We've slept in the same bed before, just not as husband and wife.

"I have all my stuff in the other room." I point at the spare room with my thumb. "I'll go change in there and meet you."

"Yeah, that sounds good," he says. The floor creaks under his steps as he walks toward me. "Do you need help getting out of your dress?" The way he looks at me, my hands get clammy and my knees almost wobble. "I can get the zipper for you." When he stops in front of me, I can barely see his face with the lights off, and I want to see his eyes.

"Do you want me to?" he whispers, and I suddenly forgot what he had to say. The only thing I can remember is that the last time he kissed me was ten minutes ago, and it's been far too long. He moves behind me, his fingers touching my arm lightly. My body is on high alert as he moves my hair from my neck. I look over my shoulder at him, his hand going to the zipper. He leans down now and kisses the back of my neck. If I wasn't looking at him doing it, I would think it was my imagination. He unzips the dress, and I want him to take it off me and carry me to his room. I want to get lost in him. I want him to get lost in me. I want to get lost in us.

"Thank you," I say to him, then turn to walk past him. I'm almost past him when he grabs my arm.

"I'll see you soon," he says, leaning down and kissing me. His lips on mine, his tongue dancing with mine. I thought that after the first couple of times we kissed that the butterflies would stop. I thought my heart wouldn't speed up, but I don't think I will ever be used to it. Just as fast as he kisses me, he is gone, leaving me holding myself up. I walk to the bedroom and hang up my wedding dress, then I get into the shower. After all, I did dance my ass off all night long. When I step out, I slip into my shorts and tank top, and I'm surprised to find Beau in my bed when I come out of the bathroom. He's on his back, the covers at his waist, and he's shirtless. One hand is propped behind his head, the other hand rests on his stomach, and his eyes are closed. I wait to see if he opens them, but when I hear small snores, I smile to myself and slide into bed beside him. I turn on my side and fall asleep fast, replaying our wedding day in my dreams.

His smile, his touch, his kisses—so much I don't want to wake up. But something on top of me is pushing me down, and when I open my eyes, I see that Beau is all over me. I'm on my side and his front is to my back, his legs are on top of mine, and his arm is around my waist. I smile to myself, trying to find a way out of his grasp when I have to suddenly pee. I move just a touch, and he holds me tighter.

"I have to pee," I whisper, and he opens one eye. "Morning," I say, and this time it's me who goes in for a kiss. Sure, it's a fast kiss, a peck on the lips, but the fact I didn't second-guess myself is huge. I think it even stuns him, giving me a chance to run to the bathroom.

"What time is it?" I ask from the bathroom after I pee, and I'm washing my hands.

"A little past seven," he grumbles. I laugh when I walk out, and he's sitting on the edge of the bed. "I must have drunk a bit too much last night," he says, looking over at me. "I didn't think I did."

"Well, do you remember we got married?" I joke, and he laughs.

"The only thing I remember clearly is us getting married." When he gets up, I look him up and down, and for once, I don't feel guilty about it since he's technically mine. "Do you want to grab some coffee and hit the road?"

He closes the distance between us, and I can do nothing but stare at him. "Yeah, that sounds good." My mouth is suddenly dry. "I can be ready in ten minutes."

"Okay, me, too." He leans in and kisses me, and unlike my kiss, this one is all tongue. His hand tangles in my hair as he turns my head to deepen the kiss. He slowly ends the kiss, and my eyes slowly open.

"I'll meet you downstairs," he says, walking away from me. I wait for him to get to his room, then lean my back against the wall and let out the huge breath I was holding. I shake my head, trying not to think of him and his kisses while I overpack for the two days we're going to be away. I do, however, pack the lingerie that Olivia slipped me yesterday when I was getting dressed. I just shoved it into the backpack without even looking at it. I put on my cutoffs and a tank top that falls just above my belly button. I slip on my flip-flops while I braid my hair and then walk out at the same time as he is walking out of his bedroom, wearing blue jeans and a white T-shirt.

"You ready?" I nod and walk downstairs with him.

"How far is this?" I ask, and he grabs his phone and puts in the address.

"It looks like a couple of hours," he says, putting on his sunglasses, and the sun reflects off his wedding ring. "We can stop at the diner in town, or we can—"

"Out of town," I say, and he just nods. "They are probably camping out to see if we walk in and if the news is real."

"I already confirmed it while I was brushing my teeth," he says. "Being mayor and all, I put out a statement."

"A statement," I repeat. He hands me his phone, and I see the statement right on the top.

From the desk of the Mayor

I am very happy to announce that yesterday I married my best friend, Savannah Harrison. We exchanged vows surrounded by our immediate family and friends. It was everything that we wanted.

We thank you for your privacy in this matter and will be sharing our official portrait as soon as we get back from our mini honeymoon.

Mayor Beau & Savannah Huntington

"Very official and very real," I say, looking back at him. He just smiles at me. "There is so much we have to talk about."

"We do," he tells me. I hate that he has his glasses on, and I can't see his face.

"What's on your mind, baby?" he says the last word softly.

"Well, where are we going to live?" I ask, trying to ignore how his term of endearment makes me feel.

"We can live at my house when you don't have Ethan," he says, "then we can stay at your house when you have him. Besides Ethan loves my house."

"You'll be okay with that?" I ask. "You didn't even bat an eye or think twice about it."

"A house is just a house," he says, looking over. "It's who is inside that house that makes a home. You're my home." I reach in my bag to take out my sunglasses so he can't see the tears in my eyes.

"For my whole life, all I wanted was a place to call home, and when I bought my house, the only thing I could think of was making a home for Ethan," I tell him, sharing another piece of myself I haven't told anyone else. But that is the way it is with Beau. He gets all my secrets and guards them. "I filled it with all the furniture I could. I hung pictures all over the place. I have his growth chart on the frame at the back door. I wanted him to feel like his home was his comfort place. I didn't even think of it the way you just said it." The tear now falls, and I look over at Beau, who grabs my hand and kisses it. "But you're right. A home isn't the house; it's the people in it who fill it with love and memories."

"That is what we are going to do. Fill whatever house we live in with love and memories," Beau says, his voice soft. "We'll make a home."

Twenty-Five

BEAU

She is quiet the whole way up to the cabin and keeps her head turned, looking out of the window. After I told her that I would live anywhere with her, she went quiet. We pull up to the house, and I look around. "When we were driving up," she says, "I wasn't sure what to expect since it is so dense with trees."

I shut off the truck and look at what Casey calls his cottage. "Only Casey could have a secret hideaway house that is brand new."

She laughs, getting out of the truck. "It's so pretty," she says, waiting for me to come around the side of the truck.

"He said that there is a lake right behind the house, but I don't know what he's talking about." I look at all the trees that surround this house. "Let's see inside."

She follows me up the steps, and I take out the key and open the door. We walk in, and it smells of pine wood right away. We take a couple of steps into the house, and I see the whole back wall is floor-to-ceiling windows. "I found the lake," she says, pointing out the windows at a huge lake. We walk past the kitchen on the left side, and I do a once-over,

168

seeing that all the appliances are brand new. The huge L-shaped couch on the right is so massive you could sit at least ten people on it. We step to the back windows and see that we are actually on stilts, something that you wouldn't see from the front of it. The dense trees are all around the lake so unless you live here or know about it, you would never know this is here. "There are the steps." She points at the steps that lead down to the lake. I turn to look up and see that there is a railing looking down into the room.

"Are you hungry?" she asks, walking to the fridge. All I want to do is grab her ass and pull her back to me, kissing her again and again. But this time, I don't want to stop until she's under me, saying my name over and over again. She opens the fridge, and we see it's fully stocked. "Do you want me to prepare stuff and then we can go and sit by the lake?"

"Yeah," I finally say. "I am going to bring our bags to the bedroom." I walk out of the room fast before she sees my cock is dying to come out and say hello to her.

Taking our bags, I go up the stairs that I didn't notice before, and I spot the master bedroom that has a view of the lake. I dump the bags right next to the king-size bed and go back downstairs. She is cutting up fruit, so I help her by finding a cooler to carry everything in. We head down to the lake, the sound of the water hitting the rocks, and spot two Adirondack chairs on a dock. I wait for her to pick a seat and then sit next to her. I open the cooler, taking out a beer for me and one for her. "I can get used to this," she says, taking a pull of her beer. "Would you be able to do this all year long?"

"Live up here?" I ask, taking a pull of the cold beer. "I mean, I'd love to vacation here, but I think I would need to be a little bit more in town."

She nods, and for the rest of the afternoon, we make idle chitchat. Both of us are nervous about what tonight will bring. We head back up to the house when the sun goes down. "What were you thinking about eating for dinner?"

"We can throw a couple of steaks and potatoes on the grill," I say. She takes the stuff out of the bag while I get the steak out.

She walks over to the wine rack and takes down a bottle. "Do you think Casey would mind if we opened a few bottles?"

I look over at her. "I don't even think he knows what's in that rack." I laugh while she comes over, opening some of the drawers to search for a corkscrew. She pours herself some wine once she gets it open and takes a sip.

"This is really good," she says. Walking over to the liquor rack, she comes back with a bottle of whiskey. I watch her while she pours some in a small glass and hands it to me. "Cheers."

I wipe my hands and grab the glass. "Cheers." I gently clink my glass to her, and we both take a sip.

"Okay, what can I do to help?" she says, walking next to me. "Do you want me to start on the salad?"

"Yeah," I say, and she touches my hip when she walks by me. I watch her grab the things in my arms, and she puts them down right beside me.

"This is fun," she says, taking another sip of wine and then looking at me. "Us preparing dinner together."

I smile at her. "We've done this before."

"Not while married." She lifts her left hand, laughing and taking another sip of wine.

"No, not married." I lift my own hand, wiggling my ring finger.

I stand beside her while I marinate the meat, and she cuts the lettuce. She leans over, and our hands slide next to each other, and she takes another sip of wine. Moving around her, I touch her just because like little touches on her hips.

Every single time I touch her, she takes another sip of

wine. She does just as much touching, and every single time she finishes doing something, she either walks by and touches me or leans into me. I see her cheeks flushing, so I lean in and give her just a little peck. Then she drinks more wine, and my stomach sinks. Is she drinking because she thinks we are going to sleep together?

I walk away from her to go to the grill. "I'll be grilling," I say, and she nods.

"I'll set the table." She turns and gets on her tippy toes and her shorts ride up, showing me her long, lean tan legs. Her shirt also rolls up, showing me her tan tummy even more. I swallow down the lump in my throat and then go outside.

I watch her set the table from outside. She drinks another two glasses of wine, and her hands are almost shaking. When the meat is done, I walk in, and she turns around with a smile. "Smells good, Mr. Mayor."

I smile at her as I walk to the dining room table that she set. I sit at the head and she takes the seat to my right. The salad bowl sits in the middle of our plates. She put another bottle of wine beside her and even put my whiskey on the table. I set the plate of steak down next to the salad, and she turns and walks back into the kitchen to grab the baked potatoes. I wait for her to sit down before taking my seat. She picks up my plate, preparing it like she always does.

"Thank you," I say, taking a sip of my whiskey.

"You're welcome, dear," she says, laughing while she prepares her own plate. "How many women have cooked for you?" I look at her. "I mean, you date a lot."

"Some would say you date a lot also," I say, and she just looks at me. "Do they cook for you?"

"Not even once. I make sure my dates are out in public so there is no gray area," she says, taking another sip of wine. "What about you?"

"No," I answer, my stomach burning. "They don't cook for me."

"Well, at least I have that one up on them then." She cuts into her steak. "Have you ever been in love?"

I take my glass of whiskey. "Yes." Her eyes now fly up, and I see that they are a darker blue.

"You've been in love?" she whispers. She looks down, and I swear I see tears in her eyes, but she grabs her glass of wine, and when she looks back at me, there are no more tears. "You've never told me," she says while cutting her steak and avoiding my eye contact.

"I've never really told anyone," I say, hoping she looks at me, but instead, she drinks another sip of wine. "Have you?" I ask as she leans back in her chair, my heart hammering in my chest as I wait for her answer.

"The steak is cooked perfectly," she says, avoiding the question. I want to press it again, but I'm not sure she'll even remember this conversation. So instead, I just finish my steak without the both of us really talking. She gets up first and walks to the kitchen, bringing her plate with her. "This was one of my best dinners I've ever eaten." She looks over at me, smiling, her cheeks pink and her eyes a light blue. She walks over. "Thank you." She bends, putting her face in front of mine. "For cooking," she says and kisses me on the lips lightly, then she moves away just a touch. "And for everything." She kisses me again. This time, her tongue slides in with mine. I want to get lost in her kiss. I want to get lost in her, but I don't want our first time to be because she's drunk.

"You're welcome," I say softly as my hand comes up to touch her face. "I would do anything for you," I say. I see her swallow and then move out of my touch. I try not to let it hurt, try not to dwell on it, but when I get up and bring the plates into the kitchen, she starts walking around me, holding my hips again. When she runs her hand up my back softly while she walks by, it takes all my willpower not to ignore the fact that she drank too much and touch her the way I want to touch her. When the kitchen is cleaned up, I lean against the counter, and she mimics my stance. "Are you tired?" I ask.

"Not really." She walks over to me and wraps her arms around my neck, getting on her tippy toes. "We can maybe go into the bedroom." My hands go to her hips, and I want so much to take her to the bedroom. I want so much to tell her all of the things, but I don't want her to have to get drunk to be with me.

"I think I'm going to take a shower," I say and see the look in her eyes change and her hands fall from my neck. Her shield is suddenly up.

"Yeah, that is a good idea," she says. "Why don't you go first?" She turns and walks away from me, and I want to call her back. I want to hold her hand and sit on the couch with her, but she has closed herself off. I saw it in the look she gave me. I walk to the shower, feeling defeated as the warm water runs down my body. When I slip on my boxers and shorts, I open the door and find all the lights from downstairs turned off.

After I walk downstairs, my eyes roam the area, looking for her, and I find her in a ball on her side. Her eyes are closed, and I have to wonder if she is faking. I stand here for a minute, and when she doesn't move, I grab one of the throw blankets and cover her with it. I sit next to her, not knowing what to do. We are both in uncharted territories, and the last thing I want to do is lose her. I put my head back, closing my own eyes, and the next thing I know, light is coming into the house directly on my face as if someone is holding a flashlight. I put my hand up to block the sun from my face and open one eye. The smell of coffee hits me right away, and when I turn to look over in the kitchen, I find Savannah moving around.

"What time is it?" I ask, mumbling.

"A little after seven," she says, and I see that she has changed from what she was wearing yesterday.

"How long have you been up?" I get up, going to the kitchen, and when she turns around, I see that her nose and her eyes are red from crying.

"I don't remember." She avoids looking at me. "I got up and took a shower." She grabs her coffee cup, bringing it to her lips. "Then I couldn't fall back asleep."

I walk to grab a cup and pour coffee in it. "You should have woken me up."

"There was no use in both of us being awake," she says, standing exactly where she did yesterday right before she wrapped her arms around my neck, and I told her I was going to take a shower.

"I came out, and you were fast asleep on the couch." I bring the cup to my lips. "It's a rough day when your wife falls asleep on the couch two days into your marriage." I can't stop myself from saying the words. I don't know what I was thinking, but what I wasn't expecting was her comeback.

She blinks and looks me straight in my eyes. "It's a rough day when your husband can't stand your touch and runs off to shower."

Twenty-Six

SAVANNAH

I don't know why I say it because I told myself for the past four hours that I was not going to bring it up. I was not going to let the hurt of him not wanting to be with me affect anything. *He married me because he had to, not because he wanted to,* the voice chants over and over in my head. The thought cuts me right through the heart, and no matter how many times I'm blinking away the tears, they fall anyway. "It's a rough day when your husband can't stand your touch and runs off to shower." I watch his eyes and then see his mouth hang open as I put my cup of coffee beside me. "There is a certain look we have to give the public." I start to say my speech that I also spent the night thinking of. "So in public, we can be all lovey-dovey, but when we are behind closed doors, it's just Beau and Savannah, best friends." The sting of the words are so much more when they are out of my mouth and not just in my head.

"What the fuck?" he says, putting his own coffee cup beside him. "What did you just say?" I look at him as he stands there, his shorts low on his hips and his chest perfect and chis-

175

eled. His black hair falls across his forehead, and his beauty makes my heart hurt.

"I just stated the obvious," I say, not even caring anymore. "I obviously wanted to."

"You wanted to what?" His voice comes out in almost a growl. "You wanted to get so shit-faced so you could muster up being with me?" His words shock me, and if I wasn't leaning on the island, I would have stumbled back.

"What?" I whisper.

"You drank all night." He points at me. "All night, you had to drink in order to actually kiss me."

"Me?" I say, pointing at my chest. "You think I drank all night because of that?" My head is spinning as I take in his words.

"Well, you start drinking, and then all of a sudden, you can touch me and kiss me," he says, looking out the window and then looking back at me with hurt in his eyes. "It doesn't take a rocket scientist to see what was happening."

"For your information," I say, my voice going just a touch louder. "I was drinking to muster up the courage to tell you all the things I wanted to tell you." I almost stomp my foot like a child having a tantrum. I don't give him a chance to say anything. I waited too long for this moment to back down now. "I sat there and asked you if you have ever been in love with someone," I remind him. "I know I asked the question, but I wasn't ready for the answer."

"Oh, well, it's better than a non-answer," he throws back in my face. "You didn't even answer the question."

"You're an asshole!" I shout. "I didn't answer the question because there was a fucking lump stuck in my throat." A tear escapes me now, and I brush it away with a vengeance. "I didn't answer the question because I didn't want to admit that I've been in love with you my whole goddamn life, and you love someone else." I finally admit it to him, and the tears make my vision all blurry. "So yeah, I didn't answer the fucking question because I couldn't stand to hear you answer it."

"You love me?" he says like he's in shock or maybe he doesn't want to hear it and maybe I just ruined the only true friendship I've ever had. "You love me," he says again, and all I can do is look out the big window at the sun shining. I look at the water, and it looks so peaceful. "Look at me."

"No," I say. "I'm sorry. I shouldn't have said anything," I say, turning to walk away and save a bit of my dignity, but he puts his hand on my arm to stop me from going.

"Look at me, Savannah," he says softly.

"I don't want to." I look down, and a tear rolls down my cheek and lands on his fingers. "I can't," I finally admit.

"You need to look at me so you can see," he says, and I feel him moving closer to me. "You need to see my eyes to know the truth." His hand slips down my arms, and he stands right behind me. I feel his heat through my T-shirt. "I need to tell you the truth." I don't move. "You gave me your side, so let me give you mine." I turn and see the tears in his eyes. "You asked me if I've been in love, and I answered yes," he says, and I'm not sure I can hear this. "But what you didn't ask me or give me a chance to say is who I love."

"I don't really want to know," I say.

"I fell in love with you when I was ten years old and you kicked me in the balls for tugging your hair," he says, and now it's me who stands in the middle of the kitchen with my mouth hanging open. "I fell in love with you even more when you were pregnant. I watched you dig so deep for all the strength to continue. I watched you build a business from scratch, and I watched you become the most amazing mother and woman I've ever seen. I've done this the whole time, falling so far in love with you that there is no one else out there for me."

"But," I finally say, "you go on all these dates."

"Yeah, because you go on all these dates," he says. "So I pretend I don't care by going on these excruciating dates." His thumb rubs my cheek. "Dates that I always end after an hour and then come in search of you." All of his words have shocked me; all of his words have left me without words. "Think back to all the dates I went on and how I would show up at the bar at nine. Because that is when business would die down and you could sit down with me." He wraps one arm around my waist. "You did your own fair share of dating."

"Well, yeah." I look down and then look up. "But if you notice, it was always after you went on a date."

"So you dated because I was dating?" he asks, smiling and I'm forgetting that I started this conversation with me being angry. I push away from him now, or at least I try, but he doesn't let his hold of me go. "Not so fast," he says. "You love me."

I roll my eyes now. "Well, you heard me say it." I want to put my hands on my hips.

"I want you to say it again," he says. I look at him, and he smiles the same smile that always makes me do whatever he wants even though I don't want to do it.

"Fine, I love you," I say. "You big horse's ass."

He throws his head back, and he laughs. "Of course she can't just say she loves me and leave it at that."

"Whatever." I roll my eyes and try to step out of his embrace.

"Oh, no, you don't," he says, pulling me back to him tighter. "You aren't running away this time." His tone is very tight and to the point. "No, not this time, Savannah. It's time to put the cards on the table."

My heart speeds up, and my stomach goes to my throat. "I think we did put all the cards on the table."

"No." He shakes his head. "I just put down a couple of

cards. I've dated all these women, and I haven't kissed one of them." He must see the shock in my eyes. "I haven't even laid a finger on them to even help them up."

"But ..." I say. "But ..."

"I didn't date these women because I wanted to. I dated them because I thought the one woman who I wanted didn't want me back." He rubs his nose against mine.

"Well, you never asked me," I whisper. "I didn't drink last night because I didn't want you to touch me." My hand comes up, and I run my finger over his collarbone. "I drank so I could have the courage to finally tell you how I felt. We were married, and you didn't even know that I love you. You didn't even know that marrying you was making my dreams come true. You didn't even know that in my whole life you were the one thing missing."

"Well, then," he says. "I don't feel bad about tricking you into marriage then. Once I put that ring on your finger, I said so many things to you in my head." He picks me up now and places me on the counter. My legs open, and he steps between them. "I said the vows, but I meant every single word and more. You've made my dreams come true, and you didn't even know it."

"Beau," I say, and he just shakes his head.

"You're mine," he says. Leaning in, he rubs my nose and kisses me lightly. "That ring on your finger means you're mine." He rubs my nose again, kissing me one more time lightly. "But now, I'm going to claim you." My breath hitches, and his hand goes to my neck, and his lips crash down on mine. I open my mouth for him right away; my hands go to his chest and then up while my legs cross at his back. His kisses before were nothing like this. He kisses me like he owns me. He takes control of the kiss and tilts his head from right to left, trying to deepen the kiss. He wraps one arm around my waist and picks me up, walking toward the stairs. Our mouths never leave each other as we make up for all those years of not saying anything. I kiss him like it's the last time I'm going to kiss him, giving him everything that I have.

"I love you," he finally says when he lets go of my lips. Burying his face in my neck, he kisses and sucks, and my senses are on overload.

"I love you," I say right before he sits on the bed with me straddling him. My hand goes to his face. "I've told you I love you so many times in my head." My finger traces his lips. "When you would walk away and I would say bye, I would whisper under my breath that I love you." I lean down and kiss him just a bit. "When you would make me laugh and hug me, there were so many times it almost came out of me."

"Every time I used to say I'll see you later," he says, "it was me saying I love you." I push him down onto his back and place my mouth on his, but he flips me on my back. "I promise you round two will be better." I laugh and then his hand pulls up my shirt. I automatically cover myself up, and his eyes fly to mine.

"I have stretch marks," I say, "from when I was pregnant."

"You don't ever hide from me. Not now, not ever." He moves my hands away from my chest, bending down and taking a nipple into his mouth, and my back arches up.

"You," he says, his voice going low. "You are my kryptonite."

Twenty-Seven

BEAU

*S*he loves me. It's the only thing that is going through my head right now. She loves me, and she's here with me, and I'm going to make her mine. I'm going to make sure that every single time she moves tomorrow, she will feel me over her.

"I hope you're ready," I say, not sure if I'm telling myself or her or maybe both of us. "Because once we start, I'm not stopping." I take her shirt off, going to roll her nipples, and her back arches up. "I've waited forever." Kissing her between her breasts, I feel her heart pounding under my lips, and I'm happy that I'm not the only one who is going through all this. I trail my tongue down her trim stomach, my hands pulling down her shorts and taking her panties with them.

"Fuck," I hiss out when I see her trimmed landing strip. I don't even think twice before my mouth devours her pussy. I lick all the way up, tasting her on my tongue and making me want more and more. Her hand goes into my hair, and I hear her moan. My tongue slides inside her at the same time my thumbs open her lips up, and I see her clit ready for me. "Fuck," I say, using one of my thumbs to rub in a circle, my tongue missing her taste. I take her clit into my mouth as my finger enters her. "Wet," I say between sucking.

"Beau." When she says my name, my cock wants out now. "I'm going to ..." She pants now, and my finger thrusts into her even faster, and then I add another one. "Right there." I look up at the same time she opens her legs even more and moves her hips up and down. "I'm going to ..."

"I know," I say, my fingers getting wetter and wetter. "Let go, baby. I have you," I say, biting down on her clit, and she finally lets go. Her legs close around my head as she thrashes from left to right, her whole body trembling. I don't let her go until she stops, and her eyes open slowly.

"Beau," she says, and it's everything I thought it would be. I crawl up her body, stopping to take one of her nipples, and then I claim her mouth again. But this time, she isn't afraid or nervous. No, she puts her leg over mine and turns me to my back, our mouths finding each other right away. Her tongue slides with mine for just a minute more. "I've played this moment over and over in my head," she says, kissing the side of my lips and then trailing them to my neck. "I'd watch you walk in and wonder what was underneath." Her tongue circles my nipple, and she nips it. "I'd go home, and I would take my toy out."

"Your toy?" I ask. My cock suddenly gets even harder, and I didn't think that was possible.

"My toy." Her tongue traces her lips. "Every single time, it was you. Every single time, I thought it was you." She straddles me now, sitting on my thighs.

"If you think the first time we do this, it's with you riding, then you don't know me like you think you do," I say, and her eyes almost light up.

"I'm okay with that." She smiles and takes her hand to rub up and down my covered cock. "Just as long as you know that

I'll be riding you." She squeezes my cock, and it's my turn to moan. "But first, I want to take you in my mouth."

"Is that so?" I ask, and she just nods her head. "You're going to take me all the way?"

"I've been dreaming of this," she says, pulling down my shorts and freeing my cock. She licks her lips as she eyes my cock. She puts her hands around the base of my cock, and my head goes back on the bed, and I close my eyes. "Bigger ..." She moves her hands up and down. "Than my toy."

"I'm throwing that toy out," I hiss when she leans down and licks my head.

"We don't have to throw out the toy." My eyes watch as she takes the tip of my cock in her mouth. "I thought that maybe you can tease me with it." Her mouth now takes a bit more of my cock.

"The only cock going into you will be mine," I say between clenched teeth. She doesn't answer me. Instead, she just moans out around my cock. I move the hair away from her face so I can see her swallow my cock. She gags a bit. "Go easy, baby," I say, her eyes looking over at me. "Take it a little at a time." She bobs her head up and down, and I could die right here. I could die watching her take my cock. Her mouth comes off, and she licks my cock right down to my balls, sucking one in and then the other.

"Fuck, I want to sit on this cock," she says, moving her hand up and down. "So bad." She puts her mouth over my cock, and I let her play for a little more, and when I'm about to come, I grab her hair and pull her head back. "I'm not done," she moans, and before she says anything else, I swallow her words.

"I need a condom," I say when I finally let her mouth go, the both of us panting with need. My cock so ready to sink in her.

"I'm on the pill," she tells me. "And I haven't been with anyone since."

"I haven't been with anyone in eight years," I say, and she just looks at me. "No one was you. I stopped trying."

She moves over to the middle of the bed, and I crawl over to her. "Make love to me." She opens her legs for me. I hold my cock in my hand and rub it up and down her slit. She's so wet and ready for me.

Her eyes watch my every single move. "Do you want to put me in you?" I ask, and she reaches out, grabbing my cock and placing it at her entrance. I slide in the head of my cock, and both of us just sigh. I fall forward, placing my hands by her head. Her hand reaches for my elbow and moves up to my shoulder and then my neck. She tilts her head back the same time I put my head down to kiss her. I slide my tongue into her mouth the same time I bury my cock into her. We swallow each other's moans, then she pulls back to say my name and opens her legs wider, but one of my hands blocks her. I sit up on my knees now, my cock not moving from inside her.

"You need to move," she says as she adjusts herself for me. "I need you to move." Her words come out breathlessly. I put one of her legs on my shoulder and fall forward again, putting my hands beside her hips and going even deeper than I thought I could.

"Beau." She calls my name again, and this time, I move in her. My hips move up and down, playing with her clit at the same time, as I pull out and slowly enter her again. I try to go as slow as I can, but when she puts her hands on my neck and looks me in the eyes, her voice comes out in a pant. "Harder." She tries to lift her hips off the bed to meet my thrusts, but I slam into her and then move my hips up and down, teasing her clit again. I bend my head, putting my forehead on hers as I slam into her over and over again. Our lips touch sometimes, and when they do, she slides her tongue into my mouth.

"Right there," she says every time I slam into her. Each time harder and harder. "I'm going to," she says, and I slam my mouth on hers. Our tongues tangle together while she spasms over my cock, and I empty myself in her. I bury my face into her neck, trying to get my breathing under control. She wraps her arms around me and hugs me close to her.

"How much time between?" she asks, and when I get up and look at her, she is smiling.

"What do you mean?" I ask, leaning down and taking her lips in a kiss.

"I mean, I could go again now." She squeezes my cock with her pussy. "From the feel of it ..." She squeezes me again. "You are also good to go."

I move out of her and slam into her again, my cock still rock hard. "I think I'm good to go also."

"Good." She rubs her hands up my back. "It's my turn to ride." The last word is drawn out in a long moan. She wiggles under me, and I take my cock out of her. She gets on her knees now in front of me and shocks me when she leans over and takes my cock into her mouth all the way to the base.

"Fuck," I say. My hand goes to her head, and my hips move on their own. I see her ass wiggling side to side, so I lean over and smack her ass. She just moans through it.

"Are you playing with yourself?" I ask. When she nods, I think I'm going to shoot down her throat. She lets go of my cock.

"Sit down with your head against the headboard," she tells me, and I look at her. "I've thought about this for many years."

"Have you?" I ask. My hand reaches for her pussy. I put two fingers in her, and she moans. "How many times?"

"Every day," she says. "Sometimes twice a day, depending on how hot you looked." She shocks me and moves her pussy away from me. "Sit." She points at the headboard, tossing the pillows on the floor.

I sit with my back to the headboard, and my cock sticking up. "Okay, baby." I take my cock in my hand. "Hop on."

"Oh, I plan to," she says, throwing her leg over my hips. "I plan on it." She leans forward, sliding her tongue in my mouth, and I feel her hand on my cock. She puts her knees by my hips and slowly slides all the way down.

"So fucking good," I say, letting go of her mouth. My hands go to her hips, and I try to help, but she shakes her head.

"This is my rodeo," she says, leaning forward. Putting her hands on the headboard, she lifts herself up and impales herself on me. "I get to ride." She does it again, leaning more into me, and I take one of her nipples between my teeth. She hisses but moves up and down faster. "How I want to ride." She lets one hand go from the headboard and brings it to her clit where she rubs it back and forth.

I push her hand away. "You can ride," I say, rubbing right and left, "but I'm going to be the one who makes you come." Her head falls back, and she puts her hands on my legs behind her, giving me room to play with her clit. I let her ride me, taking one nipple between my teeth and then sucking at the same time I play with her clit. "You close?" she puts her hands back on the headboard, riding me faster.

"Yes," she hisses as she rides my cock, not once letting go of the headboard. "I'm almost there," she tells me, and I can feel it. Her pussy tightens more and more around my cock every single time she moves up. "I'm there," she says, and I feel her come on my cock. I wait for her to finish, and when she slows down, she sits up and wraps her hands around my neck, her mouth finding mine. I kiss her while she sits on my cock.

"You done?" I ask, and she looks at me and nods. "Good," I say, pulling her up off me. "My turn." She looks at me unsure, and I flip her over. "Face down, ass up," I say, grabbing her by the hips and entering her in one long thrust. We're both panting, but I don't let off. Holding her hips, I slam into her over and over again. She comes two more times before I feel my balls tighten, and I plant myself all the way and come in her again.

Twenty-Eight

SAVANNAH

"Just one more time." I start kissing his neck as he tries to push me away with one hand while pulling me to him with the other one.

"Baby." He rolls me to the side, and the way he says my name, I know that I'm going to win this one. "It's been seven times."

"Well, that's bad luck," I say, smiling at him. Leaning forward, I kiss him. We spent the day in bed, getting up just after noon to eat something, and that went out the window when I bent over in front of him and the T-shirt I was wearing rode up over my ass, giving him a clear way to sink into me. I held on to the counter for dear life, and I loved every single minute of it. I always thought sex with him would be amazing, especially after I used to hear the women boast about him, which I know were all lies now. "Things are always better in even numbers."

"Is it now?" he says as I reach between us and grab his hard cock in my hand. "God, I don't think I have the energy."

"Oh, don't worry. I got this," I say. I laugh and go under the covers and take his cock in my mouth and by the time we finish, not only do I start on top, but it ends with him holding the headboard this time and pounding into me.

"God, I thought the last time was good," he says when he rolls off me. "I was wrong." I laugh now, getting out of bed and going over to the bathroom. "Where are you going?"

"To clean up," I say over my shoulder. "Take a shower." He throws the sheet off him and gets up to come with me. His cock is still semi-hard, and his legs thick and full of muscle. "Where are you going?"

"Someone needs to wash your back." He smacks my ass as he walks by me to the shower.

"The last time that happened, we almost flooded the bathroom." I point at the tub.

"That was your fault." He turns on the water in the shower. "I told you that it's a myth. You can't get stuck on cock in water." I throw my head back and laugh. "Now get in." He holds open the door.

"No funny stuff," I say as I walk in even though I know I'm not even going to stop him. We stay in the shower until the water runs cold. That night, I fall asleep naked in his arms, and we both wake up, looking for each other. He makes love to me slowly during the night, and when I wake up the next morning, it's with his face between my legs.

"What time are we leaving?" I ask from my side of the bed, holding the sheet up on my chest while I drink the coffee he made for me.

"We can leave after this," he says. "I'm going to have someone come and replace the bed this week."

"What?" I ask, shocked.

"He's not going to have the bed we have sex on," he says, and I laugh, leaning forward and kissing him. We get up after we finish our coffee and make the bed, then get dressed.

On the ride home, we talk this time, the nervousness of before gone. He stops at the diner on the way home, and I get out with not a care in the world. He puts his arm around me, and I slip my fingers in the hand that is hanging over my shoulder, then lean over and kiss his neck. I almost forget that it's not just the two of us. But that all changes when we walk into the diner and all the talking stops, and everyone looks over at the door.

"We aren't in Kansas anymore," I mumble and drop his hand, expecting him to drop his arm from around my shoulders, but he doesn't.

"Afternoon, everyone," he says, smiling as we walk in, letting his hand fall now, but linking our hands together. "Thought I would bring the missus in for a burger." I see some of the old ladies side-eye me and shake their heads. I put my head down, avoiding eye contact when we sit in the booth, and he looks at me. "What are you getting?" he asks, tapping his thumb on the table.

I avoid his eyes, not wanting him to see the stupid tears that have creeped up. "I don't know. I'm not that hungry," I say, and he stops strumming his finger.

"Don't let the old ones get to you," he says, grabbing my hand and bringing it to his lips. "If they know they get to you, they will keep doing it."

"It's easy for you to say." I look at him. "You haven't been the outsider your whole life." He doesn't have a chance to say anything before Mr. Lewis comes over.

"I brought you two some root beer floats." He puts the frosted mugs in front of us. "It's a wedding present." He smiles at us. "Always knew you two would end up together." He winks and walks away.

"Well, I guess it was just the two of us then," I say, grabbing one of the cold mugs and taking the straw and dunking it in. Then I grab the spoon and take a bite of the ice cream. I'm about to say something else when the door opens, and Chase comes in. "Oh, God," I say, my hands suddenly nervous. He looks around the room, smiling to a couple of people, and then when he turns and looks our way, he just glares. He walks over to the counter and sits with his back to us. "I guess I deserved that one."

"Well, if you think that is bad," Beau says, "Melody just gave me the look of death." I look around, spotting her at a table with her grandmother.

"She is still looking our way," I say, and he gets up, walking to my side of the booth and slipping in.

"Well, then let's give them something to talk about," he says right before he kisses me. Make no mistake about it, his tongue slides with mine, and I taste the sweet of the ice cream on his tongue.

"I love you," he whispers when he stops kissing me, and I'm about to tell him the same when someone fills the booth, and I look over at Liam.

"Hey there, little brother," he says, and I can feel Beau's energy change from beside me. "Heard you finally got married." His smile is creepy and leery, and I wonder how such a horrible human could have made Ethan. "Always wanted to be me." He looks around to make sure no one is listening. "Even took my sloppy seconds."

I put my hand on Beau's chest to stop him from jumping over the table and attacking Liam. "He isn't worth it."

"Yeah, listen to your woman," Liam says. "Besides, I don't want to embarrass you in front of her."

"Move." I push Beau. "I'm out. I'm not going to sit at this table with him." I point at Liam as Beau gets up. "He is a little, two-inch man, literally, and what's worse, he's also a two-pump man." I look at the table. "I feel sorry for your wife." Liam looks at me with shock. "It's no wonder she had to have Botox all over her face. How can she fake it for so long? I mean, last I heard, she said you can't even get it up anymore." I look at Beau now. "Can we stop by and see Ethan on our way home?"

He pushes the hair away from my face and tucks it behind my ear. "We sure can." He smiles. "Liam, it's been a pleasure as always." Then he looks down at his crotch. "Good luck with that." He points at his crotch and takes my hand, and we walk out.

It's only when we are away from the diner do I look over at him. "I think I'm going to be sick," I say, and he just keeps walking to the truck.

"Don't let him get to you," he says, opening the passenger door for me. "If you let him get to you, he wins." He kisses my nose. "And I refuse to let Liam win anymore."

"If I didn't love you before ..." I wrap my arms around his waist. "I would love you now."

"Good," he says. "Now let's go see our boy." I smile, getting in and making our way over to Jacob and Kallie's house.

Ethan runs out the minute we stop the truck. He runs to me first, and I don't have to bend as much to kiss him. He walks over to Beau where he gives him a side hug. "Hey, Uncle Beau."

"There they are." We hear Jacob from the porch. "The newlyweds."

I shake my head, and we walk up the steps. Ethan runs up first. "Can I watch a movie before bed?" he asks Jacob, who just nods at him. "Am I sleeping here or at your house?"

"Wherever you want," I say, the only thing Jacob and I fully agreed on was allowing Ethan to decide where he wanted to stay and when. Sure, we had a routine of fifty-fifty, but if Ethan wanted to sleep over at his house on my day, I wouldn't stop him and vice versa.

"Okay," he says, running in the house. "Kallie, my mom said I could stay if I want."

"Okay, honey." I hear Kallie say from the kitchen. We walk down the hallway into the kitchen, and Kallie is cleaning up the dinner plates. "Hey, you guys." She wipes her hands on the towel that is hanging on the stove handle.

I look at the counter and see a file that is open with the pictures of my bar. I walk over and look at the pictures of before and then after. "It's all rubble," I say, the sting of tears coming up as I go through all the pictures. "There is nothing left."

"I know," Jacob says, going to stand next to Kallie, and they share a look. "We just got the report back from Blake."

"Really?" I say to them, excited that it is one less thing standing in front of me rebuilding. "That's good news."

"I don't know about that," Jacob says, and this time, he shares a look with Beau.

"What aren't you saying?" Beau asks for both of us.

"Do you guys want something to drink or eat?" Kallie asks, but my stomach is in knots while I wait, so I just shake my head.

"They are reevaluating as we speak so it could change," Jacob says. "They are taking everything into account."

"Jesus," I say, rubbing my hands over my face. "Would you just cut to the chase and tell me what Blake said?"

"You might as well be honest with her," Kallie says. "Besides, Beau is going to get the report tomorrow anyway."

"Fine," he says. "But before I say it, I don't want you to freak out."

"Jacob," I say his name with my teeth clenched.

"Blake says that it was arson," Jacob says, and my legs give out.

Twenty-Nine

BEAU

I hear the words, and I see her going down, but I'm able to grab her before she hits the floor. "Oh my God," Kallie says, rushing around the counter. "Are you okay?"

"I'm fine," Savannah says in a whisper. "I just ..."

"She's in shock," Jacob says and then looks at me. "Bring her to the couch." I carry her over to the couch. Setting her down, I sit next to her.

"Here is some water," Kallie says, handing me a water bottle for her. She tries to take it, but her hands shake. "I'm going to keep Ethan busy so you guys can talk." She turns and walks away to the family room.

"Tell me everything," Savannah says, and I move to sit on the edge of the seat, waiting to hear what he has to say. Today started as the second best day of my life. Well, maybe the third since the best day of my life was when we got married, followed by the day she told me she loved me. Going to the diner was a stupid move, but I didn't even think. Her guard went up as soon as we stepped into the diner, and everyone looked at her, some with disgust. It made my stomach burn, but I wasn't about to

194

show them that their opinion matters, so I ignored it and sat down. Then Liam happened, and if she hadn't put her hand on my chest, I would have throttled him from across the table.

"The fire started in your office," he says, and I see the tears in her eyes. I lean back next to her and take her in my arms, kissing her head. "There was gasoline all over the bar." She closes her eyes. "Blake thinks that someone spread the gasoline and let it sit before lighting it. We found ten gas canisters in your office."

"Who would do this?" she asks. "Did you find any evidence?"

"Nothing." He shakes his head. "I don't think we will either."

"Fuck," Savannah says. "My insurance is going to be all over this. Already they didn't want to cover the vandalism. I don't even know if I have the money to rebuild the way I want."

"We are going to figure it out," I say, and she just shakes her head. "Tomorrow, we can call the insurance agent and talk to them." She doesn't say a word, and when we leave, she kisses Ethan goodbye and just leans her head on the window in the truck. When we pull up to the house, she gets out while I grab the bags and walk up the steps.

Unlocking the door, I throw down the bags and sweep her off her feet, and she gasps out in shock. "Got to carry you over the threshold."

"You had to do this the night of the wedding," she says, wrapping her arms around my neck. "I don't think it matters now."

"Our home," I say, walking in. "We make our own rules." She puts her head on my shoulder while I kick the door closed. "You hungry?"

"Not really," she answers softly, and I know that the whole

arson thing has thrown her for a loop. It's thrown us all for a loop.

I carry her upstairs, and she doesn't say anything for most of the night. The only time she comes alive is when I make love to her, and then she gives me everything she has. I wake up the next morning, and the spot next to me is empty. I sit up, and I have this sudden panic that she is gone until I smell coffee and bacon. I get up, grabbing my boxers to slip on, and then make my way downstairs to find her sitting at the island with papers in front of her. "Morning," I say, kissing the back of her neck. "What time is it?"

"A little after seven," she says, and I see her wearing one of my white robes. "I made breakfast, and it's in the oven."

"What time did you get up?" I ask, pouring a cup of coffee.

"I couldn't sleep, so I've been up most of the night." She shrugs. "I tried, but I finally gave up at around three a.m."

"What is all that?" I point at the papers.

"This is me trying to figure out how I'm going to rebuild the bar." She puts all the papers together. "It was worth some equity, but that is with the bar on it. Now it's just land." She blinks, and I see the tears in her eyes. "I'm going to go into the bank today and see what they say."

"We can figure it out," I say. "I have money. You know that."

She looks over at me. "I'm not taking your money, Beau." She shakes her head. "Not now, not tomorrow, and not next week."

"Why not?" I ask. "I'm your husband."

She avoids the question altogether. "What time do you have to go in today?"

"I should be in at around eight." I let her avoid the question. "I have to attend an event tonight. Do you want to come with me? It'll be at the mayor's house with some of my donors."

"Yeah," she says and gets up. "I'm going to head into the shower." She looks over at me and walks away, and I just watch her. "Are you not coming with me?" she asks over her shoulder, and she doesn't have to ask me twice. I walk out of the house after eight thirty, leaving her with a kiss and splayed out like a starfish in the bed.

I jog up the front steps of the mayor's house and look at the empty desk in the reception area. "Fuck, I forgot I fired Bonnie." I shake my head and walk into my office, stopping when I see my father sitting behind the desk. "What the hell are you doing?" I ask, slamming the door, kicking myself for not having the locks changed yet.

"I'm just making sure that you have everything under control." He leans back in the chair. "I heard some interesting news."

I shake my head. "I don't have time for this. I have a meeting with the accountant in a couple of minutes."

"I heard that also." He just eyes me.

"Is there anything that you haven't heard?" I put my hands on my hips. "Since you seem to know everything."

"Is she pregnant with your child?" he asks, and I glare at him.

"Watch it, old man," I hiss. "I'm not Liam. I'm not going to let you talk about my wife with anything but respect."

"Respect?" he shouts. "That whore has blackmailed me for eight years. Blackmailed us."

"She wouldn't have to blackmail anyone if your son would have taken responsibility as a man!" I shout back at him. "But being the spineless prick that he is, he made Daddy fight his battles."

"You will not choose her over this family." He slams his hand on the desk.

"She is my family." I shake my head. A knock on the door sounds, and I walk over and open the door, seeing the accountant Thomas.

"Good morning." I motion for him to come in. "Thank you for coming on such short notice."

He nods at me and then spots my father. Something comes over him, and I can't quite put my finger on it. "I didn't know you would be attending."

"He's not going to be attending anything." I look at him. "We can do this in the conference room," I say and watch him nod and walk out. I grab the files I need and look over at my father. "All my life, I looked up to you," I say, and I swear he rolls his eyes. I grab the door handle in my hand. "Now, I pray I don't end up like you."

I close the door and walk down the hallway when I'm stopped by someone who is planning the party. "I'm sorry to interrupt you, Mayor, but Bonnie isn't here."

"Yeah, I fired her," I say, and she looks at me in shock. "What can I help you with?"

"Don't worry about it," she says. "I'll handle everything. It's tonight at six thirty."

I nod and walk to the conference room, seeing that Thomas is sitting down and setting up his own papers. "Do you want anything to drink?" I ask. "I'm in the middle of hiring another assistant."

"Did Bonnie quit?" he asks, and I shake my head.

"Let's just say we didn't see eye-to-eye," I say, and he looks down.

"If you want, my daughter is looking for a job. I have her helping out at my office, but it's a pity job, to be honest. She's thirty and happily married with two kids who are now both in school."

"That would be great," I say. "Can she start today?" I'm

198

kidding with him when he pulls out his phone and types something.

"She'll be right over," he tells me. At least I can cross that off my list. "Now let's talk about why you asked for this meeting."

I sit down and open my folder. "I was going over the budget for the past ten years," I say, taking out the papers, "and I know we balanced every single year." I turn the papers toward him. "But there is something in the budget I'm not understanding. There is a miscellaneous charge every single year, and the amount gets bigger and bigger." I see him swallow and then look down. "I'm wondering if you can explain that to me."

"Well," he says, tapping his hand on the desk. "It could mean a bunch of stuff, meals that were paid for or hotel rooms. Sometimes there have been some fundraising stuff that has to be expenses."

I lean back in the chair. "Hotel rooms?"

"When you have to travel," he says, "you expense it."

"Travel?" I shake my head. "Am I missing something here?"

"Beau," he says my name in almost a warning. "Why don't you just leave it alone and run the mayor's office like you want to run it? The budget has been posted and passed in the last meeting."

"It was passed because let's be honest, five people actually attended the meeting," I say. "I'm going to be very frank with you, Thomas." I put my hands on the desk. "I'm not liking this, not one bit, and I want to see all the receipts for this." He looks down, avoiding my eyes. "And just to be clear, I have no problem moving to another firm. Your loyalty has to be to the town and its people, not who runs the mayor's house."

"I understand, Beau," he says. "It's just not as black and white as you think it is."

"But it should be," I say. "And going forward, it's going to be black and white. I'm in this office for the people, to better the town, not take from them."

"That is good to hear," he says, and a knock on the door makes me get up, and I meet Thomas's daughter, Cassandra, who I hire on the spot. The day flies by as Cassandra and I go through the list of things that needs to be done.

When I finally have two minutes to myself, it's after four, and I call Savannah who answers after five rings. "Hello."

"Hey," I say, smiling when I hear her voice. "What are you doing?"

"I was trying on dresses for tonight." She sounds defeated. "I think I have one, but I'm not sure."

"Whatever you have, I'm sure you will look beautiful in," I say, and she laughs. "What did you do today?"

"I went to the bank," she says, her voice going soft. "But I don't want to talk about it now because I have to do my makeup and get ready." I want her to talk to me about it, but I won't push her until tonight when it's just the two of us. "Is there usually food at these things, or should I make us something to eat?"

"There will be a five-course meal," I say. "It's all suits and money."

"Great," she says. "What time will you be here?"

"I should be leaving the office in about an hour," I say, looking out the window. "I'll see you then." I hang up, and something churns in my stomach, but I'm not sure what it is. When I walk into the house an hour later, I find her in the bathroom with her hair all curled and her makeup done, and my heart bursts with pride.

"Hello, gorgeous wife," I say, and she smiles so big when she turns to see me.

"Hello, hot as fuck husband," she says, and I walk to her. She's wearing my robe again. "Now before you even start." I'm already pulling the sash loose, and it shows me that she isn't wearing anything under it. "I can't mess up my hair and make-up," she tries to talk, but my hands are already cupping her pussy. She closes her eyes and opens her legs a bit to give me access. My mouth finds her open mouth and our tongues circle each other. I pick her up and place her on the edge of the counter at the same time as she unties my belt. Our mouths never leave each other while she opens her legs, and I finger her, and she plays with my cock. The only time she lets my mouth go is when I slide into her. She wraps one arm around my neck and throws her head back, giving me access to her neck, which I suck on. I fuck her as slow as I can, but with her, I lose my head, and the slowness soon turns into an over-whelming need to fuck the shit out of her. She leans back, putting her feet on the counter and opening her legs wider. "Harder." The robe slips off her shoulders, and I grab both tits in my hands, squeezing them while I fuck her until we both come.

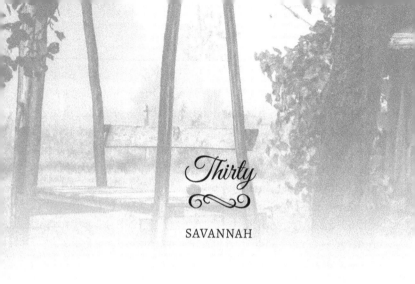

Thirty

SAVANNAH

My hands shake as I grab my purse and climb out of the truck, standing next to Beau who is wearing a blue suit that molds to him. He grabs my hand and brings it up to his lips and kisses my fingers. "You look amazing," he tells me again. When I got dressed, he was in his closet, putting on his pants. I slipped on the white and pink floral sleeveless dress and walked in to have him zip it up. The dress goes to my knees, and I matched it with white strappy sandals.

"Thank you." I smile at him shyly. I am not going to tell him what a fucked-up day I've had. I'm not going to put this on him when he has a function. So I hide it down and tuck it away. "This is nice." I look around, walking up the steps toward the house. "Remember when we were younger, we used to sit over there." I point at the tree all the way at the end of the lawn. "And watch all the people walking in."

"I hated it," he says. "I always had to dress up in a stuffy suit."

"You were handsome even then," I say, and we walk in. "I thought that everyone was a movie star back then. Dressed to the nines." I look around to see that some people have gathered near the door, and the waitress and waiter are walking around with trays of food and drinks. "Who would have thought I would actually attend one of them." I grab a glass of champagne from the passing waiter.

"You belong here," he says. He's about to say something else, but someone comes up to him and calls for his attention. He introduces me to the man who looks like he's ninety with his three-piece suit and the gold chain leading to his watch in the small pocket of the vest.

"If you would excuse us, girly," he says and pulls Beau away, leaving me standing in the middle of the room. I look around, and I get some who smile at me and some who sneer my way.

"This is going to be so much fun," I say to myself, taking another sip of champagne. I walk farther into the house, and a woman comes up to me and introduces herself as Beau's new assistant. She smiles and then runs off to speak to someone who she knows. I look around for him again as I finish off my glass and then grab another one. I try to look for Beau, and when I spot him, he looks like he is with a group of old stuffy suits.

"Savannah." I hear my name called and turn to see Mary Ellen coming toward me. She is dressed perfectly with a A-line dress that is tight on the top with a string of pearls around her neck. "Don't you look lovely?" She smiles and leans in to kiss both my cheeks, which shocks me. She's never done this before.

"Mary Ellen," I say her name and smile as fake as she is acting. I thought she liked me somewhat, but I guess I was wrong. I was wrong about so much. "You look lovely yourself."

"Thank you, dear," she says and then sees me drinking the champagne. "I would go easy on the drinks, Savannah. We have a name to uphold." I'm about to ask her what, when she grabs her own glass of champagne. "You don't actually drink it," she says. "You just hold it while you chitchat."

"Good to know," I mumble.

"So I heard the news that the two of you got married," she says, and I think maybe she might be happy for me, but when I look at her, I see her almost sneer at me.

"We did," I say, taking a sip. "It was lovely."

"I can only imagine since I wasn't given an invitation." She hisses out the last word, but she does it with a huge smile on her face. "It's a mockery is what it is," she says, and my stomach starts to burn. "Look at him." She motions with her head toward Beau, who is standing with a woman I've never seen before. Both of them are laughing, and she puts her hand on Beau's arm. "He should be married to someone like that and not—" she starts to say, and I bury down the hurt.

"Not the town whore," I finish the sentence for her. "I get it." I take another sip of the champagne, the sting of tears burning my eyes. "I'll see that it's put on my tombstone." I don't let her say another word. Instead, I walk away from her and from Beau, who hasn't once looked my way. I walk to the bathroom, ignoring everyone and pondering how bad it would be if I took off. I finish the champagne, leaving the glass in the bathroom, and when I walk out, I see that more people have arrived. I look around to see if I spot Beau, but all I see is Cassandra. "Hey, did you see Beau?"

"Yeah, he was in his office with his mother." She points at the office door and smiles at me.

I walk away from them and head to the office door, and before I knock, I can hear the yelling. "Admit it," Mary Ellen says.

"Fine, I did it to protect her. Does that make you happy?" Beau says, and the words are like a kick to my stomach. I am about to turn and walk away when the door swings open, and

I come face-to-face with Beau, who looks at me and his face goes white.

"Hey," he says softly. "I was looking for you."

I ignore the pain in my chest, and the burning in my stomach. I ignore it all and smile. "Well, you found me," I say. When he leans forward and kisses my lips, it takes everything I have not to take a step back.

"Dinner is almost served," he says, and I see Mary Ellen step up beside him. "We should go and sit."

"Go easy on the drinking, Savannah." Mary Ellen walks past us toward the backyard.

"God, that woman," Beau says, shaking his head. "She just doesn't get it."

"Well, she's your mother, and she has your best interests at heart," I say, averting my eyes.

"Are you okay?" he asks and puts his hand under my chin to make me look up. "Look at me."

I finally look at him, and I wonder if I can hide the hurt. "I'm fine. It's just been a whirlwind few days."

"I wish we could get away," he says, and Cassandra comes running to us.

"People are sitting, and they are waiting for you," she says. "Also, I'm not sure you approved it, but Savannah has been moved from beside you."

I swallow down the lump in my throat and listen to him. "I didn't approve that," Beau hisses, and I just shake my head.

"It's fine," I say. "You need to do your thing."

"I don't care," he says. "You're my wife." I want to tell him that we should talk about that, but I'm not sure now is the time to do that. Instead, I try not to make a big deal out of it.

"I already told them to fix it," Cassandra says. "I don't know about you, but I'd be pissed if my husband wasn't sitting next to me."

"Thank you." I smile at her. "That means a lot."

We walk to the seating area, and Beau holds out the chair for me, and I sit down, smiling at the men around the table. The meal is a blur, and I have no idea what is discussed, but when we walk into the house, I don't say anything to him as I follow him up to the bedroom. He doesn't even turn on the lights. He unzips my dress and kisses my shoulder, the lone tear comes out of my eye and rolls down my cheek. I make love to him, holding him in my arms as tight as I can, and when I know he's sleeping, I get up and walk down the stairs to sit on the couch. I go over the speech in my head over and over again, and when I hear his footsteps coming down the stairs, I'm ready for him. "Morning," he says, coming over to me and leaning down to kiss me. "I am going to go on the record in saying I hate waking up without you." I wait for him to be in the kitchen before I start.

"We need to talk," I say, and he turns around to look at me.

"I don't like the way that sounds," he says, smiling, and he must see that my face is probably a mess from crying all night long. "Why have you been crying?"

"It's just been an emotional couple of days," I say. "I went to the bank yesterday, and they denied me the loan," I say, and he walks to me. "He was sure to tell me that the mayor's office stands behind his decision since you will be buying the land."

"I have no idea why he said that. I haven't even had any discussion with anyone about it," he says.

"It doesn't matter, Beau," I say. "This"—I point at him and me—"was just to keep me safe."

"What are you talking about?" he says now, his voice going louder.

"I heard you," I say, and he just looks at me. "I heard you yesterday with your mother."

"Good," he says.

"I heard you tell her that you did it to keep me safe," I say, and he nods his head.

"Yeah, I did after I told her that I married you for love, and she laughed at me," he says. "You didn't hear the whole conversation, Savannah."

"It doesn't matter that I love you or that you love me," I say. "It's just too much."

"What is too much?" he asks.

"I stood in the room yesterday, looking around, and I felt like an imposter." I wipe away my tears. "I didn't belong there. I don't even belong here." I open my arms. "This town has shown me over and over again how I don't belong nor am I wanted here."

"But I want you here," he says, taking a step toward me, but I hold up my hand to stop him.

"I stayed this whole time because I wanted to show the town I could be someone else. I stayed for my bar, which I don't have anymore. It's time for me to move on."

"But what about me?" he asks, and if I was a strong enough person, I would ask him to come with me. If I thought for one minute I deserved his love, I would beg him to come.

"What about me?" I ask. "What about me walking out of my house without having people leer at me? What about going into the supermarket and hearing home wrecker at least once?" I let the tears fall. "What about being treated like I am the scum of the earth? What about that? I have a chance to walk away and start fresh." I shake my head and sit down. "I have a chance to walk out of my house and look around and smile at my neighbors. I have the chance to just be the new person in town that doesn't have so much baggage with her that I'm buried up to my knees. I have the chance to not be known as the town whore who forced Beau to marry her."

"You leaving is letting them win," he tells me. "You walking away shows them that they won."

"Then let them have it," I say. "They took everything else from me. Let them have that also."

"Nothing I say is going to change your mind," he tells me. "I can sit here and beg you to stay, but you are already gone." His voice goes low. "I can beg and plead and tell you all the things, and in the end, your mind is already made up."

"I just need to get away," I say. "Maybe I just need to clear my head. Maybe ..." I say. "I just know that I can't sit here without wondering."

"Our love means something," he tells me, breaking me. "I'm going to let you go," he says, looking down and wiping his own tear away. "Just promise me one thing."

"Yes," I say because I would promise him anything.

"That before you do anything, you let me know. Before you sign anything or make any decision, you tell me."

"I can give you that," I say. He gets up and walks away from me, stopping and turning back to me.

"For my whole life, I've loved you. For my whole life, my dream was to be married to you," he says and looks down. "It was always you. I know that I'm not the whole town"—he swallows—"but just so you know, you have at least one person." He walks up the stairs and away from me. He doesn't even come and tell me goodbye when he leaves, and I have to wonder why would he. If he did this to me, I would have stormed out and never looked back. I pack my bag and make one more stop before I head out of town.

I walk up the steps, ringing the bell, and the door opens. "Hey," Kallie says. "I didn't know you were coming over." I look down, and she must see something is wrong. "Let me get Jacob."

Thirty-One

BEAU

I walk out of the house without saying goodbye to her. I don't go to her because if I did, I would get down on my knees and beg her to stay. I would wrap my arms around her and never let her go. I don't want her to stay because I've made her feel guilty or because I forced her to stay. I want her to stay to simply stay. I want her to choose me and not have any regrets.

The drive to the office is a blur, and when I walk up to the step, I just nod to Cassie and go straight to my office. I sit down in the chair and go over everything in my head.

I don't do anything all day. I just sit with my door closed, looking out the window. I wonder where she is or what she is doing, hoping that she knows I'm thinking about her. I pick up my phone and send her a text message.

Me: *Just wanted to tell you that I miss you.*

I look at it, but then don't send it. *It's too soon*, I think to myself. I watch the sun go down, and when I walk out of my office, I walk to my truck and make it back home. I open the door, and my heart sinks when I smell her. I walk up to the bedroom where I left her this morning and see that she's taken some of her stuff.

Sitting on the bed, I feel lost. I don't eat supper because all I can do is lie in our bed and go over our conversation. How can she think that no one wants her here? Sure, there are some who hate her in this town, but I can count those people on two hands.

I sit up in bed now and grab my phone, texting the same text to everyone.

Me: Tomorrow morning mayor's office nine a.m. sharp. Mandatory.

I put the phone down, and when I walk into the office the next day, it's just before eight. I walk to the conference room and set things up. When it gets closer to nine a.m., they start filing in. Jacob and Casey are the first to arrive.

Casey looks around, asking, "Do I want to know what this is about?"

I smile and then Jacob is the one who speaks up. "How are you doing without her?"

"Horrible," I answer. "It's one day, and I swear it feels like someone died in my house."

He slaps me on my shoulder. "Love will fuck you every time," he says. "I hope you made coffee."

"I did," I tell him, "and I got doughnuts." They both take off to the conference room. Tony is the next to arrive at the same time as Sal, the town plumber.

"Whatever it is," Sal says, "I didn't do it."

I laugh at him and shake their hands, thanking them for coming. "There is coffee in the conference room."

Five more people arrive at the same time. Peter, the electrician; Jake, the carpenter; Tyler, the masonry expert that we have in town; Kaylie, an architect; and Tracy, the town gardener. "Thank you, guys, for coming," I tell them and walk into the conference room at the same time as them. "Please have a seat."

I wait for everyone to be seated before starting my pitch. "I'm sure you are all wondering why I called this mandatory meeting." I look around the table. "As you are all aware, the town bar was burned down to the ground."

"It's awful," Kaylie says. "Poor Savannah."

"It really is awful," I tell them. "It's awful, and it's a shame that one of our own has been targeted like this." I wait to see everyone's reaction to that statement. "With that said, I want to rebuild it."

Tony is the first one to speak up. "Where is Savannah in all this?" he asks, and I look at Jacob, not sure what to say.

"She went to visit her mother for a couple of days," Jacob says, lying. "She said she would be back next week." He tells me something that I didn't even know. I didn't even ask her how long she would be gone. I didn't want to think about it.

"It's a lot of work," Tyler says. "It'll take a day just to clear the mess."

"It's a big job, but," I tell them, "if we get the town to pitch in, we can do it."

"How long?" Jake asks, looking at me, slouching in his chair. "I'm assuming we are all here because this isn't a job that you want to take your time doing."

"I'd like to have it done by the time she comes back," I tell the table, and a couple of them groan.

"I can have a crew come in," Casey says. "To help with clearing the area."

"I can ask at the station. I'm sure the boys will want to pitch in," Jacob says.

"Like it or not, the bar was a meeting point in town. Many of you stopped by there on the way home from work or just to blow off some steam. It's a shame if we don't have that anymore."

"I can start clearing it right away," Tyler says, then looks at Casey. "Any extra help will be appreciated, but I'll work through the night if I have to."

"So will I," Tony says, and twenty minutes later, when they walk out of the room, I sit down.

"That was some pitch," Jacob says. "Does she know you're doing this?"

"No," I answer. "She told me she didn't think she belonged here. She thinks this whole town hates her, and I want to show her that she's wrong."

"Well, if this isn't the biggest grand gesture of life," Casey says as he gets up, "I don't know what is." He looks at Jacob. "I'm going to head over there and see if I can help do anything now."

I drive by the site an hour later and see that about forty people are working. Tyler has gotten an extra rig so they can pick up the pieces of what was her bar. I drive to the diner to get food for everybody. Tony is at the counter eating. "Hey, there." I slip onto the stool beside him. "How are you?"

"Good," he says as Mr. Lewis comes out of the back.

"Hey there, can I get about a hundred burgers?" He looks at me funny. "It's for the cleanup crew at the bar."

He nods his head. "I heard about that," he says. "I'll take care of it. I can't help them, but it can be my contribution." He turns and walks back into the kitchen, leaving me speechless.

"Hey, Beau." I see some of the older men sitting at the table in the middle of the room. "We heard that you want to rebuild the bar in a week."

"I'm going to try," I tell them.

"We may be old, but we have some good times left in us," one of them says. "We will be there tomorrow morning."

"Thank you," I tell them.

When I turn up the next day, the whole place is swarmed

with people. I park as close as I can, but with all the activity going on, it's hard. I stand at the edge and see about two hundred people ready to work. I look around, taking pictures for her. I won't tell her, but I want her to see that she matters to this town.

Instead, I send her a text.

Me: Missing you. Hope you have a great day.

I put the phone away, my heart aching in my chest when I think of her not being here. I work until I can't stand anymore, and when I go back home, all I can do is collapse in bed after my shower. I sleep on her pillow with her smell all around me, and when I wake up in the morning, I'm greeted with a text from her.

Savannah: I miss you, too. Talk soon.

I run my finger over the words, the muscles in my body aching as I stretch. I walk to the bathroom, passing the picture of us on our wedding day. I have to sit down and just stare at it while my heart beats for her.

When I show up, I'm shocked at the progress that's already been made. "Holy shit, I can't believe the frame is already up." I look over at Jacob.

"Casey hired three groups of people to rotate shifts, so there is someone here all the time," Jacob says. "Mr. Lewis hired an extra cook, and he keeps bringing food every eight hours." I put my hand to my mouth. "What if this isn't enough?" he asks, and I look at him.

"I've been without her for three days now," I tell him. "The pain just gets worse instead of getting better." I look over at him. "If she isn't going to stay, I'm leaving."

"What?" he asks, shocked.

"If she comes back and decides that this isn't the place for her, then I'll follow her wherever she goes."

"But your life is here."

"No," I say, shaking my head. "My life is wherever she is."

Thirty-Two

SAVANNAH

I watch the water crash onto the shore as I sit in the sun. It's what I've been doing for the past three days.

When I left town, I did it with a heavy heart and an even heavier mind. I cried the whole time, and the only thing I could see was Beau's face in my mind. The way he looked at me on our wedding day; the way he looked at me when we got home after the party. I shouldn't have doubted him or dropped this bombshell on him out of the blue. I should have stayed and spoke to him about it. I wipe the tear away from my face again, opening the phone and seeing the message that I sent to him yesterday, but he never got back to me.

I see a bird fly by and dive into the water and then spot a couple of people walking up toward me. I've seen these people for the past three days, and each time, they've smiled at me and said hello. Like clockwork, they walk by me, and both of them say hello to me, then smile and move on.

I get up now and walk back up the steps to the house I'm renting. I walk into the cool house and look around at its emptiness.

Three days ago, I drove into town, thinking this was it,

and I could live here. I went to the supermarket and walked down aisle after aisle, and it bothered me that I didn't see anyone I knew. It also bothered me that I smiled at people, and they just nodded at me. *God, this is what I wanted*, I told myself. This whole thing of no one knowing me is what I was looking for, yet having it makes me feel more alone than I've ever felt in my whole life.

I prepare myself a little dinner, but all I do is move it around on the plate. I miss my family. I miss everything about what was my life. Did it suck at times? Of course, but it just made it that much more special, and I see it now.

I'm about to go and lie back outside and watch the sunset when the phone beeps and my heart skips a beat when I think it's Beau. I wonder what he's doing at this moment. I wonder if he is sitting down eating, thinking of me and wishing I was there. Instead, it's a picture from Kallie of Ethan smiling at the camera.

I text her back right away.

Me: Thank you for the picture. I miss him.

I turn off all the lights and walk to the bedroom, slipping between the stark white covers and sinking into the bed. I open my pictures on my phone and go through them one by one. Most of them are of Beau and me that I never noticed before. He was always beside me at every single gathering. His hands resting on my shoulders or my arms or around my waist. I never noticed it before, or I never wanted to see it.

I fall asleep to his smile, and when I feel little kisses on my neck, I open my eyes, expecting him to be there, but he's not. I'm alone in the bed without him, and when I turn over, my heart hurts. My body hurts, my muscles scream, and my eyes leak with tears as I feel this overwhelming sense of loneliness.

Even when I was pregnant and alone with no idea of what was going to happen, I never had this feeling. I never had it because I knew that Beau would be there, that he would always be there for me. I slip out of bed and grab my robe, heading to the beach when my coffee is ready.

I watch the sunrise and send him a text.

Me: Hope you have a great day. Missing you.

I stay out here, and when my phone rings at almost eleven, I hope it's him. I want to reach out and tell him to come get me. I want to tell him that this is stupid, this whole thing is silly, and that I belong with him in my hometown. I look and see it's Kallie.

"Hey," I answer after the second ring.

"Hi," she says, and she sounds out of breath. "I don't want to disturb you for too long, but I just wanted to make sure that Ethan could stay out this weekend. He got invited to a birthday party on Friday, and then my father wants to take him fishing over the weekend."

"Um, yeah," I say, blinking. I never thought I would be able to share my son. I never thought I would be okay with a woman loving my son just as much as I do, but at the end of the day, my son is surrounded by so much love, and there is nothing wrong with that. "That sounds like fun."

"How are you doing? Are you enjoying the alone time?" she asks. A tear falls and then another one, and suddenly, I'm sobbing. "Savannah, are you okay?"

"Not really," I tell her. "I ... just miss my family."

"It's not easy," she says. She should know; she walked away from her family eight years ago because of me.

"I'm sitting on this amazing beach. I got this kick-ass house. I have people who say hello to me, and they don't even know me. Nobody leers at me or gives me a side-eye like I'm yesterday's trash." It comes roaring out of me. "And all I can do is sit here and cry."

"Oh, Savannah," she says, her voice soft. "Let's start with the first one. If you think about it, during one day, how many people said hello to you here?"

I watch the waves crash into the shore angrily. "I don't know. I never really counted," I tell her. "Plus, it depended on what I did."

"Let's just say you went to the grocery store," she says. "How many?"

"I don't know." I watch the white foam absorb into the sand while the water comes rolling in. "There is the butcher that always asks about Ethan. Then the baker always gives me a couple of treats because I helped her sister with a job."

"Okay," she says. "And how many leer at you?"

I look ahead, trying to think. "I mean, my neighbors are pretty hard-core I hate Savannah fan club members." I laugh at this now.

"Those old goats only glare at you because the missus wants your ass, and the man knows he could never get a girl like you even in his prime," she huffs, and I laugh now. "Let's be real."

"Okay, fine. You got me there," I tell her, and then my tone goes soft. "His mother doesn't think I'll be good for him." I wipe away my tear because the hurt of her words still stings me.

"He chose you," she says. "You. He knew who you were, and he chose you. He will choose you every single day of every single year because he's been in love with you since forever."

"I love him," I finally say. "I love him so much, and all I want to do is be supportive to him and be there to help him do whatever he wants to do. I don't want the town to turn their noses down on him because of me."

"You know that he doesn't give a shit, right?" she asks. "As long as you are on his side, to him, he's winning."

"Have you seen him?" I ask. "Is he okay?" I wipe a tear away from my eye with my thumb.

"He's hanging in there," she says. "You can see it bothers him that you aren't here."

"I think I'm going to just pack it in and come home," I tell her.

"Sit out the week," she suggests. "Make sure that this is really what you want."

"Thank you, Kallie," I say softly. "And I mean that in so many ways."

"You're welcome, Savannah," she says. "Go enjoy the peace and quiet of the beach. I'll see you when you get home."

I hang up, and the only thing that repeats over and over again through my head is *he is my home.*

Thirty-Three

BEAU

I walk into the house, my ass dragging, and toss my keys on the counter, then throw a piece of pizza in the microwave. I lean back, waiting for the beep, and my whole body aches. I rub my hands over my face, and see that it's almost ten p.m. I eat in the dark, chasing the pizza down with the beer I pulled out of the fridge. I don't turn on the lights as I make my way upstairs, taking off the dusty clothes and putting them in the wash. The hot water rolls all around me as the only energy I have left is in this shower.

When I collapse in bed, I smell her all around me. She spent two days in this bed, and she is everywhere. I turn to the side, and the pain in my chest is worse today. It's getting worse and worse as the days go by that she isn't here. She's texted me twice, and each time, it was to tell me that she was thinking about me. I answered her back that I missed her, but she never answered it.

Turning back over, I put one hand on my chest and another over my head. So much has changed since she left. I want to tell her everything that I've done. I let her walk away from me because I didn't want her to pity me by staying. I let her go because no matter how much I love her, no matter how much I would give to have her, I have to know that she wants me just as much. I close my eyes, and I hear it, the softest knock I've ever heard. I sit up in bed, not knowing if I dreamed it or it really happened. I'm about to lie back down when I hear it again, this time just a touch louder. I grab my shorts and walk down the steps. Turning on the lights, I wonder who it could be. Unlocking the door, I pull it open, and my heart stops in my chest. I know that whatever I did or whatever I was going to do, it would be with her by my side.

"Savannah," I whisper.

"I'm so sorry to wake you." She stands there, looking shy and uncomfortable. "I can come back, and we can talk in the morning."

"No," I say, reaching out and bringing her to me. I can swear the heaviness that was in my chest is now lighter. I take her in my arms, and she wraps her arms around my waist, and I can die a happy man with her in my arms. A tear escapes my eye, and I don't even know how long we stand here in the middle of my entryway hugging, but one thing I do know is I'm not letting her go.

"I missed you," she finally says, and I feel the wetness to where her face is. "I missed you so much." I let her go only to grab her face in my hands, my thumbs rubbing her cheeks.

"You are so beautiful," I say. "You are the most beautiful thing that I have ever seen."

I lean down and take her mouth with mine. Her tongue slides with mine, and when I pick her up, she wraps her legs around my waist as I carry her upstairs.

"We have to talk," she pants out when I let her go to undress her. "Things have to be said."

"I know," I say. "I know." I kiss her again. "And we will. I just need you."

When she lies down and I slide into her, I'm home. "I love

you," I whisper in her ear, wrapping my fingers with hers beside her head. "I love you more than life."

Her legs wrap around my hips. "I love you," she says. "I love you," is all either of us can say at this moment. I lose myself in her over and over again, and she does the same. The sun comes up, and we are still wrapped in each other. She lays her head on my chest with the sheet pulled up over us.

"I used to get up every morning," she says, "and watch the sunrise." She looks up at me.

"I can't do this lying down. I need to get up." She rips the sheet off her and then grabs one of my shirts and puts it on. "Okay, I'm good," she says, and she takes a huge breath. "I drove to this town about forty minutes away from here."

"Was it pretty?" I ask, and she smiles so big her whole face lights up.

"It really was," she tells me. "I had this house right on the beach, and I would get up every morning." She moves her hands the whole time. "I mean, I didn't really sleep, but I would grab a cup of coffee and sit on the beach and watch the sky turn from dark to a light pink to a blue. The whole time I did that, I wanted you next to me. I didn't even care if the neighbors would come out and wave to me before they left for work. Then I spent time walking around the town, and not one person said anything to me. Not one person cared or looked my way, not a sneer, not a leer, and not even any words under their breath. I smiled at a couple of them, and they nodded politely, but that was it."

I get up now, tossing the sheet to the side. "Will you come with me?" I ask, putting on my own shirt. "I mean, after you put pants on. Will you come with me?"

"Where?" she asks, and I look at her.

"It's a surprise," I say, and she just looks at me. I walk to her, taking her cheek in the palm of my hand. She tilts her head to the side, pushing into it. "But it's a good one."

"Okay," she whispers. After she puts on shorts, we walk to the truck. She climbs in, and I turn to her before I start the truck.

"Can you do me a favor?" I ask, and she looks over at me. "Can you close your eyes? I want you to see it when it's time."

"I hate surprises," she tells me, leaning back and closing her eyes. "Like I hate it more than coriander." I laugh because she really hates surprises. One time, I wanted to throw her a surprise party, and she didn't even show up. I had to go and get her at home.

"I know but trust me," I say, "you'll love this one." I make my way over to the place where I've spent the past seven days. The number of splinters that I had removed this week has to surpass one hundred. I pull up and finally see it in the sunlight. I get out and walk over to her side of the truck, opening the door and grabbing her hand. "Keep your eyes closed," I say, and she walks slowly with me. "Almost there," I say, and when we are finally in the right spot. "Okay," I tell her, watching her face. "You can open your eyes."

Her eyes flicker open, and I see them take in the building that everyone has spent the whole week working on. "What in the world?" She looks at what she last saw as a pile of rubble. "How did you ...?" She looks at her bar in shock.

"God," I say, looking down, "I had this whole speech set up for when you came back home, and now, I don't know what to say. When you left, you said that you didn't feel at ease in this town. You said that everyone always looked at you with a sneer or a leer." I turn to look at her. "But the town made this possible."

"What are you talking about?" she asks, walking toward the new bar.

"I'm talking about how the whole town came together to rebuild Savannah's Bar," I say. "Every single day, almost twenty-four hours a day, people would show up to help rebuild this place." I look over at the sign that we just put up last night that says Savannah's Bar. "People would go to work and then show up at night to offer help."

"You did this?" She blinks away tears. "You made this happen."

"I want to take all the credit, but I couldn't have done it without everyone coming down and helping. Let's go look inside."

I grab her hand and walk over to the door, opening it and stepping in. "Anything that you don't like can be returned," I say. The bar that was old is now in a shape of an L, and there are more stools than there were before. New tables and chairs are scattered around as well as high-top tables. "There is a bigger stage for the bands." I point at the big stage against the wall. "There are also six pool tables and two dartboards." I point at the raised level. "There are two steps so they can watch the dance floor."

"This is ..." she says, looking around. "I don't know what to say," she sobs.

"You mentioned when we got married that a house is just a house, and it's who is inside that makes them a home. This ..." I put my hands out. "Savannah, this is your home. It's what you built. You may think that people don't like you, but there are more than you know who will stand up with you and not against you."

She puts her hands to her mouth and starts to shake with tears. "I can't believe this."

"If you don't want it and don't want to stay here, we can go wherever you want," I say, and she looks at me shocked. "I'm nothing without you, so if you say the word and decide that this isn't what you want, then we will find a place where you want to be."

"You would do that?" she asks. "You would walk away from everything?"

"I'm empty without you," I say. "This whole week just proved to me that my heart beats just for you, and only when you're around. I was empty, a shell of a man." I walk to her. "You, Savannah, where you are is my home. Beside you, holding your hand, kissing you, laughing with you, fighting with you, making love to you. That is where my home is." I get down on one knee in front of her. "I know that this is late, and technically, we are already married, but ..." I take a huge deep breath. "Will you marry me? I mean, this time for real."

"I came back here, and I was expecting to have to beg you to forgive me. What I did to you by leaving was uncalled for. It hurt you, and I didn't even think how you would feel having me leave. It was selfish, and I promise to never do it again."

"Does that mean you're staying?" I ask, the hope filling my heart.

"It means that this ..." She opens her arms. "This bar, this town, Ethan, you ..." She grabs my face, bending over. "You are my home, and I'm not going anywhere." I smile through my own tears. "And to answer your question, yes, I'll marry you again."

Thirty-Four

SAVANNAH
FOUR DAYS LATER

"Where do you want us to put all of these red Solo cups?" I hear a voice behind me and turn around. "The table out there is full."

I look at one of the volunteers who has come to help us set up for our grand opening. "Is there space under the table?"

"Good idea," he says and walks away from the bar toward the door.

"Are you done ogling other men?" I hear Beau coming out of my office and looking at me. I throw my head back and laugh.

"I have enough man at home that I don't need to go out looking for another one," I say, smiling. It's been four days since I've been back home. Four days that I've cried only happy tears. "Are you ready for your speech, Mr. Mayor?" After Kallie and Olivia came over, they told me about all the men and women who came out. I didn't know how else to say thank you to everyone, so I thought we should throw one epic party.

I brought it up to Beau, who thought it would be amazing if we did family day there also, so my parking lot is now set up with barbecue pits. There are a couple of ponies that Casey has donated for the kids to ride. There are some inflatable rides also. "How is setup outside going?" I ask as he walks to me. "It's good. The bands are setting up."

"I can't believe it's going to be so big," I say as the door opens, and I see Billy, Charlotte, and Cristine walk in.

"Give me a kiss," he says in a soft voice. I lean my head back, and he kisses my lips. "I love you."

"Love you more," I say, and I hear Charlotte squeal.

"This is so nice," she says, looking around. Beau takes my hand and walks me around the bar. "Savannah, this is wonderful." She envelops me in a hug when I get close enough to her. "So, so wonderful."

"It's filling up out there," Billy says. "But I thought we could whip up a special sweet tea."

"No!" Beau and Charlotte yell at the same time.

"Why don't you come down on a Saturday night, and we can have a Billy's Special?" I suggest, and I see him smiling so big. "We can even set you up behind the bar."

He takes his cowboy hat off his head and smiles. "Well, I reckon I can do that."

"You just made his day," Charlotte says, and I'm about to tell her that it's the least I can do when the door opens, and Ethan comes running in.

"Mom," he says. "The bull just got here."

"The bull?" I ask, and see Olivia and Casey come in the door followed by Kallie who is dragging in Jacob.

"I told him it was a bad idea," Olivia says. "But Mr. Rodeo King over here thought it would be a good idea to get the kids excited about the new rodeo courses he is going to be offering at the new farm."

"If they last on the bull, they get free lessons," Casey says. "It's a win-win for everyone."

"We should get out there," Beau says. I look at one of the

waitresses inside and motion that I'm going outside and she should take over the bar. We have the bar open for anyone who wants to get out of the heat.

We walk outside, and I have to stop. There are so many people, and it looks legit like a carnival. "Look at all these people." I look around.

"Mom, I'm going to go ride the bull and see if I can win the lessons," Ethan says, running toward the fake bull.

"If he breaks anything," Jacob says, putting his hands on his hips. "Casey, you are taking him to the ER."

"If he breaks anything," Beau says, "I'm blowing it up." My heart fills with so much love to see how much my son is loved. I watch Billy walking with him, his arm around his shoulder while he holds Cristine's hand.

"Shit," Beau says from beside me. "I forgot the ribbon at the house." Another thing he wanted to do was the official cutting of the ribbon for the bar. "It was on my desk, and I even told myself not to forget it."

"You can call Grady," Jacob says. "He's on duty now, and he said he'll be swinging by when he can."

"Great idea," Beau says and sends him a message. "Okay, Mrs. Mayor, it's time to greet the people." He grabs my hand, and we walk around, saying hello to everyone. Beau poses for some pictures while people actually talk to me. It is nothing like the dinner that I attended.

I get more hugs that day than I have ever gotten in all this town. I have men coming up to me, telling me they miss the bar and that they are excited it's reopening. I have the women asking me if I would ever think about having ladies' night where some of them are talking about having dancers come in.

I laugh and look over at Beau, who is looking down at his phone. "What's up, Grady?" The smile on his face disappears. "What? Where?" He looks at me, and then I see Jacob running over to us.

"Don't make a scene." I hear Jacob beside Beau, my eyes going from one to the other.

"What's happening?" I ask, and Beau looks at Jacob.

"We have to go, and it has to be quiet," he says, and the two of them are walking away. I run to keep up with them, and it's like we are young all over again. Me chasing them.

"You are not coming with us," Jacob says over his shoulder, and then Beau looks over his.

"You stay here, and I'll call you as soon as we know something," he says, and I glare at him. "Don't look at me like that, Savannah." He stops right next to Jacob's car, and now Kallie is walking over to us followed by Casey and Olivia. "You have all these people here." He points at the crowd. "You can't just leave."

"One-half of these people are here to meet the 'hot mayor' as one of the women said. Two, there is something going on, and you are hiding it from me, and ..." I fold my hands over my chest. "I don't like it."

"What's going on?" Kallie asks from beside me.

"I have no idea," I say to her. "But these two got phone calls and were off running to leave."

"Listen," Jacob says. "We don't have time for this." He looks at Kallie. "I have to go; it's police business."

"Then why is Beau going?" she asks the question I want to ask.

"It's better for everyone that you just tell them or else ..." Casey says. "I'll be the one left here with three pissed-off ladies." He looks at them. "I can barely handle that one." He points at Olivia who just shrugs. "I can't handle the other two as well. Especially Kallie who will get back at me, and Savannah, well, she pours my drinks when I come here. I don't want her to poison me."

"Oh my God," Beau says, pulling at his hair. "We need to go, so get in the truck."

"You could have saved all this time," I say, getting into the back and squeezing in when Kallie gets in followed by Casey and Olivia sits on his lap.

"This is so illegal," Olivia says, but she flies back when Jacob backs up and speeds off.

"Where are we going?" Kallie asks, and Beau looks over at me, and my stomach sinks.

"What happened now?" I ask him, ready for whatever good that was coming my way in the past two weeks is now going to be taken away from me.

"Someone was just caught trying to burn down the mayor's house," he says, and the gasps in the truck are mostly from the back seat. I feel Kallie's arms around me. "Grady was there to pick up the stuff I forgot. He thought he saw something but wasn't sure, but when he walked into the house, he smelled the gasoline." The tears are now just running down my face.

"The good news is that after a little bit of a chase, he got the guy," Jacob says. "But before we get there, you have to promise," he says and then looks at me through the rearview mirror. "The both of you." He looks now at Beau. "That you will not fly off the handle when we get there. This is still a police investigation, and we don't really know anything right now."

"Who is it?" Beau asks between clenched teeth. My body starts to shake, but I don't have to wait long because we pull up to the mayor's house, and there are five patrol cars with their lights all going. I get out of the truck as soon as he puts it in park, and I walk around. Beau grabs my hand before I can run and see who it is. I don't have to see him, but I can hear him shouting at the top of his lungs.

"Get these fucking cuffs off me, you pig," he says. My body starts to shake, and it takes Beau putting his arms around me to feel safe. "You can't pin this shit on me. I didn't do anything." We walk just a few steps, and he sees us.

"She was supposed to be mine!" he shouts. "She was always supposed to be fucking mine."

I just watch him as he's being led to the car, his hands cuffed behind his back. He wears all black, and his face is streaked with dirt.

"Oh my God," Kallie says from beside me. "It's Chase."

Thirty-Five

BEAU

"Chase." I hear her voice next to me, but my eyes are glaring at him. I take a step forward, but Jacob pushes me back.

"This is a crime scene." I look at him. "If you touch anything, the whole case can be thrown out due to tampering." I am shaking with rage. This man dated Savannah, he pretended he cared, and all along, he was the one who tried to hurt her.

Grady bends him down and puts him in the back of the car. "You guys don't have nothing on me!" he shouts just as Grady closes the door and then walks over to us. Chase is still yelling in the car, but I don't understand what he is saying.

"What do you have?" Jacob asks Grady who looks down.

"I was here picking up the stuff you forgot," Grady says to me. "I saw this movement on the side, and then he tore through the house. I had to chase him all the way through the back fields." He looks at his arms that are all scratched up. "I spotted his car while I had him on the ground. He fought like a banshee," he says, and it's only then I notice that his mouth is bleeding from the side. "I haven't checked out his car yet."

"I'll do that," Jacob says. "You get him down to the station and get him booked. Read him his rights."

"Or not," Casey says, and everyone looks at him. "You caught him on the premises, and he started a fire. You pretty much have a slam dunk case."

"This goes by the book." Jacob glares at Casey.

"Got it," Grady says. Walking back to the car, he gets in and you can hear Chase yelling and screaming now.

"Okay, you three," Jacob says to Kallie, Olivia, and Casey "You need to head back to the bar and make sure that no one knows what's going on." Then he turns to me. "You two." He points at Savannah and me. "Are not going to listen to anything I have to say, so get in the truck, and we'll go check out the car."

Grabbing Savannah's hand, we rush to the truck. "Are you okay?" I ask her quietly before Jacob gets in.

"No," she answers. "If it wasn't for my stupid dating to try to make you notice me, none of this would have happened."

I brush away the tear on her face. "If I didn't have my head so far up my ass, I would have told you I loved you a long time ago." I smile at her when she smiles and then looks down. "So I am the one to blame."

I put my arm around her shoulder and pull her to me, kissing her head. Jacob gets in the truck, and we head over to the truck. "There it is." Savannah points at the silver truck. "That's Chase's truck." Jacob pulls over and parks in front of it. I open the door and wait for Jacob to go ahead of us.

"Don't touch anything," he says, putting on a pair of gloves. He opens the driver's door, and it looks normal. There is no mess anywhere. It's a clean truck. Jacob leans in and presses the button of the trunk, and we walk around. When he lifts the lid, we all gasp.

"Holy shit." I look down and see that there are gasolines cans, sticks of dynamite, and binoculars.

I'm about to lean in and move things when Jacob's phone rings. "Yeah," he says and then looks over at us. "Okay, we can be there in ten." He closes the phone. "Chase wants to talk, but he will only do it with Savannah there."

"Fuck, no!" I roar out when she says, "Let's go."

"You are not going in there," I say, and it's her now who puts her hand on my cheek.

"He has the answers to all of our questions," she says quietly. "I need to know why."

"She is not going in there without me." I look over at Jacob who just nods.

We get to the station, and I walk in holding Savannah's hand. Grady is there waiting for us. "He is waiting for you guys. He has quite a story for you." I follow Jacob into the room where Chase sits behind a brown table with his hands cuffed in front of him.

He looks up and gone is the cocky guy who got arrested and in his place is a guy who knows his time is up. "Good," he says. "The gang is all here."

Jacob sits down in front of him on the chair. "Well," Jacob says. "We're all here. What did you want to say?"

"I suggest you sit down because this is going to be a long one," he says, looking over at us, and neither of us move. "Suit yourself. I guess I'm going to start at the beginning," he starts. "Before I say anything, I only did this for you," he says to Savannah.

"For me?" She points at her chest. "How is any of this for me?"

"When I first stepped into town and took one look at you, I knew that you were perfect for me,"

Chase tells her. "I'd come into the bar and watch you all night long." He looks down. "But he would show up." He points at me. "And ruin it. Then you didn't come one night, and I waited in the parking lot, and I followed her home."

"What?" Savannah whispers. "Oh my God."

"I stayed out there watching until all the lights were off, and then the next day, I did it again," he says. "This time, I waited for you to leave, and then I snuck into your house."

"You were in her house?" Jacob says, shocked and his hands go into fists. "My son lives in that house."

"I never would touch your son," Chase says. "I liked being in your space." He looks at Savannah, and I want to yell at him to look away. "Anyway, I finally got the courage up to talk to you more, and then I asked you out and you said yes." He smiles. "I thought I had a chance."

"One date, officially" Savannah says. "Half a date at that. Coming to visit me at work is not really a date."

"You didn't give me a chance!" he yells, and it takes everything I have not to jump over the table and attack him. "Anyway, I started following you more and more, and it just became a habit. I tried to get you to see me. I was right in front of you the whole time, but you were so in love with Beau you didn't see me." He looks down. "So I had to do what I did in order for you to see me." His eyes fill with tears. "Can't you see I did it all for you?" He goes on and on with the story, and when I walk out of the station, I'm raw.

"You need to calm down," Savannah says, and I just shake my head. "What do you want to do?"

"The only thing that I can do," I say, waiting for Jacob outside. He looks at me and tosses me the key. "Thank you."

I sit in the truck, and she doesn't say anything until we get there, and I shut off the truck. "You don't have to do this," she whispers, and I look over at her. "You don't even have to say anything about it."

"Then I'm just as bad as he is," I say to her and look forward. "It ends now."

I get out of the truck and walk around, and Savannah waits for me. There is a party going on not too far from here, where we should be, but now we are here. She links her fingers with mine, and we walk up the steps, and I ring the doorbell. I hold my breath when I hear the locks open and I come face-to-face with my mother. "Beau," she says, smiling. "We didn't know you would be coming."

I push past her and look around. "Where is he?" I ask, and she turns and pretends to be confused. "I know he's here, Mother. I saw his truck outside."

"Now is not a good time." She looks at me and then looks at Savannah. "Perhaps ..." She continues talking, but I walk to my father's study and push the door open. He sits on the couch leaning back while my brother's wife sits in front of him on the single chair, and my brother stands looking out the back window.

"This is great," I say and walk into the room with my mother behind us. "Family meeting time."

"She isn't family," Liam says of Savannah, raising his hand to point at her. I notice now the empty glass in his hand.

"Is that the way to speak to the woman who had your child?" I say and look over to my mother to see if she knew about it. But her wringing her hands gives me my answer, and I shake my head. "It's over." I look at my father who just leers at me.

"I don't know what you're talking about," he says, glaring at me. "But if this is another tantrum you're going to throw, I suggest you watch your tone with me."

I laugh now bitterly while Savannah squeezes my hand. "Beau," she says my name. "You aren't one of them."

"You," my father says to her. "You need to learn when to talk and when not to talk."

"I love you," I whisper and lean forward to kiss her lips.

"What the fuck is this?" Liam says. "You barge in here acting all high and mighty and what?"

"The police just arrested Chase." As I say his name, my

eyes are on my father, but just like the poker player he is, he doesn't even bat an eye. "I'm assuming you have no idea what I'm talking about."

"Not a clue," he says, his eyes never leaving mine. "Should I?"

"Well, considering you were going to pay him a million dollars to take out Savannah and Ethan." I say the words that taste like acid in my mouth. My brother looks at me, his mouth open, and then looks back at my father. "You should know his name."

"I have no idea what you're talking about," my father says.

"Well, here is a surprise." I let go of Savannah's hand. "Chase said you might say that so he gave us this." I take my phone out of my pocket and press play on the video that Chase secretly recorded of my father and him.

"That can be doctored. That proves nothing," he says, and I want to grab him by his throat.

"The thing you did wrong this time," I tell my father, "was hire someone who was unhinged to begin with." I shake my head. "You see, you hired Chase to do a job, but what you didn't know is that Chase was already forming a case on you, Father. He has meetings of the two of you. He has all of the names of the women who you have fucked over during the years." I look over at my mother who doesn't say anything,

"I have a clean-cut record." He leans forward now. "That man is on drugs."

I laugh. "Twenty-five abortions. Twenty fucking five. Money taken to pay for these abortions. Money paid for apartments to keep your women close. Fifteen women all around the town all set up. That isn't even counting the ones he keeps in town. Taking the town's money to make sure your dick stayed wet." I look at him. "You're fucking pathetic. The thing you did wrong. Paper trail."

"Okay," Liam says. "So what? He cheats on Mom. That isn't a surprise to anyone." He looks at my mother, who is standing there with her hands to her mouth and tears running down her face. "Sorry, Mom. So what are you going to do, rat on your father? He's your father."

"Your wife," I say, looking at him and then my sister-in-law, who sits there with a shocked look on her face.

"What?" Liam whispers.

"You see, dear old Dad," I say to him, "I found the files." He glares at me. "The files that you hid under the floor in my office."

He slams his hand on the desk. "That's enough of this shit. This is my house!" he shouts.

"My wife ..." Liam says almost in shock.

"You are lying," she finally says, getting out of her chair.

"You see ..." I look at Liam, "what dear old Dad does is he gets what little dirt you have hidden away, and then he blackmails them. Pushes them until they have no choice but to give in. He's been doing it for years."

"My wife ..." Liam says. "You slept with my father?" She turns and runs to him.

"Is it mine?" Liam asks, and she looks at him and then looks down, her hand going to her stomach. "God," he says, holding his chest and looking over at my father. "How could you?"

"Oh, please," my father says. "You were too drunk to get it up," he says, and he's about to say something else when a shot is fired. Liam grabs his wife, and I grab Savannah, but my eyes are on my father as blood starts to seep through his shoulder.

I look back to see my mother standing there with his gun in her hand. "I gave you everything," she says, walking to him, and he groans, holding his shoulder. "Everything. I stood by you when I caught you with my best friend on our wedding day." She points the gun at him. "When you chased the staff around. When I had to spend my birthday alone because you were with one of your whores!" she screams, and you see that she is broken. "I did everything for you." She sobs. "Everything." I get up now and walk over to my mother who stands over my father, and her hands are shaking. "Everything!" she yells, and I call her name.

"Mom," I say, and she turns her face to look at me.

"He ruined everything," she says.

"I know he did, Mom," I say, "but this is not going to help anyone. Give me the gun. Let him stand there in the courtroom and let everyone know what he did. Just give me the gun," I tell her, holding out my hand. "Just give me the gun."

Her hands shake as she holds the gun, and a sob rips through her. "I'm so sorry," she says, handing me the gun. The front door swings open, and I hear boots running down the hallway.

"Beau!" I hear Jacob scream my name.

"In here," Savannah says, her own sob coming out of her. "We're in here."

The door swings open, and Jacob runs in and sees my father on the floor. "Shit," he says.

"I shot him," my mother says. "I shot him."

It takes an hour for them to take my father out on a stretcher, and my mother is sitting down on the couch, her composure is just like it always is. She sits there with her feet crossed at her ankles and her hands on her knees. "Is she going to be arrested?" I ask Jacob.

"Not unless your father presses charges," Jacob says. "Right now, he's not saying anything."

"How are you doing?" Savannah says, coming over to me and hugging me around the waist.

"I'm doing okay, baby," I say, kissing her head.

She looks up, and the clouds suddenly start to roll in. "Looks like a storm is coming."

I look up and see the black clouds start to roll in just as fast as the white clouds chase it away. "Looks like the storm passed us," I say, kissing her. "And we are still standing."

Epilogue One

SAVANNAH

One year Later

"This is silly," I say, looking around the room at Olivia and Kallie. "We are already married."

"But this time," Kallie says, coming to me, "you got to pick your own wedding dress."

"Even if we had to have it altered since your baby bump kept growing," Olivia says, and I put my hand on my lace wedding dress over my little baby bump. We were not trying to get pregnant, but when it was time to renew my pills, Beau told me to maybe not take them, and let's see what would happen. Well, it took one month, one month of trying or not being careful, and I was carrying our baby.

"She looks like she has a basketball under there," Kallie says, smiling. A lot has changed in a year. After Mary Ellen shot Clint, he was sentenced to twenty-five years in jail, but after a month, he had a heart attack in his cell. I felt sorry that Beau lost his father, but I didn't shed a tear for that bastard. When the truth came out, I found out that my own mother had to have two abortions at two different times.

She also decided that she wasn't going to let any man dictate her life, so two months later, she married her landlord. I shake my head, hoping that she lives a happy life. Chase got off with doing only five years and now lives far away from us.

"The baby just kicked me." I laugh. Taking Kallie's hand, I put it on my stomach so she can feel it. "She likes you." Kallie just smiles at me, and that, too, has changed quite a bit. This rivalry that we had when she first got to town is now gone. I know that she would do whatever she could for my son, and to me, that means everything.

"I don't know if I could have done this without you," I say. My eyes fill with tears, but I am going to blame them on the baby. "You didn't have to do anything for me." I put my hand on hers on top of my stomach. "I made you lose eight years of your life. I can never give those years back to you."

"It was meant to happen this way," she says. "Besides, who knows if I would have ended up with Jacob had I stayed." She winks at me, and I roll my eyes. "You never know."

"You were his missing piece," I say. "I know it's silly and all that, but I wanted to know if you would be my maid of honor." I dab the tears that are running down my face. "It's fine if you don't want to."

"It would be my honor," she tells me, grabbing me and bringing me in for a hug.

"If you guys continue with the waterworks, there will be no more makeup left, and your pictures will have to be edited," Olivia says. "God, I can't wait until you both stop with the hormones."

"Is it still a secret?" I ask her of her own little bump, and she nods her head.

"We are still waiting for the twelve-week mark." She puts her hand to her stomach. "So yes, it's still a secret."

"Mum's the word," I say with a smile. I'm about to say

something else when a knock comes on the door, and it's pushed open by my tall boy.

"Mom, Uncle Beau said if you don't get out there now ..." He smirks just like his father and uncle. "He's throwing you over his shoulder and dragging you out there." He laughs, and I look at him. He has grown so much in one year that the suit he had the last time had to be replaced.

"Tell your uncle to hold his horses," Olivia says as she walks to the door. She walks out with Ethan, no doubt to scold Beau.

"I see she got her country down." I shake my head.

"It's like she was born with it," Kallie says, picking up the flowers. "Now let's go and get you remarried."

I grab the small bouquet and walk out to meet my husband. I walk with Ethan who just smiles and high-fives all the guys once he hands me over to Beau, who kisses me right away. "I think that is supposed to be for after," the officiant says.

"She's already mine." He winks at him, then he bends and kisses my stomach, something that he does all the time, which makes him even more special and makes the women swoon even more.

"I can go on." The officiant smiles at him, and Beau just nods. "Since the two of you are already wed in holy matrimony, I'm going to go straight to the vows," he says. "I believe that you two have your own vows."

"We do," Beau says. "I'll go first." Making everyone laugh and just like our first one, the wedding is our closest friends and family. "Savannah, I was sitting down the other day, and I tried to think back to when we were younger to try to pinpoint when I fell in love with you." When he starts talking, my tears just don't stop, and I don't even try to stop them. "My whole life I've loved you from afar. I waited for the right moment to tell you how I felt, and I prayed that when I did this, you would feel the same." He turns to the crowd. "She did." Making everyone laugh. "Walking hand in hand with you through this life is so much more than I knew it would be. Thank you for making my dreams come true each and every single day by holding my hand and being the best friend and mother to our children." He grabs my face in his hands now and kisses me. "I love you."

"Another kiss," the officiant says, shaking his head. "Savannah."

"Right," I say, my hands shaking. "Beau," I say. "For my whole life, I've wanted to fit in." I look down, not sure if I should have started with that and let everyone know how vulnerable it has made me. "I used to walk with you in town when we were teenagers, and I would make pretend that you were my boyfriend and that we were together. It was everything that I dreamed of and more. You have held my hand and been my protector since I can remember, and every single day, you show me how much you love me and our children by putting us first." I'm almost sobbing. "My heart is yours, and you were my missing piece. You were my everything. Thank you for taking our house and making it a home."

He kisses me now, grabbing my face and not letting go, not even when the officiant talks above the cheering that is going on around us. "Mr. and Mrs. Beau Huntington."

Epilogue Two

BEAU

Ten Years Later

"I have to get going," I tell Cassandra on my way out of my office. "It's our anniversary, and I'm sweeping her away to our cottage." I smile, thinking about having Savannah all to myself for two straight days. There will be no carpool to ballet or soccer practice. No cheerleading, no rodeo. Nothing but me, my wife, and a bed.

"Have a great weekend." She smiles at me, and I rush home. I smile when I see Ethan's car in the driveway. He loves coming home for the summer.

I walk up the steps and walk in just in time to hear our daughter, Chelsea, yell at the top of her lungs. "Mom, Ethan has a girlfriend, and she gave him a red mark on his neck!" I close my eyes. Ethan is very much loved by the ladies, and his father and I have both given him the sex talk. I just hope he listens to us.

"Ethan." I hear Savannah say his name. "What did I tell you about the hickeys?" I walk into the room while he stands in front of her.

He grew to six feet four, and he is all cowboy. He beat Casey's record at the rodeo not too long ago. "Mom, it's not my fault if the ladies can't control themselves around me." He turns to Chelsea. "You're not allowed to date until you're twenty."

"You were playing tonsil hockey with Emily when you were fifteen." She points at him. She just turned ten years old, and she has already had five "boyfriends."

"Hey," I say, walking to my wife and kissing her on the lips.

"Gross," Ethan says, giving me a hug. "I'm surprised you guys still have ..." He raises his eyebrows.

"All the time," Chelsea says, looking at us. "You guys need to keep it down a touch."

I look over at her with my mouth hanging open, but Savannah answers her. "If you don't like to hear it, you should go to bed when I tell you to."

"Don't worry, squirt," Ethan says, picking her up and tossing her over his shoulder. "I'll get you some earphones."

"I'm back!" I hear our eight-year-old son, Toby, shout from the front door. He came into this world as quiet as can be, and he's even more quiet now, but don't let that fool you. His happy place is being on the farm with Billy and Casey.

"Take off the muddy clothes in the mud room!" Savannah yells to him. "What time are we leaving?"

"As soon as we drop them off at Jacob's house," I say.

"I can take them," Ethan says. "I promised Dad and Kallie I would drop in and spread my love."

"Like you spread it with—" Chelsea says, and he blocks her mouth.

I wrap my arms around my wife and kiss her neck. "Do you want to head out?" I ask her as Toby comes into the house and goes to the fridge. "Wash your hands," I say before his mother does and he groans. "Where is Keith?" I ask of our six-year-old son.

"He's already at Kallie's," she says. "Charlotte came over to drop off pie," Savannah says when Ethan pops his head into the kitchen.

"Grams brought pie?" He smiles and goes to the fridge. I feel a twinge of sadness when I think of my brother and my mother. They both moved away as soon as my father died. My mother couldn't stand the town knowing her business. My brother, on the other hand, went to rehab for ninety days, came out a reformed man, and now sells insurance. She miscarried the night my father was shot, but they have two kids. We talk occasionally, but it ends there. I look around the kitchen now at my almost twenty-year-old stepson eating pie directly from the plate while his sister argues with him about germs. My wife's yelling at both of them to knock it off. *This is what content feels like*, I think to myself, looking around and seeing all the family pictures hanging on the walls throughout the house.

The sound of thunder rips through the house. "A storm is rolling in," Savannah says, looking outside.

"The storm already arrived," I say, repeating the sentence we always say.

"And we are still standing," the kids finish for me.

Books By Natasha Madison

Southern Wedding Series

Mine To Have

Mine To Hold

Mine To Cherish

Mine To Love

The Only One Series

Only One Kiss

Only One Chance

Only One Night

Only One Touch

Only One Regret

Only One Moment

Only One Love

Only One Forever

Southern Series

Southern Chance

Southern Comfort

Southern Storm

Southern Sunrise

Southern Heart

Southern Heat

Southern Secrets

Southern Sunshine

This Is

This Is Crazy

This Is Wild

This Is Love

This Is Forever

Hollywood Royalty

Hollywood Playboy

Hollywood Princess

Hollywood Prince

Something Series

Something So Right

Something So Perfect

Something So Irresistible

Something So Unscripted

Something So BOX SET

Tempt Series

Tempt The Boss

Tempt The Playboy

Tempt The Hookup

Heaven & Hell Series

Hell and Back

Pieces of Heaven

Heaven & Hell Box Set

Love Series

Perfect Love Story

Unexpected Love Story

Broken Love Story

Mixed Up Love

Faux Pas

Printed in the USA
CPSIA information can be obtained
at www.ICGtesting.com
LVHW092246280324
775804LV00031B/616